A Body Tidy

A Clara Fitzgerald Mystery
Book 21

By
Evelyn James

Red Raven Publications
2021

© Evelyn James 2020

First published 2020
Paperback edition 2021
Red Raven Publications

The right of Evelyn James to be identified as the Author of this work has been asserted in accordance with the Copyrights, Designs and Patents Act 1988.

All rights reserved. No part of this book may be reprinted or reproduced or utilised in any form or by any electronic, mechanical or other means, now known or hereafter invented, including photocopying and recording, or in any information storage or retrieval system without the permission in writing from the author

A Body Out of Time is the twenty-first book in the Clara Fitzgerald series

Other titles in the Series:
Memories of the Dead
Flight of Fancy
Murder in Mink
Carnival of Criminals
Mistletoe and Murder
The Poisoned Pen
Grave Suspicions of Murder
The Woman Died Thrice
Murder and Mascara
The Green Jade Dragon
The Monster at the Window
Murder on the Mary Jane
The Missing Wife
The Traitor's Bones
The Fossil Murder
Mr Lynch's Prophecy
Death at the Pantomime
The Cowboy's Crime
The Trouble with Tortoises
The Valentine Murder

A Body Out of Time

Chapter One

Tommy Fitzgerald sat in the parlour concentrating on teaching Pip, his Labrador puppy, how to shake paws. So far, the dog was succeeding in outfoxing him into giving her bits of dog biscuit without actually performing any trick at all.

"That's it, just lift the paw a fraction."

Pip tipped her head on one side and wagged her tail with the enthusiasm of a creature that has no idea what is expected of it, but that realises showing willing is the best way to earn another dog biscuit.

"You have been at that half an hour," Clara Fitzgerald, Tommy's sister, entered the parlour and flopped down onto the sofa with the day's post.

Between them the Fitzgeralds ran a private detective agency, Clara had been the founder of the business and had made her name as being a woman daring enough to take on 'men's work'. Three years later, Clara had seen her fair share of dead bodies and solved more crimes than many a humble police constable. She confessed to herself, though only in private, that she rather enjoyed her work. Not the grisly bits, not the poor mutilated victims or seeing how low humanity could stoop, but puzzling out a mystery,

1

joining together sometimes rather random dots and, ultimately, bringing justice to those who had been wronged.

Of course, she was not always solving murders or serious crimes. Quite often she was tasked with more mundane duties, such as the recent case supplied to her by the town mayor who wanted to know who was putting out food for the seagulls on the town hall roof. The birds had created quite a colony up there and had taken to divebombing certain people as they entered the building. It happened that those certain people had also gone up on the roof and smashed some eggs. Clara could not blame the seagulls for holding a grudge and was quite impressed by their ability to not only remember these people, but to identify them out of the many souls who went into the town hall.

Seagulls, in all their varieties, had been a protected species since 1918. It was technically against the law to disturb or destroy their nests while in use (Tommy had discovered this through the Brighton Ornithology Society, who were making a fuss about efforts to dislodge the colony), nor could the gulls be killed.

The mayor was beside himself but had latched onto the desperate hope that if they could stop food being put out for the gulls, they might move on. Clara felt it was cruel to dash his hopes and duly set about trying to find the culprit. The mayor had become very quiet when she came back with the news that the perpetrator happened to be a member of the nobility who was renting a property next to the town hall for the winter season. He had a title and a love for birds, especially seagulls.

The matter was duly dropped, and certain people informed they best start coming to work under umbrellas and never set foot above the third floor if they valued their hair.

"You are not getting anywhere," Clara remarked to her brother.

Pip glanced her way and in the process of turning

A Body Out of Time

slightly lifted her left paw.

"Look, she is doing it!" Tommy said in delight. "Good girl, have a biscuit!"

Pip chomped her biscuit, happily oblivious to whatever she had done to earn it. She was onto a winner here.

Clara glanced through her letters.

"Ah, more bills, as usual," she groaned. "When did we find ourselves owing Harris & Sons the art dealers money?"

"That was the Melton case, when they were convinced someone had been switching out paintings in the family home for fakes. The son was responsible. He had gambling debts," Tommy said, absorbed in his dog training.

"I only walked into their shop and asked a couple of questions!" Clara declared. "They have sent me a bill for £5 saying it was a consultation!"

"I think art dealers' premises are called galleries, not shops," Tommy said idly.

"Well, I am not paying that! Next they shall want to charge people for viewing their paintings on the shop floor."

"Gallery floor."

Clara glared at him, but he was not looking her way. Instead, he had moved on to attempting to teach Pip to roll over. This was because the pup had grown tired and flopped down to have her belly rubbed. Tommy was convinced this was evidence that their training from the day before was producing results.

Clara flicked the ridiculous consultation bill onto the floor, feeling it deserved nothing more than her deepest disregard and turned to a curious letter with an Irish postal mark.

"Who do we know in Ireland?" she asked her brother.

"No one," Tommy replied without looking up. "I've never even been to Ireland."

Clara opened the envelope and produced a thick letter in familiar handwriting.

"This is from Susan Campbell," she informed Tommy.

A Body Out of Time

"She hasn't written in a while, not since Christmas."

"How is the baby?" Tommy asked casually.

"According to Susan's last letter he is thriving. She was studying for her archaeology degree last time she wrote me. Remember how when we first met her, she was so despondent about her future and what she would do with it. She was convinced she was not hardworking enough to have a career."

"And now she is firmly tucked up in the world of academia," Tommy smiled. "Why is she writing to you from Ireland?"

Clara unfolded the letter and started to read.

Dearest Clara,

First, I must apologise for my dreadful lapse in correspondence, but life has been so very busy. Baby Austin is going through the terrible twos, I had thought that was a nonsense, but I see it is very much a reality! He tries nanny's patience something awful, but he can be such a dear boy as well.

All the family are hale and hearty. We had a peaceful Christmas and were well rested for returning to regular life. Which brings me to what you are no doubt curious about, why this letter was sent from Ireland.

As you know I have been studying for my archaeology degree and my university was recently given permission to operate a 'dig' in an historic site in Ireland. All us second year students were offered a chance to participate in the dig and get some hands-on experience during our spring hols.

Well, it seemed such a delightful idea and a fine chance for a break from things! All the family decided to come, and we have rented a nice little cottage with sea views. It is positively darling!

Now, Clara, we have all discussed it and agreed that you must come and join us and make it a proper family holiday. We have not seen you in over a year and we did so promise to keep in better contact. I am sure you will love it here and the dig is already producing some interesting things.

We may even find a body! Ancient, of course, and deep in a bog. That is why the university wants to excavate the site as they believe it was used to bury the bodies of human sacrifices or maybe criminals in the long distant past. Peat diggers are always coming across mummified remains.

I thought to myself, why, here are some very old murder victims and if anyone ought to be able to unravel what became of them it would be my cousin! You see the archaeologists are all very good at identifying things and dating them but can't figure out the hows and whys of the way anything died. They are making such a faff of it. I thought what they need is a real detective to show them how it is done.

Please do come over Clara, bring Tommy and Annie, and do bring darling Captain O'Harris. I have not had the chance to meet him yet, though you write so much about him.

Please respond swiftly (and do agree to come) for I cannot abide to wait too long for your answer. This is so exciting Clara, and you must be here. They are saying this will be one of the most important archaeological discoveries in Ireland this century, how amazing is that?

I eagerly anticipate your reply.
Yours Sincerely (and with dearest wishes)
Susan Campbell.

Clara read out the letter to Tommy.

"Ireland," he mused. "Well, we could do with a holiday. We haven't had one in over a year."

"But Ireland, in the spring?" Clara had visions of wet fields and choppy seas. Ireland was a beautiful emerald green isle for the reason it received a lot of rain, especially in the early and late parts of the year.

"It's April, time for some sun," Tommy chivvied her.

"April showers, you mean," Clara glanced out the window where a glorious sunny day belied the fact that if you walked outside without a coat on you would soon feel the tail end of winter nipping at you.

"I bet Ireland will be beautiful this time of year," Tommy mused. "The lambs and calves will be in the fields.

A Body Out of Time

The flowers will be blooming and the trees starting to blossom. And you can bet this cottage the Campbells have rented is the biggest cottage ever to bear that name."

Clara smiled. She had to admit it did sound tempting to get away for a while and she had always had a curiosity for history. Bog bodies. They were a new one on her, not that she hadn't dealt with the odd mummy in her time as a detective.

"Well?" Tommy asked.

"I suppose it would be rather pleasant," Clara grinned at him.

"And Susan wants to meet the darling Captain O'Harris," Tommy chuckled. "You know what that means."

Clara looked at him blankly. He tutted.

"The Campbells clearly are beginning to think they hear the sound of wedding bells, and not the ones that will hopefully be ringing for me and Annie soon," he explained.

Clara was aghast.

"John and I... we haven't even discussed..."

"Let's just say we all have a good idea of where you two are headed," Tommy laughed at her. "Even if you don't."

Clara blushed, which was a rarity in itself.

"What are you two gabbling about?" Annie entered the room with a cup of tea in her hand. She had been baking and was looking slightly hot and flustered.

Annie had started her association with the Fitzgeralds when she took on the role of nursemaid to Tommy and a helper to Clara around the house. Before long, however, she had realised that what the Fitzgeralds really needed was a housekeeper with the demeanour of a lion tamer. The Fitzgeralds were the sort of folk who were full of good intentions and ideas but tended to leave most of them unfinished and with a mess to clean up. As Annie would say, it came of thinking too much and not being practical.

Annie had taken charge of the house like a benign overlord and now ruled over it to everyone's contentment when it came to domestic affairs. At some point fairly early on she had gone from being an employee to being a devoted friend. Now she was engaged to Tommy and they planned to wed in the summer. No one was as yet quite sure how this would change things between them all, though Annie stoutly maintained that everything would be exactly the same as before, just she would have a different surname and a ring on her finger. And you didn't argue with Annie about these things, she had a 'look' she could give you that made all your words dry up in your mouth.

"Our cousins, the Campbells, have invited us on holiday to Ireland," Clara explained.

"In the summer?" Annie suddenly looked worried.

"No, they know the wedding is then," Tommy reassured her. "They want us to go over now."

"But it is only April?" Annie remarked. Her vision of a holiday was something that occurred on a hot Bank Holiday and lasted only a few hours, a day and night at most, then you could get safely back home very relieved it was all over and done with.

"Susan is working on an archaeological dig as part of her degree," Clara explained. "It sounds very interesting. We are all invited."

Annie contemplated this for a moment.

"Well, if you want to go…"

"They have some very unique cakes in Ireland," Tommy tossed into the conversation casually. "I do believe I once read they make a form of bread from potatoes. I don't suppose anyone around here has recipes like that. Historic, traditional recipes."

He had caught Annie's attention, as he knew he would. She was a glutton for new recipes, especially ones no one else in Brighton knew so she could show off her culinary knowledge. If there was one weakness in Annie's usually robustly down-to-earth demeanour, it was the pride she had for her cooking skills.

"Potato bread?" Annie turned the idea around in her head. "Is that possible?"

"You'll only find out in Ireland," Tommy shrugged. "No one over here would know how to make it properly."

"There is an 'unusual breads' category in the baking competition at the annual summer fete," Annie said with a dreamy look in her eyes. "I don't think they have ever had Irish potato bread entered."

"There you go," Tommy said. "Coming to Ireland Annie? Got to keep up your reputation for having the most unusual and diverse recipe collection in Brighton."

Annie was convinced, they both knew it, but she was going to fight them a bit longer, so it did not look as if she just gave in that easily.

"It will require a bit of packing and I shall have to leave some of my work unfinished here," she said. "I'll need to find someone to take care of the chickens."

"I'm sure one of the neighbours would," Clara said.

"Oh yes, plenty would for the extra eggs, but who do I trust to shut them up properly at night?" Annie retorted. "I suppose I could find someone suitable."

"Are you coming then?" Tommy pressed.

"You'll need some new wellingtons if you are going to be stomping around a place people are digging," Annie continued. "And we ought to bring over plenty of tea."

"I do believe they have tea in Ireland, Annie," Tommy assured her.

"But is it the right tea?" Annie responded quickly.

"Taking into account all these arrangements," Clara interjected, "Do you think you would like to come?"

Annie gave Clara a firm look, then Tommy. She had folded her arms. They knew her answer already, but she was going to make them wait. With a grudging tone she said.

"I suppose I ought to. You two will get into no end of trouble without me."

Chapter Two

In the end it only required a few days to pack and prepare for their unexpected trip. Captain O'Harris was delighted by the invitation. O'Harris ran a convalescence home for servicemen who had suffered mental trauma in the war. There were many of those about, sadly, and he only had so many rooms, but he was making a small dent in the vast problem and there was hope that others would follow his example and set up their own homes on similar lines. O'Harris was also very close to Clara, they had not quite admitted to themselves that they were more than friends, but everyone else knew it.

O'Harris sometimes felt overwhelmed by the work at the home, he had taken on a lot of challenges and was breaking some quite rigid barriers to help the men in his charge. At times he was utterly exhausted to the point of feeling almost paralysed by the amount of things he had to do. A holiday would do him good, especially a holiday with Clara.

So, there they were, early one morning, boarding the train that would take them to the ferry, that would then carry them to Ireland. The milk had been cancelled, the chickens placed in the care of a neighbour, the coalman informed they would have their delivery a week later than usual, and a card pasted discreetly on the door of Clara's office informing any potential clients she was currently absent and please call back another time.

Annie had packed the sort of provisions and clothing an invading army would have been proud of. Clara had only just prevented her from packing a teapot, convincing her after several minutes of intense debate that there were teapots in Ireland, and she did not need to fret. Annie was acting as if they were going to a foreign land where things were suspiciously un-English. But then Annie considered London another country and any venture 'up North' was liable to bring her out in a fluster, for Northerners were, to Annie's mind, near enough savages.

Tommy informed Clara that he blamed it on the magazines Annie bought and read with the sort of fervour she usually only reserved for her cleaning.

"Every story about a woman being mistreated is set somewhere in the North," he explained. "And you know Annie thinks that each of those fictional tales is based on a true story somewhere along the line."

"One of these days we shall have to go to Durham or Northumberland and prove to her that people in the north are no different to those in the south," Clara replied stoutly.

"Good luck with that," Tommy smirked. "She'll probably envision us all being eaten by Lancashire cannibals."

When they were finally on the train and settled in a compartment, Annie produced a thick package wrapped in brown paper from her substantial handbag. It proved to contain jam sandwiches, which she handed around as if she were issuing out gold coins.

"To sustain us," she informed them.

"Annie, how long do you think it takes to get to Ireland?" Tommy asked her with a hint of laughter in his voice.

"Too long," was Annie's instant response. "I shan't have anyone fainting on my watch."

"I was not aware that was a risk," Tommy said.

Annie glared at him. O'Harris took a bite of his sandwich to show willing and rested his hand on his knee as he munched. He soon discovered that this put his sandwich in the ideal reach of Pip, who carefully extracted it from his hand in one deft move. She then looked at him and wagged her tail, as if she were doing him a favour.

"Ah, sorry!" Tommy said. "Pip, get out of it! Bad girl!"

Pip turned her deep brown eyes upon him, and he felt guilty at once.

"Well, not bad girl, that was harsh of me."

"Thomas Fitzgerald, when are you going to get your dogs under control?" Annie demanded. She was referring to Bramble, Tommy's small black poodle, in her complaint, as well as the Labrador pup. Bramble was currently perched between Tommy and Annie, his eyes fixed on Annie's sandwich as if it were some holy item he could not bear to be parted from.

"She is only a pup," Tommy protested.

"What of this one?" Annie pointed at Bramble and nearly lost her sandwich as he went to dive for a bite.

"Bramble!" Tommy scolded the poodle. "Look, give me the brown paper for Pip to snuffle, then she'll be happy."

Annie handed over the brown paper the sandwiches had been in, still berating Tommy for his ill-mannered dogs. O'Harris gave a sideways glance to Clara. They were sitting side-by-side, opposite the feuding pair.

"Did they get married without telling anyone?" O'Harris joked.

"They argue like it," Clara chuckled back. "But this is normal."

"I dread to think what it will be like after they are wed then!"

"Oh, they rather enjoy it I think," Clara winked.

At that moment the war was won decidedly in Annie's favour and to show her superiority, she broke a piece of her sandwich off, placed it before Bramble with the firm imprecation to 'leave' and then when he had duly performed this trick, she told him he could have it. Tommy, who had yet to master this skill himself, looked on with a frown.

~~~*~~~

They reached the ferry station after dinner (more sandwiches produced from Annie's apparently endless store, this time cheese and pickle, with a quarter each of a pork pie she had bought the day before) and boarded with anticipation. The bright sunlight of the morning was fading to a grey and rain laden sky, just the sort of weather you did not want to be crossing the Irish Sea in.

They settled inside the passenger deck and watched the grey ocean swelling beneath them as they crossed.

"Tell me about the Campbells," O'Harris said when they were settled, this time he was sitting next to Tommy, opposite the girls.

"Hogarth Campbell is my father's first cousin," Clara explained. "His father and my grandfather were related by marriage. Hogarth has three children from his first marriage, Andrew, Peg and Susan."

"Peg can give you a bit of a start on first sight," Tommy interrupted. "She styles herself like a man, unless she has reinvented herself again since last we met. I rather like her, but waters run deep with that one."

"Hm, and she poisoned her uncle," Annie said with an unhappy look on her face.

O'Harris looked surprised.

"It was not clear if Eustace died directly from poison, or from a heart attack he had around the same time," Clara said. "Peg had been poisoning him systematically, I am afraid. It was the sort of case the police can't decide what to do about, so they let it drop."

"Just don't drink anything she offers," Annie said darkly. "And if there is water in your room, don't touch it."

"Annie, that is going too far. She had her reasons for lashing out at the old bully," Tommy said. "And she has been redeeming herself ever since, working with charitable organisations and really being selfless with her time."

"If anyone should be worried about her presence, it ought to be Glorianna," Clara pointed out. "Glorianna is Hogarth's second wife and she has never gone down well with his children."

"That age-old gripe," O'Harris raised an eyebrow. "The wicked stepmother."

"Hogarth married Glorianna rather swiftly after his first wife's death. Some unkind souls even spread rumours Glorianna had poisoned the poor woman. Unfounded, of course, Mrs Campbell was very unwell."

"Glorianna is prickly because she feels the outsider," Annie added. "She seems abrupt and cold. I like to think there is a warmer soul beneath the exterior."

"You are willing to think that of Glorianna, but you have Peg down as irredeemable," Tommy said to her.

She gave him a glare.

"Glorianna has not poisoned anyone."

"So, which of the family is the archaeologist?" O'Harris asked before a new row could start.

"Susan," Clara replied. "She is the youngest of the siblings. She got herself into a spot of bother back in 1920, a case of naivety getting the better of her. Anyway, she now has Austin as a consequence. He shall be three in the autumn."

"Susan is the gentlest of the family," Annie said. "She is a sweet but fragile girl. I really worried about her when we were last there."

"She has done a lot of maturing since Austin was born," Clara countered. "She was lost back in 1920, but she found her path quite by chance. In the summer of 1921, Hogarth was asked by a local archaeology society if they could dig up some of his land where there were the remains of a suspected Roman fort. He gave his permission and all that summer they were active. Susan became involved in the dig and discovered she had a real passion for hands-on history. She enrolled on an archaeology degree soon after."

"Quite something," O'Harris nodded. "And here she is in Ireland."

"I am worried about this bog bodies business," Annie muttered. "I mean, I know they are long dead, and no one is looking for them now or anything, but is it right to lift the poor souls up from their resting place?"

"If the archaeologists don't do it, the peat diggers will, in pieces," Tommy reminded her. "At least this way their deaths will not be in vain. We shall learn about them, about the age they lived in and how they died. They will tell us their story, instead of getting chopped up and lobbed onto a fire."

"Were they murdered?" Annie asked.

"That seems the case," Clara said carefully, knowing Annie could be sensitive about such things. "Alternatively, they might be executed criminals. Susan thinks I might be able to offer my opinion on the subject."

"A bit of detective work on your holiday?" O'Harris reproached her.

"Only for fun," Clara corrected him. "I shall be mainly going on lovely long walks to admire the scenery."

"With me, I hope?" O'Harris teased.

"Well now, if you must tag along," Clara teased back.

"Did Andrew ever marry that young lady, what was her name?" Annie paused thoughtfully as the name of Andrew's betrothed drifted tantalising out of reach of her memory. "Oh bother, what was her name?"

"Laura," Clara said.

"Of course, Laura Pettibone!" Annie declared. "Pretty as a painting, but with a head full of air."

"The marriage never happened," Clara said, elaborating to O'Harris. "Our cousin Andrew was precariously close to committing bigamy when his actual wife walked into the wedding ceremony and made her presence known. It was a messy business. It was a wartime wedding that should never have happened. In any case, Laura was heartbroken and ultimately she could not resolve her feelings of betrayal well enough to consider marrying Andrew."

"She married an American, last year," Tommy added. "Susan was rather upset over it all as she and Laura had been friends."

"Andrew rather rolled with the punches," Clara snorted. "I don't know if he ever really loved her. Though he is hard to read, keeps his cards close to his chest."

"You can try and analyse him while we are there," Tommy said to O'Harris. "You've picked up a lot of tips from your psychiatrists at the home."

O'Harris laughed.

"I am hardly qualified for that! Besides, a man is entitled to be who he wants to be, without people analysing him."

"I just hope Andrew is a little more friendly this time around," Clara said.

"We haven't seen the Campbells since the disaster of Andrew's wedding," Tommy drilled his fingers on the table they sat at. "We said at the time we would go back for Christmas and things, but you know how it is."

"That first Christmas we had the case of the Berkeley Square ghost hoax," Clara said. "After that, we just seemed to get caught up with one thing or another. It shall be nice to see them all again and catch up."

"You actually mean that," Tommy said, looking at her in astonishment.

"I do," Clara defended herself. "I know the Campbells are complicated, and our last visit was not ideal, but they are family. Besides, I want to see Austin."

"I knitted him a cardigan for last Christmas," Annie said proudly. "And Clara made him a little hat."

"I was safer with the hat than the cardigan. I tend to have trouble keeping the arms the same length," Clara added.

"I sent him a wooden toy horse on wheels," Tommy said with a grin on his face. "And I did not make one bit of it. It was all bought from that toy shop in town."

O'Harris started to laugh aloud as Tommy preened in his complete inability to make something handcrafted for his infant cousin. Before long Annie and Clara were laughing too.

"You are hopeless," Annie said with a warm smile.

"It was a very nice horse," Tommy objected. "The wheels were painted red."

They were all distracted by the sound of retching and as one they looked down to the floor where Pip was gagging in that heaving, dramatic way dogs can. Bramble was watching her with anticipation as she brought up, largely intact, the jam sandwich she had stolen earlier and then stared down on it forlornly.

"Oh dear," Tommy said, inserting a finger into Bramble's collar before the poodle could attempt to consume the mess.

"I think your dog is seasick," Annie got up with care, stepping around the pup and the mess.

Pip was whining to herself, clearly not happy.

"I'll take her for a walk on deck, see if that helps," Clara offered, as Annie waved over an attendant to explain what had happened.

"I'll come with you," O'Harris offered.

They cajoled Pip into movement, and she plodded half-heartedly with them out onto the deck. The rain had not yet begun, but there was a stiff breeze whipping over the sides of the ferry and throwing saltwater in their faces. They started to take a turn around the deck, going slowly for the sake of Pip.

"Thanks for inviting me, Clara," O'Harris said a little shyly as they walked. "It will be nice to spend some time with you."

Clara almost said that it had been Susan's suggestion, then changed her mind.

"It will be very nice."

O'Harris reached out and took her hand. She stepped a little closer to him and they both smiled contentedly at each other. Down at their feet, the fresh air and ability to see the sky was doing wonders for Pip. She started to bark at some seagulls passing over the ferry.

"Someone feels better," O'Harris said. "Do you want to

go back inside."

"No," Clara said with a smile. "I want to stay right here, with you."

He slipped his arm around her shoulders and they stared out at the ferry's wake, both utterly content to be exactly where they were.

Chapter Three

Susan Campbell attempted to leap across a narrow trench in her rubber boots. The ground sucked at her feet and instead of gracefully flying over the gap, she barely made the jump, slumped down to one knee on landing and watched her right hand vanish beneath layers of mud. Despite that, she arose with a smile on her face, her excitement to see her cousins undaunted.

"Clara! Tommy!"

They had found the dig site after some considerable difficulty. After leaving the ferry they had taken a bus to the nearest town, following instructions Susan had supplied in a telephone conversation to Clara. They then asked for a gentleman by the name of O'Leary who was supposed to act as their escort.

O'Leary, according to the locals, had not been seen in some time. Not since, in fact, he became embroiled in a skirmish with the Civic Guard over a spot of rabbit poaching. Local opinion was that he was either hiding somewhere or had been arrested and was currently locked up in the gaol in the great old castle east of the town. Neither of which assisted Clara and the others.

They asked around for an hour before they found

A Body Out of Time

someone who knew about the dig and was prepared to stop what they were doing and show them the place. It proved to be an older gentleman with a donkey cart. He had been bringing a load of old potatoes into town, most were past the stage where a person would eat them unless driven by desperation. He was selling them as animal fodder.

His route home happened to take him past the dig site, and he was happy to offer the little troupe a ride in his now empty donkey cart. His view of the excavation was that it was a strange fancy of rich English folks with too much time on their hands.

"They're dead, aren't they?" he said of the ancient bog bodies. "What good does digging them up do?"

There was no point in dissuading him from his pragmatic view and they just smiled and nodded and explained they had been invited for a holiday. When Clara mentioned the cottage, they were staying at the man brightened considerably.

"That'll be the old writer's house. Back before the war, this author fellow lived there, wrote some lovely poems, he did. He signed one of his books and gave it me as a gift. I like to read a poem before going ta bed."

He talked the rest of the way about these poems, reciting odd excerpts that particularly appealed to him. They seemed to be almost exclusively about this corner of Ireland and the ways of life the poet had observed. Ways of life that were fast disappearing and had only been preserved in verse. No one pointed this out to the older man as they feared it would offend or upset him.

He deposited them alongside a stone wall and pointed in the direction of some distant figures who could be seen bending down or walking around. Then he glanced at them and whistled through his teeth.

"You'll be regretting those shoes," he said, before prodding the donkey with a stick and heading up the lane.

Annie looked at her feet anxiously.

"What is wrong with my shoes?"

And now they had traipsed across what had proven to

be less of a meadow and more an imitation swamp, had considerable amounts of water and mud up their legs and in their shoes and were feeling a little fraught over the whole affair. Susan's smile and warm greeting pushed some of the thoughts of her discomfort from Clara's mind.

"Susan!" she said, as they embraced. "You look well."

Susan looked radiating with health and vigour, which was a far cry from the grey-faced, maudlin girl Clara had met back in 1920. She had put on a little weight, which made her prettier to Clara's mind, and she had a colour to her cheeks.

"I am very well," Susan smiled, then she clasped Tommy in a big bear hug.

Tommy was somewhat startled.

"Clara has said in her letters you are walking again. I am so delighted!" She stood back and took a good look at him. When last they met Tommy had still been struggling with the war injury that had confined him to a wheelchair.

"I still have a limp," Tommy told her. "And I feel the cold in my knees, but apart from that I am sound."

"Glorious!" Susan said with joy. "And Annie, I am so pleased you could come. I am dearly looking forward to the wedding."

Susan hugged Annie next, much to Annie's dismay. Annie was not the hugging sort.

"Now, that just leaves this gentleman," Susan turned her attention to the fourth human member of their party. "You must be Captain O'Harris."

"Pleasure to meet you," O'Harris grinned.

A brief glimmer of the old Susan appeared at that moment and she blushed a little, then she slipped her arm through Clara's and remembered herself.

"There is so much to see! I could talk about it all day, but, of course, we are starting to lose the light. A quick tour will have to suffice."

She took them to the nearest trench. The men standing in it, working through the thick, peaty soil, were invisible up to their waists.

"This is trench one, it started as our test trench. We think there must have been a pool or maybe a spring here in the past. We have found a lot of little objects that seem to have been thrown in, including a very ancient sword. It was broken. They always broke things before throwing them in."

"Maybe they were just getting rid of things," Annie said, peering into the trench and giving a little shudder at the sight of so much black mud.

"Oh no, these things, even broken, would have been very valuable. We believe they were offerings to pagan gods, or maybe to water sprites. Appeasing nature and asking for good fortune, that sort of thing."

Annie did not look convinced.

"Trench two is where things get a bit more exciting," Susan led them on. "I mentioned in my letter that a lot of bodies have been found in this area, well, we think we have one in this trench. They have found this dark leathery object they think is a person's hip sticking out of the ground. Aside from being black from the soil, the skin is perfectly preserved. We are carefully excavating it to see if the whole person is down there. Unfortunately, all too often, these bodies have been hacked in half or have lost pieces when the peat diggers have been at work. Only one man in a dozen reports finding body parts, the rest just thrown them away or burn them. So much history lost!"

They peered into the trench. Two men were huddled over what looked like a black lump sticking out of the slightly lighter ground. It could have been the heel of a boot, or a bag, it was hard to tell at this point whether it was part of a body.

"Lastly we have trench three," Susan moved them on again. "This one is proving a disappointment so far. We had it on good authority that a lot of smaller items had been found in this area. We were hoping for another deposit of sacrificial objects. So far, we have not found much at all."

Unlike trenches one and two, where the diggers had been older men who looked experienced at their job, trench three was occupied by two young men who were diligently scraping at the soil with trowels. Clara guessed trench three, proving somewhat unpromising, was being used for the training of the archaeology students.

One of the young men looked up as they approached and brushed back a strand of fair hair that fell into his eyes as he looked up with a muddy hand.

"This is Jason," Susan introduced them. "He is from America but is over here because he wants to study British archaeology."

"Hi," Jason grinned at them. He had very white, very straight teeth.

"Jason these are my cousins," Susan added.

"Nice to meet you," Jason nodded.

Next to him the other young man, a dark-haired fellow who had not even bothered to look up, slapped at Jason's arm.

"Pay attention, we have to get this section done before nightfall. Especially as Susan has abandoned us."

Jason pulled a face for the benefit of the visitors and went back to work. Susan was nonchalant about the reaction of the other young man. As she led them away once more, she explained.

"That was Rufus. He is terribly odd. Obsessed with his work and no notion of how to be polite to people. I am not even sure he was raised by human beings sometimes," Susan chuckled to herself. "Jason and I are convinced he was raised by some wild animals, like wolves, which is why he is so appalling around people!"

"Jason seems nice," Clara said, carefully.

Susan sighed, then her face flushed again.

"Do you think? He is very sweet. He is kind to Austin too. Austin adores him."

"What about you?" Clara asked.

Susan hesitated.

A Body Out of Time

"Once bitten, twice shy," she finally admitted. "I do like him, but I am in no rush."

Clara nodded and said no more.

They were heading towards a large canvas tent, the sort you sometimes saw at summer fetes housing the refreshments or the baking competition entries. It was at least sixteen feet long and one of the flaps in the middle was raised up on posts to form a covered entryway.

"Reminds me of a campaign tent," Tommy remarked as they stepped inside.

The tent was full of tables covered with boxes and objects. Three sides had tables lining them, while a further large table was set in the middle. Nearly all the space was filled. There were heaps of books with titles such as Archaeology in Ireland 1910-1912, Irish Prehistory, and The Preservation of Bodies in Bogs. The tables around the walls appeared to have been set up to serve as different stations for workers. At one, items were being sorted and washed, at another a woman was diligently drawing detailed pictures of each cleaned item that came her way. At the last table, the items were being sorted, catalogued, and labelled accordingly before being stored away in boxes.

At the middle table, an older man was sitting peering at a selection of objects that had been through the processes of cleaning, drawing, and cataloguing already. He was studying these items with a magnifying glass and making detailed notes in a ledger by his side.

"This is Professor Peabody," Susan introduced them. "He is my tutor at university."

Professor Peabody raised his head from the examination of what appeared to be a coin. He gave them a look that might have been considered full of disregard, if you were not aware that the man was clearly utterly fixated on his task.

"I take it this is where everything comes when it is found," Tommy said.

"Oh yes," Susan agreed. "Here we sort and identify

everything and note which trench it was found in. We are meticulous in our work."

"Archaeology is a growing discipline," Professor Peabody spoke. "You may have heard of the work of Howard Carter in Egypt? His methods are to be admired. Everything is photographed in place and also once it has been removed. He has a visual record of all the finds. We are following those principles as best we can. I have a dark room set up behind this tent in an old van we have bought for the purpose. We are taking pictures of everything."

Professor Peabody spread his hands over his table, encompassing the many precious things on the surface.

"You must be Susan's cousins?" he added.

"They are," Susan said brightly. "I was just showing them around."

"Have you any excavating experience?" Peabody asked them.

"None," Clara confessed.

"Pity, we can always use extra hands in the trenches. Perhaps we shall get you trained up. Trench three has space."

"They are here on holiday," Susan told him firmly. "However, Clara is the private detective I told you about."

"Ah! Susan thought you might be able to offer insight into the way any bodies we find have died," the professor said. "She says you are good at solving mysteries."

"I certainly can try," Clara replied. "If you find a body."

"We are working on it," Peabody chuckled. "This place is supposed to be riddled with them. Must have been an execution ground or a sacrificial site back in the past. You cannot imagine it, can you? People being brought here to die, sometimes in quite gruesome ways. The meadow looks so peaceful now."

They all found themselves looking out the tent door, across the rolling grass, which dipped and rose in strange ways. Once this area had been extremely boggy, the water considerably higher so that some of those dips would have been submerged. Now it was just squelchy, with some deeper parts in places where an unsuspecting foot might go down and become stuck.

"Ever found signs of where people lived in these parts back in those days?" O'Harris asked.

"At a nearby hill there are circles in the ground. You can see them better in the summer when the crops are growing. We think that might have been a Bronze Age fort or settlement, but the farmer has never allowed the area to be dug," Peabody shrugged.

He was going to say more, but a shout came up from the dig site and they were all distracted. Peabody stepped outside, heading towards the raised voices and the others followed. A man in tweed plus-fours was marching across the dig site.

"You are ruining my life's work!" he yelled at Peabody.

"Go home Lethbridge," Peabody sighed. "You had your chance."

A man from a nearby trench clambered out and took the intruder by the arm, gently but firmly leading him away. Lethbridge did not fight him but turned back and waved a finger at Peabody.

"You have not heard the last of this!" he cried. "I shall have my vengeance!"

"Madman," Peabody tutted to himself.

"What was that about?" Tommy asked Susan.

"I'll explain later," she said, some of her good humour gone. "Perhaps we should go to the cottage now?"

"Yes please," Annie said with just a hint of a wail in her voice. "I want to dry my feet."

They all glanced down at their ruined footwear, not one of them had dry feet. Susan sighed at them in the sort of voice you use on sweet but tiresome children.

"I did say to bring wellingtons, didn't I?"

Chapter Four

The cottage, as Clara had anticipated, was a grand affair, less cottage and more rustic mansion. It was about a mile from the dig site and the walk was made unpleasant by everyone (excepting Susan) having wet feet. There would be blisters aplenty to complain about that evening.

"This used to be the home of a poet by the name of Edward Tennent. The locals around here adore him because he wrote lots of very insipid and nostalgic poems about the way of life in these parts. As far as I can tell, he lacks a following much outside of this small part of Ireland," Susan explained as they walked down the drive to the house. "Before that it belonged to an Anglo-Irish noble who preferred to stay in London. It was rather neglected, by all accounts, before Tennent took it on, did it up and made it into some fantasy of the past."

The drive was lined with rose bushes, currently hunkered down from the winter cold that had barely gone and not showing a single bud. In summer they must be glorious, though Clara took a count of the number of them and reflected that the upkeep of so many roses must be labour intensive. Roses were not the sort of plant you could leave to get on with things. They needed the tenderest and most diligent of care.

As she was thinking this, she noticed an older man hoeing a patch of soil in what was most likely a flower bed in better months.

The cottage had the appearance of a rich man's summer holiday home or hunting lodge. It was Victorian, with a lot of mock Tudor timbering thrown into the mix, but whoever had built it could not resist two matching sets of enormous bay windows that were definitely not Tudor. The great front door was studded with iron and had ornate brackets. A door knocker in the shape of a growling lion's head glared at them as if it would actually bite if they reached for it.

"Tennent had some money behind him," O'Harris noted.

Clara could see he was counting the chimneys and working out in his head how much a place like this might cost to keep in good repair. His experiences with his own ancestral family home put him in good stead for working out such things.

"Tennent was old money. He certainly didn't make it from his writing," Susan replied. "His niece owns the place now and rents it out to folks such as us. It is absolutely gorgeous inside."

She opened the front door and was swiftly proven to be speaking the truth. Tennent had gone in heavily for the arts and crafts movement of the latter part of the nineteenth century. The wallpaper, if not actually designed by William Morris, was most certainly inspired by him. The furniture was of a similar calibre and where there was wood panelling it was often delicately ornamented by carved details of roses. Susan wanted to take them directly through to the airy sitting room with its immense fireplace, another imitation of something Tudor. Clara halted her.

"I think we can all agree we need to sort our footwear out first."

Susan cast her eyes down at their feet and remembered.

"Ah, yes. Let me show you your rooms."

A Body Out of Time

The house was spread over three floors and there were plenty of bedrooms for guests. Tommy and O'Harris had rooms on the north side of the house, while Clara and Annie were opposite on the south. The rooms smelt freshly aired and the bed linen held a faint fragrance. Clara felt a little awkward walking in with her wet shoes.

Susan also showed them where the nearest bathroom was. It must have once been a bedroom, because no one made a bathroom that big on purpose. The bath sat slap bang in the middle of the room and a tall, wide window illuminated the space. There was a slight lack of privacy, Clara felt; anyone wandering past in the gardens could easily see a person in the bathroom. She opted to fill a jug from the tap with hot water and retreat to her room to wash and dry her feet. Her shoes, she concluded after she had stripped them off, might not be possible to salvage.

Dry-footed once again, the foursome headed back downstairs to see the rest of the family and make their presence known. Susan was waiting for them in the sitting room. Andrew Campbell had joined her. He looked as Clara remembered, handsome in a severe way, with a faint sneer always lurking on his lips. The war had damaged Andrew as it had damaged almost every man who had served. His damage was to his personality.

He nodded to them all as they entered.

"Susan was saying you had arrived. Was the journey all right?"

"My Labrador puppy gets seasick," Tommy declared. "But otherwise, it was a fine journey."

Andrew gave him a faint smile; it was not a common sight.

"Good to see you on two legs."

"It's good to be on them."

This gentle comment broke the ice and Andrew almost seemed to be warming to them, or at least as much as he was capable of warming to them. Andrew hid so much away behind mental walls, it was hard to know quite what was going on within him.

"Are you interested in this dig, Andrew?" Clara asked him politely.

"Not really," he shrugged. "I'm spending my time driving around, sightseeing. I bought a camera recently and I am trying it out on all the views."

"I imagine the landscape around here is quite magnificent," Captain O'Harris said. "Captain O'Harris, by the way."

He held out his hand for Andrew to shake.

"If you ever want to come for a ride, just ask," Andrew said amenably. "It's good to have company."

"Are your feet all right?" Susan turned to Clara.

"Better than I feared," Clara replied. "And the wellies are on standby for tomorrow. Now, you were going to tell us what that fuss was at the dig."

"Fuss?" Andrew asked casually.

"Mr Lethbridge turned up again," Susan sighed.

"That old eccentric? Why don't they get him banned from the area?"

"Professor Peabody thinks he is harmless, just a nuisance."

"Care to tell?" Tommy asked.

Susan shrugged.

"It is not terribly complicated. Mr Lethbridge is a self-taught archaeologist. His speciality is ancient folk carvings, like the Uffington White Horse, or the Cerne Abbas Giant."

"What are those?" Annie asked.

"They are enormous figures carved into hillsides, usually where there is chalk so that the figure stands out in white once the soil is removed. They have to be continuously re-cut to stop them disappearing again," Susan elaborated. "While some are thought to be relatively modern, others are believed to have been first carved in ancient times. We do not know their symbolism or purpose. They might have been the identification of the tribe or a tribute to a god."

"They are fascinating things, I can see why Lethbridge would be intrigued by them," Tommy said.

"Obsessed, more like," Andrew huffed.

"Mr Lethbridge has dedicated his academic career, if you can call it that, to seeking out these sorts of folk carvings that have been lost to time and nature. There is a theory, though not everyone agrees with it, that at one point there were hundreds of these carvings all across the British countryside, marking out boundary edges, perhaps, or indicating who ruled the territory. Only a handful have survived, the rest have disappeared beneath grass and trees, and in some cases houses and roads," Susan added. "Mr Lethbridge has written a dozen books on the subject. He has attempted to excavate these lost carvings in other places with debatable results."

"Is that why he is here?" Tommy asked.

"Exactly," Andrew replied. "He is convinced there are folk carvings hidden away in the meadow where they are digging. He is furious because he thinks the dig is destroying any chance he might have had of tracing those old carvings."

"You have to understand, if there were carvings, they would be the first ever to be discovered in Ireland," Susan said.

"Good money spinner for him," Andrew snorted. "Another book to write and lots of publicity."

"You are sceptical about the existence of these carvings," O'Harris had seemed to be only half-listening before, now he had his full attention on Andrew.

"I have read one of Lethbridge's books and his methods are so naïve as to almost be laughable. The man hammers iron rods into the ground until he hits hard soil. His theory is that in the areas where a figure was carved the soil will be less compacted and the iron rod will sink further before hitting hard soil. By this crude method he has plotted out suspected folk carvings."

"Surely his results could also just be a product of natural

geography?" O'Harris said.

"Precisely why few in the archaeology community take him seriously," Susan nodded. "A couple of years ago he actually invested time in a dig searching for a golden chariot supposedly buried beneath a hill in Cambridge. There was this local legend about it and Lethbridge decided it could be based on a true story."

"Did he find anything?" Tommy asked.

"Not even some old coins for his trouble," Susan shook her head. "But he writes well and even though the dig was a failure, people bought his book by the thousand."

"How come he has never dug up the meadow then, if he thinks there are carvings there?" Clara asked.

"The landowner wouldn't give him permission. He is a funny sort. Took a good deal of negotiating on the part of the university to persuade him to let us excavate here. He had no time for Lethbridge who is not backed by an institution and does not even have a degree," Susan looked relieved about this. "We have been very lucky. If Lethbridge had gone about that meadow in his usual fashion, we could have lost so much archaeology."

"Silly old coot is not thinking rationally," Andrew said with his familiar sneer. "Who would have carved anything in that meadow when it must have been a bog in the past?"

"I suppose he must have his reasons. He hasn't just picked the spot for nothing," Tommy frowned.

"Oh, it's the same as with the Cambridge dig," Susan said. "He came across a pamphlet in the British library printed sometime in the 1600s and recording a legend from this area that a wealth of gold was buried in the bog and a ghostly white horse would rise from the area where it was hidden. Lethbridge thinks the horse part is an analogy and that what was actually there was a carving in the ground to mark this as a sacred spot. The gold was part of the sacrificial offerings, rather than buried treasure. He is not so wrong about that either. We have been finding lots of small items, mostly bronze, but a couple are gold. They are bracelets, brooches, that sort of thing."

"No one with any sense believes the ghostly horse part, however," Andrew interjected.

"Professor Peabody thinks that is just a story put about to scare people away from the place and stop them looking for the gold."

"Considering what happened in that meadow, back when it was more of a bog, I am not so surprised that people might have thought of it as a bad place, cursed or haunted. Thinking of the poor souls killed and dumped there, for what purpose, we are not sure," Clara mused. "I think any normal person would gladly avoid it."

"Well, that is the saga of Lethbridge," Susan leaned back against the tall arm of the sofa. "He is harmless, just a nuisance really."

"What did you think of the dig site?" Andrew asked them. "Aside from the mud, obviously."

"It intrigues me," Clara confessed. "It appears that a body has been discovered."

"Peabody will be happy," Andrew chortled. "Broken swords and old coins are all very well, but what a fellow needs to make his academic name is a body."

Susan slapped him playfully on the arm. He grinned at her and Clara was warmed to see this unabashed teasing between them. Andrew had been so repressed, so withdrawn after the war. At last, he seemed to be coming out of that.

"What about trench three?" Andrew asked his sister. "Found anything yet or is it still a fool's errand to keep you out of mischief."

Susan rolled her eyes.

"Not all trenches can throw up wonders. Archaeology is as full of disappointments as it is triumphs."

"Meaning you haven't found a thing?"

"Howard Carter had several seasons finding barely anything and nearly gave up before the discovery of Tutankhamun's tomb."

"As long as you don't go bringing a curse down on us all."

Susan waved a hand dismissively at him.

"There is no curse of Tutankhamun. Just people enjoying a good story too much."

"As you say," Andrew smirked.

"Where are the others?" Tommy asked when the conversation lulled.

"Father and Glory went out for a long ramble," Andrew answered. "Father's doctor is rather insisting he take some exercise. Says he needs to lose weight too. It's really upset the old man. Glory thinks getting him out in the fresh air will do him good. Peg went off into town, don't know what she is up to and she certainly won't tell me unless she wishes to. She hasn't been herself lately."

"Oh dear," Clara said sympathetically.

"Peg is just feeling a little lost," Susan corrected her brother. "I remember how that feels. She is not sure where her life is going. For a short while she seemed to have found her path, she became involved with a lot of charity work after…"

Susan found her words drying up. She did not want to mention her Uncle Eustace's death. She quickly skirted around the issue.

"She was doing all sorts of fundraising, was out every day at meetings or helping to make things for good causes. She seemed happy. Then it all fizzled out."

"We are all rather lost sheep in this family," Andrew said. "None of us have made our way in the world, except Susan who is now trying to do so. I am trying to pursue my racing, but it's still early days for the sport in England. A lot of racetracks have been abandoned because of the war. Anyway, I rather feel I am doing that just to pass the time."

"That's rather gloomy, old man," Tommy said softly.

Andrew shrugged.

"It's honest, that's all."

The happy conversation had grown sombre and everyone found themselves falling silent. Andrew had sunk into himself again, and the news about Peg made them feel solemn. It was a great relief when they heard the front door open and someone hurry in. There was a scurry of small footsteps.

"Austin!" Susan cried out in delight.

Chapter Five

Little Austin was a precocious child with his mother's looks and, presumably, his father's personality. He certainly did not act like Susan who had always been a bit shy and reserved. Austin was outgoing, bubbly and, above all as Clara later reflected to herself, spoilt. Austin had been overindulged by his doting step-grandmother Glorianna. Though she had initially been horrified at the news her stepdaughter was pregnant outside of wedlock, she had rapidly come around to the idea and had stepped into the role of pandering, pampering grandparent with remarkable ease.

Whatever Austin wanted he got, and Clara found herself, much to her shame, disliking the small boy who wailed or made demands in equal turns to get what he wanted. Five minutes into the child's arrival he had grabbed Bramble's tail and yanked hard before Tommy could intervene. Austin came perilously close to being bitten, which would have served him right, Clara considered, but would have got Bramble into a lot of trouble.

Bramble was rescued. Austin wailed at losing his new plaything. Glorianna tried to suggest Tommy let the boy play with Bramble or, worse, young Pip and things looked likely to get very heated very rapidly. Clara declared the dogs needed a walk before their dinner and they extracted themselves as politely as they could.

"What a ghastly child," Annie said the moment they were outside in the cottage garden. "They have utterly ruined him, and he isn't even three yet."

Tommy was still fussing over Bramble, who he was carrying in his arms as if he would never let him down on the ground again. The poodle looked less perturbed by his misadventure.

"My Auntie Flo would have whipped me if I had done something like that to an animal," Captain O'Harris said. "Children these days."

They all made murmurs that indicated that children were much more disagreeable nowadays than they had been when they were children themselves.

They were coming around the corner of the cottage, Pip gambolling across the lawn when they saw someone approaching them.

"Who is that fellow?" O'Harris asked. "Another of the family?"

"That would be Peg," Tommy remarked. "I did say she can take you by surprise."

Peg had lost her fiancé during the war. How much bearing that had on her transformation was hard to tell. Clara suspected there had always been something of the rebel within Peg, even when she still wore dresses. These days she cut her hair short and styled like a man's. She wore trousers and a shirt and had even managed to develop a male swagger as she walked.

Clara was vaguely aware that some women felt more comfortable portraying themselves as men. She was also familiar with women loving other women, living together as if they were husband and wife. It was not something you talked about, but there were some ladies in Brighton who lived unconventionally, though very discreetly. People mostly turned a blind eye.

Whether Peg was inclined towards her own sex in that way Clara was not sure and felt it was not her business to ask.

"Hello all," Peg said, looking rather glum as she made her way towards them. "Are the old folks back?"

"If you mean Glorianna, she has just arrived with young Austin," Tommy said.

"Ah, you have met our household imp, have you?"

"Briefly," Clara said tellingly.

Peg grinned.

"He is somewhat of a horror. Actually, he is not so bad when Glorianna is not present. He plays up for her. But then most of the time she is around, so that does not really help," Peg shrugged. "Who is this?"

"Captain O'Harris, may I introduce my cousin Peg," Clara said.

O'Harris held out his hand for her to shake and Peg's smile broadened.

"Oh yes, I like him!"

"What have you been up to?" Tommy asked Peg, he had always been fond of his masculine cousin, even after he discovered she had been poisoning her uncle.

"Wandering the hills," Peg shrugged. "This place is so dull, Tommy, I quite despair. I thought a little break away would do me good. I feel so strung out most of the time. I reasoned a bit of peace and quiet would help. Instead, out here with all this solitude my thoughts seem even louder."

Peg looked wistfully across the garden.

"I have hiked all the routes I can find. Been to every town and village, most are not worth the visit, I might add. Now I am worried I might actually have to spend some time without distractions, which seems to me a terrible thing, indeed."

"Not interested in the dig?" Tommy asked.

"Oh no, too many dead people. Too much mud. It makes me shudder," Peg wrapped her hands around her arms as if a physical chill had come over her.

"Still, it is good Susan has found something she enjoys at last," Clara said.

"No doubt about that," Peg agreed hastily. "I am very glad for her. She gave us quite a scare back when we last saw each other. I am happy that she has found something she can be passionate about."

"What about you, Peg? Have you not found something to be passionate about?" Tommy asked.

Peg shrugged.

"I think I keep looking in the wrong place."

They were strolling back to the front of the cottage, from here they could see they were atop a slight hill and the fields fell away before them. In the distance was just visible the cream square that indicated where the tent at the dig site stood.

"Why did you come?" Peg asked abruptly as they found themselves at the door of the cottage.

Clara looked surprised.

"We were invited."

"You could have turned it down, you have before."

"Well, we needed a break, and, I suppose, I was curious."

Peg turned her head in the direction of the dig site.

"Have you met Jason?"

"Susan introduced us," Clara replied. "I sensed there was something between them."

"Oh yes, she likes him a lot. Wouldn't surprise me if she married him and went to America, you know," Peg tipped her head on one side thoughtfully. "Would do Austin good to get out of his grandmother's shadow if that occurred. Did you also meet Rufus?"

"Sort of," Tommy said cautiously.

Peg laughed.

"Rude and brusque, isn't he? I rather like him."

They were distracted by O'Harris.

"Is that Professor Peabody?"

The professor was stumbling up the drive, looking fraught.

"His head is bleeding!" Annie declared.

As a group they rushed towards him and met him halfway. He came to a swaying halt and O'Harris took his arm firmly to stop him falling over.

"What has happened?" Clara asked him.

Peabody grimaced and touched gingerly at his head.

"I fell into a trench," he said. "Smacked my head on a trowel edge."

"We need to get you looked at immediately," Clara started to take his arm to lead him inside. He resisted.

"No time. I need help securing the dig site. Came here because Susan is the closest…" he sagged on his feet and barely remained upright.

"You really need to sit down," O'Harris commanded.

"I need people to secure the dig site!" Peabody persisted doggedly. "Lethbridge has been there, rifling through things. I don't trust him!"

"All right, look, I shall fetch Susan and we shall go down to the site and check everything is where it should be," Clara told him.

"Thank you," Peabody said weakly.

"We can look after him," Annie said, nudging O'Harris away so she could take Peabody's arm. "If there is trouble, its best you have Tommy and O'Harris with you."

"Who did you mean by 'we'?" Peg asked suspiciously.

Annie gave her a pointed look.

"Yes, that's what I thought."

Clara hastened indoors and found Susan still in the sitting room.

"There has been some bother at the dig site. Professor Peabody is here. He wants us to go to the dig site and make sure it is all safe."

Susan jumped up in alarm.

"Is the professor all right?"

"He has fallen and cut his head," Clara said.

Behind her, in the front hall, Peabody was being carefully escorted towards the kitchen where his injury could be treated. Susan's mouth opened, but the next moment she realised it was time to be pragmatic rather than to ask lots of questions.

"We should take torches, it is getting dark," she said heading into the hall and grabbing her coat. "Did he say what sort of bother?"

"He mentioned Lethbridge," Clara replied.

"Great," Susan sighed. "That man is a dreadful nuisance."

"I think I ought to come too," Andrew said. "Just in case."

No one argued and shortly they were on the drive and hurrying towards the dig site.

Everything seemed peaceful when they arrived. Susan went straight to the tent first and stepped inside to see if anything had been taken or damaged. As far as she could tell everything was where it should be. Professor Peabody's thick book of notes was still sitting on the table where he had left it and all the artefacts appeared to be present and correct. If Lethbridge had come to cause trouble, it was at least not in the field tent.

They moved on to the trenches, which had been covered by oilcloth to protect them from any overnight rain. Susan pulled back the cloths one by one, revealing the trenches exactly as they had been left. In trench three they noticed a trowel that had been recently wrenched from the soil. It was easy to conclude this was the sharp object Peabody had cut his head open on.

"There is nothing here," Susan said with relief once their search was concluded. "We should go back to the house."

She had flicked on her torch, now evening had fallen. The muddy dig site was full of hidden dips you could wring an ankle in if you were not careful. Susan flashed her torch across the site and for a moment they were all sure they saw a figure, but the next instant it was gone.

"Probably the shadows of a tree," Tommy said.

"What if this Lethbridge fellow is just hanging around waiting for us to leave?" O'Harris countered. "He looked the sort."

"Would he cause damage to the dig site?" Clara asked Susan.

"I don't know," she replied. "He seems a little mad."

She cast her torch beam across the meadow again. There was no sign of anyone.

"I don't feel like I can just leave the site unguarded," Susan added. "I would never forgive myself if something were to happen."

They were all feeling worried now. Lethbridge had seemed just the right combination of instability and righteous indignation to do something terrible, such as destroy the dig site, or at least all the finds. It seemed wrong to leave them unguarded.

"How about this," O'Harris said. "Susan and Clara go back to the cottage and see Professor Peabody. Tommy and I will stay here and keep a watch on things. Once Peabody has been informed, he shall have to take responsibility for having a guard placed on the site."

Clara was torn, she wanted to speak to the professor, find out exactly what had happened, but she also wanted to remain at the dig site and act as a watchdog. She also didn't like to think she was being sent out of harm's way by O'Harris. She was as tough as any of them, and they knew it.

"I'm not sure I should go," Susan said. "It feels wrong for me to leave."

"Someone has to inform the professor of all this," Tommy reminded her.

Susan did not budge. Clara gave a sigh.

"You three remain here, I shall go up to the cottage," she said at last.

O'Harris looked horrified.

"Alone?"

"What precisely is going to happen to me?" Clara said. "Lethbridge is interested in this dig site, not in me. It is only a mile, you will be able to see my torch glow all the way."

Reluctantly, O'Harris agreed. It seemed the dig site was more in danger than Clara and he should stay here and keep an eye on things.

"You could take Bramble, he will bark at strangers," Tommy offered.

Clara looked at the poodle who was sitting at Tommy's feet.

"I shall be just fine," she said.

Then she walked away, using her torchlight to find the road. She was wondering if Lethbridge had come to sabotage things, or to talk with Peabody. Had their talk turned into an argument? Had Peabody really just fallen into a trench, or had he been pushed?

All this over a boggy meadow, Clara reflected. Well, it wasn't really a boggy meadow. It was a symbol of a person's career and future prospects. Lethbridge and Peabody were both fighting over it because it could be a turning point in their careers. Lethbridge might be eccentric, but he was also acutely aware of when a situation could be turned to his advantage. If he had found the first folk carvings in Ireland, he would be a hero of the archaeology world.

Well, maybe...

There was no one on the road, no one in the fields. Most people were already home, sitting around their fires, eating and drinking and contemplating what tomorrow might bring. Only crazy archaeologists and interfering Englishwomen were out on a cold night like this.

Clara headed up the drive. For a brief instant she felt as if she was being followed. She spun and shone her torch across the drive. It had a powerful beam and illuminated the dainty rose bushes several feet away. There was no one else. Clara was pretty certain she was getting jumpy now.

She turned back to the house, the sensation of eyes piercing into her back refusing to fade.

She was drawing close to the door, thinking she would be glad to get back inside, when someone stepped from the shadows. In her surprise Clara came close to throwing her torch at the new arrival. The person held up their hands.

"It's me, Lethbridge."

Clara groaned.

"What do you want?"

"Is he all right?" Lethbridge asked. "Professor Peabody?"

"Did you push him?"

"No! We were arguing, he went to walk off and he caught his foot and fell into a trench. He screamed blue murder at me when I tried to help and he shouted I should clear off, so I did."

"Seems to me you have caused a fair bit of bother," Clara said folding her arms across her chest.

"I never meant anyone any harm. Might I see Peabody to apologise?"

Clara considered this for a moment.

"You best come round the back," she said.

"Thank you," Lethbridge said gratefully.

Chapter Six

Professor Peabody was less than pleased to see Lethbridge. He had a cloth pressed to his forehead, while Annie was trying to locate an ice pack to soothe the bruising.

"What is he doing here?"

"Be nice," Clara scolded him. "He is here to apologise."

Lethbridge certainly looked remorseful. He was holding his hat in his hands, wringing the brim in a way that was likely to leave it permanently misshapen.

"I am very sorry for what occurred," Lethbridge said. "I feel awful that you were injured."

"Yeah, well, it only hurts all the time, so..." Peabody grumbled under his breath. "What were you doing at the site anyway?"

"I wanted to see if you had interfered with the area I suspect my white horse to be in," Lethbridge said with an air of hurt pride. "I found that site first, you know."

"I rather think it could be argued the peat diggers found the site first," Clara remarked.

Lethbridge cast her a dirty look.

"I've told you already Lethbridge, there is no chalk beneath the ground, or even sand that could be used to make a carving. The land is so wet, all you get when you dig is water," Peabody puttered.

"That, dear boy, is the point. I do not believe the horse was defined by chalk as is the case with the white horses and giants in England. I believe they cut the outline of its body to be filled with water! It would glisten in the sunlight, ripple with the wind, freeze icy white in winter! Imagine it."

Lethbridge's eyes had grown glossy as he envisioned this, it was clearly something he had spent a lot of time dreaming about.

"Why all this fuss about horses carved in grass?" Annie said looking fed up with the whole notion. She had failed to find ice but had a suitably soaked wet cloth to hopefully achieve the same effect. She handed it to Lethbridge.

"Have you never heard of the Uffington White Horse, Annie?" Clara asked her.

"Sounds like a pub," Annie said with a tut.

"The Uffington White Horse, dear lady, was etched into the earth centuries ago by our distant ancestors," Lethbridge said, rather elated to have someone he could educate on the subject, most people ignored him the second he began to talk. "A long time ago, people took up the top layer of the soil on a hill to reveal the white chalk beneath. They cut away the turf in a careful pattern to create a stylised outline of a running horse. It is a truly remarkable example of ancient art. How did they work out the pattern, for instance, when the horse can only be properly seen from a distance or when atop something tall? Why did they do it is another question we all ponder. But the most amazing thing is that over the intervening centuries, though people forgot the purpose of the horse, they continued to recut it again and again. There have been some adjustments to the lines in the process, but the overall horse would be familiar to our ancestors."

"Archaeologists believe there were other similar figures," Peabody added, to balance out Lethbridge's bubbling enthusiasm. "They have been lost to time, the grass growing back over them. Rediscovering them is near

A Body Out of Time

impossible."

"Unless you have my techniques, which I have perfected over many years," Lethbridge said stoutly.

Peabody did not look impressed, but he bit his tongue.

"Are they all horses?" Annie asked.

"Horses seem to be the main focus for the carvings," Lethbridge nodded. "Certainly, there are more horses than anything else. Again, we do not know why, though it is possible the horse symbolised a goddess or nature spirit our ancestors were fond of. It might also be a case that only the horses have survived, other symbols were perhaps a little too earthy for our prudish forebears. Take the Cerne Abbas Giant, for instance."

"What about him?" Annie asked innocently.

"I am not sure Annie would be interested in him," Clara tried to interrupt.

"The Giant is either a god or maybe a Wildman, we don't know. He is standing up, waving a huge club and is utterly naked. He also appears to be rather excited by everything," Lethbridge explained with surprising tact.

"Excited?" Annie said. "Why should that trouble me Clara Fitzgerald?"

Clara was starting to go red.

"We must assume he was a fertility symbol, considering his phallic depiction," Lethbridge was saying thoughtfully. "It is really quite amazing our Victorian ancestors never gave him a fig leaf or something, considering how enormous his erectio…"

Clara gave a sharp cough, duly interrupting Lethbridge before he revealed all the Giant's secrets to Annie.

"It was most kind of you to drop by Mr Lethbridge," she rose. "But it is getting late and we must see Professor Peabody home."

"Oh," Lethbridge glanced at the injured man. "Of course. Once again, my full apologies, it was never my intention for such a thing to happen. If we could only work together…"

"I'll think about it," Peabody said in the sort of voice

that indicated he had no intention of doing anything of the sort.

Clara saw Lethbridge out and waved him off. The man seemed harmless, if eccentric, she didn't think he would cause any damage to the dig site. When she went back in the cottage, Peabody was getting himself together to go on his way.

"Thank you for your assistance," he told Clara.

"Captain O'Harris has remained at the dig site to ensure no one disturbs it," she replied.

"Once I am back at my accommodation, I shall send Rufus to take over. We shall have to arrange a watch system," Peabody scratched his chin.

"Not that I think Lethbridge is a danger to the site," Clara added swiftly.

"Maybe not," Peabody said. "Thank you again."

He departed looking rather jaded. Annie sighed as he left.

"Men do make such fuss over silly things," she said. "Why would there be a horse underwater, anyway?"

"I don't think that was quite Mr Lethbridge's point."

"That's what it sounded like to me," Annie huffed. "Oh dear, I hope Tommy and O'Harris are able to get back for dinner!"

As it happened, both men were safely back at the cottage in time to settle down to a pleasant meal of Beef Wellington. It was the first occasion since Clara's arrival that the entire Campbell family had been present together, excluding young Austin, who had been sent off to bed with his nanny, much to the guests' relief.

Hogarth had finally appeared, having spent a pleasant morning trout fishing. He had caught absolutely nothing and that was precisely how he liked his fishing. Catching things spoiled the whole process of sitting quietly with nothing to do. Clara was pleased to see he looked fit and well. After his brother's fatal heart attack, Glorianna had undertaken the task of keeping Hogarth in tip-top shape. She watched his diet, had him take regular exercise and was encouraging him to switch tobacco brands to one she had seen that was supposed to promote good health. Hogarth seemed happy to indulge his wife's concerns and it was noticeable that he had lost weight and toned up as a result.

"I am so glad you could all come," Hogarth said as they tucked into a feast fit for kings. "We are really making a holiday of everything. Susan has her archaeology, Peg is developing a passion for hiking, Andrew is sightseeing in the car and Glorianna and I are just enjoying relaxing. It is so nice to have everyone together and happy."

Hogarth had a remarkable ability to completely fail to see when other members of his family were not as content as he was. In this instance, he was sure Andrew and Peg were enjoying themselves as much as him. Since neither sibling seemed inclined to discourage this thinking, Clara said nothing.

"I am thinking of sponsoring a museum wing, or something, for Susan's finds," Hogarth added. "The Campbell Collection."

"Father, you know the university secures all the finds," Susan told him lightly.

"Well, I expect you to get credit," Hogarth said firmly. "You are doing remarkable things. Up to your knees in mud, scraping around on the ground. It isn't everyday a Campbell becomes an archaeologist."

"I just wish it was not so messy an occupation," Glorianna said weakly.

Everyone ignored her.

"This is a team effort," Susan told her father gently. "But I am sure my name shall get a mention in the dig reports."

"I should hope so!" Hogarth said with that air of self-assurance and pride only those who are very rich and very secure in the knowledge that they are rich can muster.

Clara picked politely at her Beef Wellington. Annie was observing it with a look of silent horror. The meat was pink inside, extremely pink. Only the outside was brown. Annie had not said anything as no one else seemed to be bothered, but she was quietly appalled that cook would allow raw meat onto the table.

"What are your plans for this holiday?" Hogarth asked Clara.

"A bit of walking, a bit of sightseeing," Clara shrugged. "And keeping an eye on the dig, that looks very interesting."

"Did I tell you we think we have found a body, Father?" Susan spoke up.

"Oh, how horrible," Glorianna winced.

"A very ancient body," Hogarth consoled her.

"But if it is like the other ones, well, it is all so ghastly!"

"Other ones?" Clara asked.

"Six bodies have been pulled out of the bog," Susan informed her. "There may have been more than that, but no one reported them. Not all of the bodies are complete. Mostly we either get legs or torsos."

"Oh dear," Glorianna said, having gone distinctly pale.

"That is a lot of bodies," Tommy said.

"It is. This area must have been very significant. And the bodies have been dated to various time periods. The oldest was almost certainly put there in the bronze age, but we have a torso we believe is from the seventeenth century. Most likely he was a victim of crime. Someone robbed him, killed him and shoved him in the bog thinking he would never be found."

"But the others were not so secretly buried?" Clara asked.

"No," Susan nodded. "Of course, we are not sure precisely what happened to them. Professor Peabody believes they were sacrificial victims, ceremonially killed and buried to appease some god or gods. Jason, however, is more inclined to the theory they were criminals who were elaborately executed for their crimes. I, personally, think there could be a third variation where the victims are both executed criminals and human sacrifices. After all, why kill a productive member of the tribe when there is a man facing death anyway?"

"Can we talk about something less horrible?" Glorianna begged.

Though Susan thought little of her stepmother, she was kind enough to agree to drop the subject of human sacrifices at the dinner table.

"What I am curious about is why Lethbridge thinks there was a horse carving here," Tommy interjected. "I mean, from how you described it to me Clara, it sounds like it was some sort of primitive water feature, like those ornamental ponds people dig in unusual shapes."

"The celts, who were the ancestors of the Irish and who many around here still identify with strongly, had a strong horse culture," Susan elaborated. "We don't know anything for certain, because nothing was written down until much later, but we think they may have believed in a horse goddess called Epona. We only know about her through the Romans, who adopted her into their own pantheon of gods. The only Celtic deity they adopted, in fact.

"She was the protector of horses, ponies, donkeys and mules, as well as being a fertility goddess. We do not know a lot about her worship in the British Isles. Some say the Uffington White Horse was associated with her. We know the horse was incredibly significant in Ireland and associated with kingship.

"Considering the significance some give to the Uffington horse and other horse carvings in England, there is a strain of scholarly thought that there should be a similar thing in Ireland. That is what Lethbridge certainly believes and it has become a quest for him to find the remains of an Epona folk carving like those in England, here in Ireland."

"Sounds like he could be onto a wild goose chase," Clara reflected. "Considering what Professor Peabody said about the soil hereabouts."

"It is true the soil has to be a certain type to make carving into it worthwhile," Susan agreed. "Chalk is obviously the best as it is so vivid when exposed. But I have heard rumours of horses carved into other soils."

"But this mad idea about a water horse," Tommy said, "where has that come from?"

"Ah, well I can answer that, and I am not an archaeologist," Hogarth said gleefully. "You see, there is a little-known legend in this area that once, a very long time ago, a fairy, or maybe she was a pixie, was lured from the waters of the bog by a handsome man. He convinced her to marry him, but on the condition that should he strike her three times, she would return to the bog she came from.

"All was happy for a while, but then they had an argument one day and the husband lashed out and slapped her. That was the first blow. Sometime later, he was saddling his horse, swung around with the bridle and caught his wife in the face with the reins. That was blow two."

Hogarth was counting them off on his fingers as he spoke.

"Lastly, the husband grew drunk one night and started to brawl with other men, his wife tried to drag him away and he accidentally hit her. That was the third blow. A terrible wind whipped around them all and the woman transformed into a white horse and galloped all the way to the bog from which she had first come and vanished within. Her husband tried to summon her back every day after until his death. Some say she was the goddess Epona, and the story is an allegory of kingship and needing the goddess' favour to rule successfully."

"And because of that Lethbridge thinks there is a horse carving in the bog?" Tommy said, astonished, but not that astonished.

"He dug up a hill in Cambridge because of a legend about a golden chariot," Susan reminded them with a shrug. "He has explored other sites in Ireland, but this one holds his attention, I guess because of the bog bodies. He desperately wants to look for his white horse there."

"And instead, Professor Peabody gets to excavate the bog," Clara said thoughtfully.

"Well yes," Susan replied. "I suppose we can all see why he is upset, can't we?"

Chapter Seven

The next morning dawned with glorious sunshine. The sort of fragile sunshine you sometimes get in spring, which is very white and glaring, and altogether too fleeting. The Campbells came together as a family to have breakfast, it was rather like dinner to them, an occasion to be with each other, to discuss the day ahead, all before they departed on their own separate ventures.

Naturally, Clara's party was invited to join them. Breakfast was served at eight, as Susan was going to rush down to the dig site as soon as she was done. This did not suit everyone, Peg, in particular, was not an early bird and endured the early breakfast hour out of dedication to her sister.

"Back home we don't do this," she confided to Tommy over eggs and bacon, waving a fork at the table. "Honestly, half the time Andrew doesn't turn up for dinner even. This is all for the sake of the holiday. We still remain terribly dysfunctional."

Tommy did not know how to reply to that, so he merely nodded and smiled.

Suitably booted up, now they were familiar with Irish mud, Clara, Tommy, O'Harris and Annie followed Susan

A Body Out of Time

down towards the dig site. Pip and Bramble bumbled along with them, happy to be out on a fine day. There was not a cloud in the sky, which Clara considered remarkable for the time of year. It was promising to be a good day.

"Of course, trench three is just to keep us busy," Susan said as they walked. "Everyone really wants to be on the body in trench two, but Professor Peabody won't let any of us second year students touch it, in case we make a dreadful mistake. Rufus is very hot under the collar about it."

"Rufus struck me as someone who can be very hot under the collar about anything," Clara remarked.

"Well, yes," Susan said, trying not to smile.

"And what about Jason? I hear talk you are quite enamoured with him," Clara asked.

"I can't think what you mean. He is very nice, but I am I already told you I am in no rush," Susan said innocently, though she went red in the face. "Oh look, bluebells!"

She briskly walked towards a clump of blue flowers as if they were the most fascinating thing in the world. Tommy gave his sister a nudge.

"Hardly subtle!" he scolded her, teasingly.

Clara raised an eyebrow at him.

"Wasn't meant to be," she replied.

When they reached the dig site it was already a hive of activity. Archaeologists, Clara observed, were early birds. Jason and Rufus were in trench three, trying to look as enthused as it was possible to be when forced to dig up a load of barren earth for the sake of having something to do. Every now and then they cast envious glances at trench two. In fact, everyone was constantly casting surreptitious looks that way. It seemed progress was being made, for Professor Peabody was sitting on a camp stool at the side of the trench, his attention rivetted on the excavation.

"I better join Rufus and Jason," Susan said to the others and drifted away.

Annie squelched her feet on the boggy ground and sighed to herself. Clara elbowed Tommy. He looked up and recognised the situation. Poor Annie who had no interest in old bones, especially old bones sitting in mud, had been very forbearing about the whole excavation and had even restrained herself from saying anything about her ruined shoes. She deserved a bit of consideration.

"I say Annie, why don't we go for a walk into town?" Tommy suggested. "See if we find a bakery or something where you can ask about traditional Irish recipes."

Annie brightened up.

"Don't you want to see them dig up that body?" she waved her hand in the direction of trench two.

"It isn't going anywhere, is it? Been there several centuries already. I think it can wait until we have been into town."

Annie's smile broadened and she headed off with Tommy much happier already.

"You'll be eating soda bread for life once she has the recipe," O'Harris grinned at Clara.

"I might quite like soda bread, can't say I have ever tasted it," Clara replied lightly. "Are you happy to stay, or would you prefer we go for a walk ourselves?"

O'Harris pulled a serious face.

"If you don't mind Clara, I would much prefer to see the emergence of a bog body," he said, as if this was liable to cause Clara great consternation.

"You are terrible," Clara snorted. "I half want to say we should go for a walk just to repay you for that."

"And miss out on this?"

Clara gave a small huff.

"Am I developing a reputation for being obsessed with corpses?"

"I think that is a foregone conclusion," O'Harris said.

"At least this one doesn't need a detective," Clara retorted. "His murderers being long dead and out of the way themselves."

"I am sure that makes him feel better."

They walked over to the trench still talking in the light-hearted teasing way people who are very fond of one another do. They became silent at the sight of the body in the pit as it was slowly exposed. Yesterday it had looked as if a corner of a leather bag was sticking out of the mud and it was difficult to say what part of a person the object being excavated was, or even if it was a person. Archaeologists were better at these things than those not experienced at finding remains but even Peabody and his team would have had a hard time the day before saying what precisely they were digging up.

The situation that morning was becoming clearer. With great patience the team in trench two had pulled the soil further and further away to reveal the torso of the person. It was now obvious the victim of the bog was lying on his right side. They could see his left shoulder and all the way down his arm to the left elbow, which was bent, the arm being held close to the body. The left hip had also been exposed and the left thigh. The head, however, was still too deep down to be seen, except for where the neck snaked into the ground. Considering the speed the team was now operating, though still with great care, it should not be much longer before the body was fully exposed.

Peabody looked up at Clara and O'Harris as they drew closer.

"This is what I was hoping for," he said, gesturing at the corpse. "You can never be sure, you know. They say bodies have been found in the bog, and I have seen examples of parts of them preserved in other museums. But you think to yourself, what if all the bodies have been found? What if they are no more?"

Peabody lowered his voice.

"Quite frankly, I was slightly concerned all the trenches might turn out to be as barren as number three."

Clara twisted her head to look over at the failed trench, where Susan and the other students were diligently aerating the mud for the sake of thoroughness.

"I've never seen anything like this," O'Harris had crouched down and was staring into the trench. "I have tried to picture it. Best I could do was conjure up the muddy corpses I saw on the battlefields during the war.

This is very different."

He leaned further into the trench.

"It looks like he just laid down and went to sleep. Is that cloth around his chest?"

"We believe so. Some sort of fine linen," Peabody nodded. "More usually we find them naked. We don't know if this was how they were when they were dispatched, or whether the same waters that preserve flesh destroy clothing. The discovery of cloth on this body indicates we shall have to revise our thoughts on the subject."

"He is dreadfully thin," O'Harris added.

"That is the effect of the mummifying process," Peabody hastened to add. "It sucks out all the moisture from the body, so the skin sinks back onto the bones. It really is a fascinating process."

"Can you tell how he died?" Clara asked, she was finding it hard to separate the man from the historical artefact. She kept staring at the corpse and wondering what his last moments were like. How frightened had he been? Or had he accepted his fate? Was it a swift departure from this life, or full of torment? All those centuries in the ground and Clara could still feel empathy for him.

"Hopkins, can you explain your theory again about the way the fellow died?" Peabody called out to a man in the trench.

Hopkins was a man in his thirties with a bristly beard and very thick glasses. He had been in the process of excavating a foot, now he paused and looked up.

"It is too early to say for certain," he placed an instant caveat on his statement, "but there is a gash on his side that could have been from a knife. Of course, it might also be from a peat shovel. We shan't know for sure until we can take a proper look."

"Stabbing is not as common a method of disposal for these victims," Peabody added. "Usually they are either throttled to death or their throats slit. I read about one bog body where both legs had been broken to prevent the victim trying to run away."

Clara winced. Distance of time did not make such news any easier to swallow. It might have all happened centuries ago, but at some point someone had suffered.

"This fellow has no broken bones," Hopkins said with a quick glance up.

"At least that is something," Clara said.

Peabody was about to speak again when he spied something in the distance. His good mood evaporated at once.

"Why is he back?"

Clara looked up and saw Mr Lethbridge lurking around a distant hedge. For once he did not seem in a rush to come closer.

"Maybe, when you are finished, you could let him have a little look for his missing horse," Clara said in a whisper to the professor.

"Do you say that in seriousness?" Peabody looked appalled. "The man's a complete idiot."

"Misguided, perhaps, but that does not mean he should be denied compassion."

Peabody did not look impressed.

"Think about it," Clara suggested.

Peabody gave a long groan, then he came to a surprising decision. He stood up and walked over to Lethbridge. The eccentric academic did not know whether to run or not as he was approached by his rival. Peabody spoke quietly and Lethbridge noticeably relaxed. After a moment he hopped the hedge and followed the professor back to the trench. He peered in with eager curiosity.

"Well, well, another sacrifice to Epona!" he declared, for Lethbridge was, if nothing else, dedicated to an idea.

Peabody started to mutter something then caught Clara's eye. He had the victory here; it was the right time to be gracious.

"A sacrifice to something," he admitted.

By now the trench was drawing everyone's attention and slowly but surely, the other diggers abandoned their own excavations to witness the revealing of the body.

Peabody had his sketchbook out and was drawing a detailed image of the discovery. He was a skilled draughtsman, Clara observed.

Hopkins had exposed most of the legs and feet. His colleague was still attempting to find the head.

"What if it doesn't have a head?" Susan declared.

Peabody was so struck by this idea he paused in his sketching.

"A decapitation," he said dreamily, as if this was a very romantic notion.

At that moment, the archaeologist in the trench gave a grunt of triumph.

"I've found his chin!"

Slowly a face was revealed. The head was rather round, and the features looked older than Clara had expected, though that might have been a product of the mummification. The eyes appeared tightly shut and the mouth pulled into a grimace. It was not a peaceful, slumbering face. It was the face of someone who had gone to their death unwillingly.

"Is there rope or cord around the neck?" Peabody asked eagerly.

"No," Hopkins said, now assisting in the excavation of the head.

"Oh," Peabody looked disappointed. "There are usually the remains of a cord used to garrot the victim somewhere about. Sometimes it is still knotted at the back of the neck."

Clara felt that was a small mercy for the poor man in the trench. Imagine being throttled and stabbed? How horrid!

The head was now completely visible, and it had a worryingly 'alive' feel to it. Though blackened by the peaty soil, it still retained the roundness of life, and the expression on the face added to the sense that the man could wake up at any moment and demand to know what they were up to. It was safe to say they were all in awe.

Hopkins had begun working outwards from the neck in search of the victim's right arm, which was the only limb still to be discovered. He dug around the shoulder to find the upper arm and then followed its line through the soil. Instead of being bent into the chest, the right arm was flung up alongside the head, as if the poor man had been trying to save himself from the waters.

"Have you ever thought what our ancestors would think of us digging up these men?" Lethbridge said solemnly. "These sacrifices were meant to appease the gods by resting in these waters forever."

"Nothing is forever," Peabody said. "Anyway, forever is relative. They were probably only hoping to appease the gods long enough for their lifetime and maybe their children's."

"The gods appear to have been very fickle, considering the number of sacrifices dropped into bogs for them," O'Harris said. "You would start to get fed up about it."

"If they were sacrifices," Peabody said cautiously. "That is still up for debate."

Clara was watching Hopkins' trowel picking away soil with great concentration. The arm was nearly completely visible, he was now working on the forearm and the wrist. He flicked back dense soil with the tip of the blade, working with immense care. Clara saw something that made her frown.

"Did you see that?" she asked Hopkins.

He looked up at her with a hint of concern.

"What?" he said, but she had the impression he already knew and just didn't want to think about it.

"I saw what appeared to be a glint of sunlight hitting something reflective," Clara pointed to the wrist of the body.

Hopkins sucked in his lip.

"Yes, I saw that too."

He kept scraping away and the wrist emerged from the earth. He gently revealed the hand, which was clenched into a fist, then paused. He called out for someone to hand him some water and then poured it over the victim's wrist.

"Oh dear," he said, the colour draining from his face.

"What is it?" Peabody asked urgently.

It was Clara who replied.

"Your Bronze Age human sacrifice appears to be wearing a wristwatch."

Chapter Eight

They stared a long time at the corpse, no one touching it, all just frozen in shock. Then Peabody spoke up.

"It could be a Celtic bracelet?"

Hopkins gave him an odd look, then he scraped around the wrist ornament a little bit more, before sitting up and shaking his head.

"It is definitely a wristwatch."

That threw them all back into silence.

"The police shall have to be summoned," Clara said at last.

"Oh, no, no," Peabody said hastily. "They would trample all over the excavation site. They might tell us we have to stop altogether! I can't have the police here."

"A man is dead," Clara pointed out. "Murdered."

"Yes, but five minutes ago he was also dead and murdered, but because we thought he was over two thousand years old we weren't fretting about calling the police," Peabody retorted firmly.

"That is different," Clara answered, trying not to sigh at his stubbornness.

"Hardly," Peabody responded. "This fellow could have been in the ground years."

"Wristwatches have not been worn that long," O'Harris pointed out. "They became popular after the war."

"But some people were wearing them before the war," Peabody said, determined not to lose the argument.

"Well, we have to do something with him," Hopkins declared. "We can't just leave the poor fellow here."

"The police must be informed," Clara insisted. "This is a murder, and the murderer is likely still at large and should be caught."

"I've already had enough trouble here," Peabody snapped, his eyes briefly glancing at Lethbridge though he refrained from saying anything. "I don't need more with the police. Besides, what would the landowner think if the police came on his land after a body? He has been very sensitive about us digging here as it is. He shall have a fit if the police turn up."

"Do I keep excavating him?" Hopkins asked.

"Yes, keep at it Hopkins," Peabody called down. "Now, Miss Fitzgerald, I can see you have a bee in your bonnet, so I am making myself plain. Under no circumstances are you to go to the police and report what you have seen."

"That is a crime," Clara reminded him.

Peabody actually hesitated at this, and stared down into the ground forlornly, seeing all his hopes and dreams for making the discovery of the century, in Ireland at least, evaporating.

"I have a suggestion," Susan said, slightly tentatively at first. When everyone looked her way, she started to hesitate. Susan had never been big and bold, and though her newfound confidence was carrying her further these days than she had ever been, it still had its limits.

"What is it, Susan?" Peabody asked gently.

Susan cleared her throat awkwardly.

"It seems to me we can't avoid telling the police about this eventually," she said quickly before anyone could interrupt, "but we need not say anything just now. The poor man is not going anywhere, and he is so perfectly preserved that if we wait a week or so to tell the police, once the dig is finish, what harm will there be?"

Clara went to say something, but Susan hadn't finished.

"And, in the meantime, Clara could make some quiet enquiries regarding this man. She is a private detective, after all."

Peabody's attention swung back to Clara. He seemed to be looking at her properly for the first time.

"Why yes! That had quite slipped my mind! That settles it. You can investigate this matter while the dig carries on, as soon as we are finished the police shall be notified. Does that suit you Miss Fitzgerald? After all, this man has laid in the earth years waiting to be found, what will a few more days matter."

"And Clara is much better than the police," Susan added with familial pride.

"Excellent!" Peabody clapped his hands together and Clara knew she was defeated, for the moment. Not that she much liked it.

"Get him out of the ground, Hopkins," Peabody said to the fellow in the pit. "Then we shall put him in the finds tent. I shall have to clear a table."

It was at that moment Peabody remembered Lethbridge's presence. The eccentric academic had a strange, glazed look on his face. It was impossible to know what he was thinking, but his far-off expression suggested he was contemplating something.

"Lethbridge!" Peabody snapped.

Lethbridge blinked and looked at him.

"You understand we are not saying anything to the police just yet?" Peabody said to him in a very clear and loud voice.

Lethbridge gave him a peculiar smile.

"Of course."

Peabody did not look pleased.

"Remember Lethbridge, if the police stomp all over this place, the odds of you getting to excavate at some point are worse than pigs taking to the skies!"

"My odds are not precisely great at the moment,"

Lethbridge said, his grin looking more and more self-satisfied, the grin of a man who has just seen an advantage in a battle he has been badly losing. "Seems to me it would not make life any worse for me if I were to say something. Not when I have already been refused to dig at this site."

"Lethbridge…" Peabody pointed a finger at him, his temper rising.

"Of course," Lethbridge hastened to add, "we could come to an agreement. Something along the lines of letting me dig a few sample pits, hammer in a few test poles, that sort of thing."

Peabody's expression of fury and frustration had frozen on his face. Clara was sure she saw him twitch, as if his lips and eyes were linked to invisible strings, then he came to an inevitable decision.

"Fine, Lethbridge, let's talk about this in the tent," Peabody was not gracious in defeat, he sounded as if someone was pulling the words out through his gritted teeth. "Everyone get back to work!"

He waved his hands at his team and shooed them away like they were clucking hens. Lethbridge still had that alarming grin plastered on his face as he followed Peabody to his tent to discuss their new arrangement.

Hopkins gave a long sigh after they were gone, his relief palpable. Aside from his fellow digger, the only people left at the trench were O'Harris and Clara. Hopkins cracked his back, rolled his shoulders, and set to work excavating the body.

"Well?" O'Harris asked Clara.

She looked at him morosely.

"Well, what?"

"Are you going to do as he asks?"

Clara huffed.

"It goes against my better judgement, but I came here for Susan and if I ruin this dig for her, she shall be so upset," Clara glanced over at her cousin who seemed to have a renewed vigour for digging in barren trench three after the discovery of the murdered man. "She would understand, of course, but she would be so disappointed. And Peabody has a point. The second we go to the police this whole dig will be ruined."

"And the fellow has been down there a long time," O'Harris added. "Nothing is going to change in a week. Not as though you are going to find any fingerprints on him, or anything like that."

Clara stared into the pit. It went against the grain to delay reporting a murder, even if the delay was unlikely to do any harm.

"You know, in a quiet place like this, I don't suppose the police have much experience with murder," O'Harris continued. "You, on the other hand…"

"You are saying that even if the police were informed, they might not be of any use?" Clara asked him, wondering what Inspector Park-Coombs would say to such a thing.

"I mean they would probably have to send to a bigger town or city for detectives, maybe to Dublin. Now, if you could give them a head start, wouldn't that be good?"

Clara wanted to groan at him, but she didn't. It seemed everyone was against her going to the police immediately. She knew that not all police stations were manned with capable men such as Park-Coombs and in a remote location like this, where the population was scattered about so spartanly you could walk for a whole day and see no one, the chances of there being anyone sufficiently experienced to know how to deal with a murder were pretty slim. They police would need all the help they could get, in fact, they would likely need Clara, though whether they would be happy about that was another matter.

"A few more days," O'Harris added. "So, they can finish this dig."

"Is no one on my side?" Clara grumbled.

"We are being practical," O'Harris grinned. "Besides, has it not occurred to you that if the murderer was still in the area, he would have heard about this dig and attempted to prevent it to keep his crime hidden."

Clara had considered that, and it raised various

possibilities. It might be the killer was no longer living in these parts, maybe they had never lived here. It might be they had somehow missed the news of the dig, even though it was about the only interesting thing being discussed in the region. It had been a quiet winter and the only gossip was about this excavation. It could be the killer was dead also, in which case nothing could be done to bring them to justice. Lastly, it might be that someone had been influencing the landowner – the reason why he had refused Lethbridge access to the site – but had finally failed and conceded defeat, maybe hoping the body would be long decomposed or the archaeologists would not dig where it lay. Not everyone appreciated the peculiar preservative properties of the bog.

"First things first," she said, deciding to stop thinking about her forced agreement not to go to the police, she was already considering breaking her word, "we need to find out who this man was."

They looked into the trench, where the body was close to being freed from the soil.

"Apart from the watch, does he have any other personal items on him?" Clara asked Hopkins.

Hopkins had nearly removed all the soil around the man's wrist and hand and was working down his arm.

"I haven't seen anything else," he said.

"I think the clothes he is wearing are a pair of cotton pyjamas," the other digger in the grave said. "It is hard to say until we examine them properly, but that's what they remind me of."

"He died in his pyjamas," O'Harris said. "Possibly."

"Have you seen any wounds other than the cut in his side?" Clara asked the diggers.

"No, there is nothing around his head," Hopkins said. "At least from what I can see."

"Stabbed once and pushed into the bog?" O'Harris suggested.

"Or dumped here after he was dead," Clara replied. "I suppose it seemed a pretty good place to hide a body."

A Body Out of Time

"We have been monitoring this site for a few years, trying to get permission to dig here," Hopkins looked up from the trench. "Some years back there was a big flood, and this area was deep in water. Compared to now, it would have been more like a lake."

Clara looked across the muddy meadow. A drainage system had been dug to cause the water to run off, thus enabling the peat diggers to get to the rich earth easier. In the process, the bog had been transformed to more of a water meadow. It was still not somewhere you would walk if you could help it, maybe in the height of summer it was almost dry, but the rest of the year you were still ankle deep in water. The trenches had to be bailed out regularly, trench two even had a hand pump to aid the process as it was deemed the most important. The sides of the trench had been lined with boards to keep the soil from crumbling and the diggers had put down boards to kneel on, not that it helped much, as they soon sank into the damp earth.

If Clara had ever seen the trench system employed in the last war during the worst winters, she would have recognised the similarities. Anyone dumping a body in this bog would have assumed it would never be found. What must they have thought when the drainage was put in place and the peat diggers moved in? Had they lain awake at night imagining the discovery of the body?

Hopkins sat back on his heels, wiping one muddy hand across his forehead.

"I think we might have freed him enough to lift him. Professor Peabody will want to be present."

He dragged himself out of the trench to fetch the professor, this also brought Lethbridge back to the scene. Clara watched on with interest as the body was very carefully prised from the soil, a wide board being gingerly inched beneath him until he was completely out of the ground. Then the two diggers lifted him out and laid him on the edge of the trench.

It was their first clear view of the man out of the soil. He lay huddled on his side, rather as if he were asleep, except for his unhappy expression. He was a consistent dark brown colour from the ground, even his clothing was that colour. He looked like a sculpture in bronze rather than a person. He did not remain in the open for long but was covered by a clean sheet and taken into the finds tent. Not that there was anyone around to see the discovery.

Clara watched the body being ferried away and then turned back to Hopkins.

"Would you excavate the trench further? In case any other items are down there?"

"Certainly," Hopkins smiled at her. "You are really a detective?"

"I am," Clara said with a hint of pride.

"Good job you were here when we found the fellow, then. Maybe you can solve this before the police have to be told."

Hopkins went back to his trench. Clara and O'Harris wandered over to the edge of the field, where there was a stile in the hedge which they could sit upon.

"Clara, don't take this the wrong way," O'Harris grinned at her, "but do you ever go anywhere without a body showing up?"

"Well, we knew a body would probably be here," Clara countered. "Just not a new one."

O'Harris chuckled.

"Always an adventure with you."

"I'm sorry John, I really don't want to get involved. This was meant to be a holiday."

O'Harris reached out for her hand and squeezed it.

"Nothing to be sorry for. I was wondering how we were going to pass the time, anyway," he told her firmly.

"I don't deserve you," Clara replied, a smile now coming to her lips.

"Here now," O'Harris chuckled, "of course you do!"

Chapter Nine

Annie and Tommy discovered that the nearest town was barely a village. There was a single shop selling everything people might need, or rather, everything the shopkeeper decided they might need. If something was required that was not in stock, he might be persuaded to try and order it in, then again, he might not.

When they enquired about whether there was a bakery in the area, the shopkeeper gave them a strange look and informed them bluntly that people baked for themselves in these parts. If you wanted something fancy, you sent off to the next town which was ten miles away. Annie was downcast at this news.

"English, are ya?" the shopkeeper asked them in his lilting voice.

"That's right," said Tommy. "We are here visiting our cousins who are involved in the bog dig."

"Ah, that be on Murphy's land. He is a rare ole beggar. Doesn't see a soul from Sunday to Sunday if he can help it."

"What happens on Sundays?" Annie asked innocently.

"He comes to Mass, of course," the shopkeeper looked at her incredulous.

"Of course," Annie blushed, not a churchgoer herself,

she had forgotten the strong religious sentimentality in Ireland, and also that they were largely Catholic.

"You'll be staying at the big cottage," the shopkeeper continued. "Mrs Kelly cooks for you."

"Yes, she does," Annie agreed.

"Why would you be needing a bakery then? Someone got a birthday you want a cake for?"

"No, actually, I was hoping to learn some traditional Irish recipes," Annie revealed. "I did attempt to ask Mrs Kelly, but she was too busy."

The red-faced, stout Mrs Kelly had proven to be a harridan in her kitchen. It was her domain and 'guests' were not welcome, in the same way that a lost hunter looking for shelter is not welcome in a bear's den. One misjudged encounter with Mrs Kelly had convinced Annie that she was not a woman who might supply her with cookery lessons.

"No, I can see that being something of a problem," the shopkeeper nodded sympathetically. "Mrs Kelly has always been that way. She's buried three husbands, you know, and at least two were already dead."

He chuckled at his own joke.

"Well, Annie, I guess you won't be learning any new recipes this trip. Sorry about that," Tommy said to her.

Annie looked crestfallen; she had been looking forward to bringing Irish cooking to Brighton. Alright, she just might have been considering how a certain fellow cook she was rivals with would react to her new delights, especially if she was the only one with the secrets to Irish soda bread and so forth, but that hadn't been the whole reason for her interest. Annie collected recipes like some people collect stamps, or seaside novelty ornaments. It was the closest thing she had to a hobby – though Annie was generally against the notion of hobbies. She considered that if a person had time to waste on pointless activities, they must have time to spend doing something useful, like blacking the stove.

"Now, now," the shopkeeper said quickly when he saw

A Body Out of Time

Annie's expression, "no need to despair, I know just the person to put you in touch with. Mrs Lynch just down the road is a fine cook and very traditional in her recipes. She has recipes passed down to her from her great-great-great grandmother."

The shopkeeper looked exceptionally proud of this revelation. Annie grew interested.

"Will she teach me?"

"Bound to," the shopkeeper nodded. "I shall personally escort you there."

He paused for just a split second.

"Will you be bringing the dear woman a gift on your visit? It is traditional."

Tommy saw the way things were going, but the man had been very helpful, and he was not against supporting local business.

"What would you suggest?" he said, instantly giving the shopkeeper free rein to supply them with whatever he cared to.

The man's smile expanded until it looked likely to cut his face in half.

A short time later they were being escorted to Mrs Lynch's home, a box in Tommy's arms containing more 'gifts' than the old lady could possible find use for. Among homemade fudge and a jar of local honey, there was a bottle of Irish whisky and a carved wooden coaster that bore the name of the village. Tommy was certain the coaster would not be wanted by Mrs Lynch, but the shopkeeper had been so determined to sell it to him.

They arrived at a dilapidated cottage with a garden overrun by nettles and brambles. Annie looked on with grave misgivings.

"Mrs Lynch doesn't get into the garden much in winter," the shopkeeper said as if he recognised the alarm the garden could cause. "And her grandchildren all live away. It's not like it used to be. Time was the younger generation took care of the old folks, now they all cart off to America, or at least to the next town to get better jobs.

They have no consideration."

He knocked on the cottage door, then opened it and yelled loudly.

"Mrs Lynch, it is just Mr Doyle from the shop."

"What?" a voice yelled from within.

"Mr Doyle," the shopkeeper repeated very slowly and clearly. "I have some people interested in traditional Irish baking."

From the dark depths of the cottage an old woman emerged, hunched over a walking stick so badly she seemed to be permanently staring at the floor.

"What?"

"Irish baking," Doyle repeated. "They are English."

Mrs Lynch hobbled closer and managed to lift her head and look weakly at Tommy and Annie. The fog of old age cleared from her eyes as she registered what Doyle had just said. A smile graced her lips.

"They've come to the right place, then."

Doyle left them with the old woman. She shuffled towards the back of her cottage and they followed, entering a tidy kitchen. Every pot and pan had its place, every surface was scrubbed clean, there was a sense of order and good housekeeping in the room that was lacking in the rest of the house. Annie approved.

"Can you bake?" Mrs Lynch asked Annie

"Yes," Annie said firmly, before deciding this needed to be clarified. "I have been highly placed in our local baking competitions. Scones are my specialty."

"Not scones as I make them," the old woman grinned mischievously. "Tell me why you want to learn Irish recipes. An honest answer now."

Annie started to open her mouth, then hesitated. An honest answer? There was only one.

"I like to learn new recipes."

Mrs Lynch considered this.

"Good enough," she said. "Now, I have to decide where to begin. There is so much I could teach you. These recipes, you understand, have been passed down through the many generations of my family. Not that my own children and grandchildren are interested. Traditional cooking, they say, is dull and stodgy. They want all these new quick foods, bought in tins, or bread ready baked for them. They don't understand what they are losing."

"That is a shame," Annie said, her words heartfelt, she could think of nothing worse than an ancient recipe being lost because people simply could not be bothered to cook.

"You sound like just the right sort of person for me to teach," Mrs Lynch looked satisfied. "I shall impart to you all the knowledge I can, then at least someone shall be carrying on my family's knowledge."

While this conversation was occurring, Tommy was looking out of the window into the back garden, which was as overgrown as the front. He noted that a drainpipe was leaking, even though they had not had rain for a few days. It must be seriously blocked and was holding water, which could only seep out through the smallest of gaps. When it really did rain, the water would gush over. He wondered what other parts of the house must be in a similar state of ill-repair and then his gaze fell on the hunched up old woman. He came to a decision.

"Mrs Lynch, I am not a cook like Annie, but would you accept my assistance around your home as a thank you for allowing us to intrude on you?"

"Oh," said Mrs Lynch, unsure how to respond.

"I could sort out some of the things that need fixing about your cottage. It would be no bother, and since you are showing us such kindness, it seems only fitting we should offer something in return."

Mrs Lynch was still too amazed to respond.

"The alternative is me sitting up a corner of the kitchen watching you two bake, and Annie hates it when I do that," Tommy concluded.

"I do," Annie admitted. "I feel as if his eyes are pressing into me."

Mrs Lynch took several moments to contemplate what she was being offered, then she came to a decision.

"I would be extremely grateful, young sir."

"Call me Tommy," Tommy smiled. "I would be glad to do it."

"I can't say the last time anyone did any repairs to the place. I got too old a lifetime ago," Mrs Lynch chuckled to herself at the words. "I do believe there should be tools and things in the little shed next to my peat store."

"I shall take a look," Tommy said. "Don't worry about a thing."

Then he left Annie and the old woman to discuss all things flour and egg related, feeling good to have a purpose. Not so very long ago, he was the one people were doing things for because his legs wouldn't work, now here he was returning the favour. He might have a limp, but he could certainly repair some guttering and that made him feel a sense of worth and contentment.

He found the shed, after fighting through some brambles that could have been auditioning to shroud Sleeping Beauty's castle in thorns. Tommy came to the conclusion, after getting scratched several times, that brambles were bigger in Ireland. It was probably all the rain.

He discovered some old tools, a little rusty, but serviceable, and he went about his first errand which was to clear the guttering. After fighting through more brambles, he discovered a ladder hanging on the stone wall from hooks. He took it down, tested each rung and, satisfied it was not rotten, set to work.

Tommy had never been much of a handyman, but he could muddle through most jobs. The gutter proved to be clogged by slimy leaves and a disintegrating bird's nest. It was a messy task removing the debris, but also deeply satisfying. He started to hum to himself as he worked, strangely content.

He was so absorbed that it was several moments before he realised he could hear a voice he recognised. He paused in the process of trying to pry a lump of moss from the downpipe and listened harder.

"No one can see us."

"Who shall see us here?"

One voice was male, the other female, and he knew them both. After all, in a village where everyone had the musical southern Irish accent, English voices stood out pretty starkly. There were only so many English people about the area and Tommy was certain he had met all of them. In any case, he knew the voices of Andrew and Glorianna Campbell, he would recognise them in his sleep.

"I don't like being so... exposed."

"I'm not walking up into the hills again. There is a chill wind. Besides, Hogarth took Austin to see the sheep up there."

"We should find somewhere indoors."

"Oh, stop making such a fuss. There is no one to see us."

Tommy had completely frozen in his work. What could Andrew and Glorianna be conspiring over? They were supposed to be arch enemies, at least that was how things had seemed when the Fitzgeralds had last been present. To hear them speaking together like this had Tommy's curiosity piqued.

He peered cautiously around the edge of the roof and could just see the pair standing before Mrs Lynch's cottage. They had their backs to him and were looking across the road, perhaps keeping an eye out for anyone coming.

"I preferred it when we went to that old barn," Andrew said. "It felt private there."

"Well, now there are cows in that barn, and I don't intend to share with them," Glorianna said tetchily. "I agree its damn inconvenient, but there is no one about. Susan is deep in her trench. Peg has gone walking towards the coast doing whatever it is Peg does."

"What about Clara?"

"She went to the dig too," Glorianna shrugged. "Stop being so paranoid."

"If my father found out..."

"He won't."

Tommy watched in amazement as Glorianna slipped her hand into Andrew's.

"I would not want to hurt my father," Andrew said.

"We are hurting no one. Not when he knows nothing." Glorianna drew closer to him.

"I know you have been hurt in the past and that it still stings. That silly girl should never have jilted you, you know? She had no notion of what she had."

"She couldn't abide the fact I had lied to her."

"She had her head full of cotton wool, that one. Everyone lies about their past, just think what she has missed out on."

In that moment Glorianna turned to Andrew, popped up on her toes and kissed him. Tommy sank back behind the wall breathless at the sight. He knew he had gone red, not so much from embarrassment, but horror. Andrew was having an affair with his stepmother! Clara would never believe it! He was not certain he believed it and he had witnessed it.

"You are a good man, Andrew," Glorianna said softly. "Never doubt that."

"Good men don't cuckold their fathers."

Glorianna laughed sadly.

"Life is never so simple."

Tommy heard footsteps as they started to walk away in the direction of the shop. He remained tucked behind the wall, worried in case they saw him. Glorianna and Andrew! How could that have happened? They hated one another, or at least they had seemed to hate one another.

Tommy was feeling shaken by the scene and hurried down the ladder to solid ground. It was not every day you saw such a sight. Hogarth would be heartbroken if he were to discover this.

Tommy ran a hand over his face, a little too late remembering what he had just been doing. He cringed and his immediate problems shook him out of his daze. It was not his complication, he told himself. He was not going to start slinging about accusations, for no good would come of it. He wouldn't even tell Clara. If Glorianna and Andrew wanted to be so foolish, well, they would have to abide by the consequences.

He still could not believe what he had seen, but there was a gutter to finish clearing and nothing quite distracted the mind like rotting leaf matter stuck down a pipe. He took a deep breath, then pretended he had not seen anything at all.

Chapter Ten

Clara walked around the body as it rested on the main table in the finds tent. It had been cleaned up and was resting on a white sheet. Out of the ground the position of the figure was clearer to see. The man had rested on his side in the bog, legs slightly drawn up and bent at the knees, feet crossing over one another. One arm was nearly folded to the chest, the other stretched up over the head. He had rested on his right cheek, and this had left folds in the mummified skin. He still had that grimace on his face which made Clara uncomfortable. It looked like he was accusing them for their neglect in summoning the police.

Professor Peabody stood to one side, watching.

"Where do you begin?" he asked her, after she had prowled around the body for some time.

"I begin by garnering every possible clue I can from the body," Clara answered. "There is always something you overlook first time, but if you can get the majority of facts straight off it helps enormously."

"So, what is the body telling you?" Peabody pressed her.

"I imagine it is telling me much the same as it tells you. After all, an archaeologist searches for clues about how the ancient body he has unearthed died and who they might have been in life."

"A fair observation," Peabody nodded. "Shall I offer my thoughts?"

He didn't wait for her to answer before he did just that.

"I see a middle-aged man, running to fat, but still relatively fit. Hair is thinning, that can't be blamed on the bog mud, as it is very good at preserving hair. Considering his appearance, I would hazard a guess that our man is not a casual labourer. His fingernails are very neat, and his hands are not calloused as might be the case with a person who did a lot of manual labour. I also noted there were no injuries to them. Labourers are always damaging their fingers and hands, it is the nature of the work.

"The pyjamas are another telling clue. Where they remain, they are compressed against the skin, but it is possible to see they are made of a fine weave, suggesting a very soft fabric. It appears to be good quality cloth. The watch, of course, is a prime sign that our man had money. I don't know a single peat digger around these parts who could afford a wristwatch."

"All valid observations," Clara agreed. "Unfortunately, as far as we can tell, our victim has no distinctive features to aid with identification. In a regular post-mortem, the coroner would look for things like scars or tattoos to offer a means of determining who the person was. We don't appear to have anything like that and the cloth sticking to the body makes things even harder."

"How do you propose finding out who he was, then?" Peabody asked. "Normally that is not a question an archaeologist asks, unless we are looking for a specific individual at a site."

"My starting point will be to find out if anyone has gone missing from the area in the last decade or so. The watch offers a means of fixing a rough date for when he vanished. It is pretty modern in design. I don't suppose many people around here have watches like that."

"Supposing he wasn't local to the area?" Peabody

suggested.

"Well, if he was a visitor, he must have been staying somewhere, at least overnight, since he was clearly dragged from his bed," Clara waved vaguely at the pyjamas. "If he was staying in the area, there are only a handful of places he could have been. That includes the cottage where I am staying."

Peabody studied the body for a while longer.

"What are you going to do now?" he asked Clara.

"I'm going to head to the nearest town to find where the local newspaper is printed. When someone goes missing, and they are of a well-to-do appearance as this gentleman is, there is usually an appeal in the local press."

"You'll want to head to Little Limerick," Peabody said. "That's what the nearest big town is called, and they publish a newspaper that covers most of this area. It comes out every Friday."

"You sound like a regular reader."

Peabody shrugged.

"I have to read something when I am eating my breakfast."

Clara found Captain O'Harris and briefed him on her plan. He had been watching work in trench two, where they were still digging in the hopes of finding a genuine bog body. The discovery of the murdered man had cast a pall over the excavation, there was an air of disappointment concerning the whole thing. It wasn't that the diggers were callous towards the poor man they had found, they were just upset he had not been from the Bronze Age.

Little Limerick was a long walk and neither of them fancied it now the sky had grown grey and was edging towards an April thunderstorm. O'Harris suggested they head back to the cottage and see if they could borrow a car. Andrew and Hogarth had both brought their cars with them, and it seemed likely one would at least be available. They walked back across the field, attempting not to lose their boots in the mud.

They were just arriving at the cottage when Andrew rolled up in his car.

"Just the man!" O'Harris declared.

Andrew gave him a piercing look, some of his old surliness returning, then he lightened up.

"What is it?"

"Can we borrow your car to go into Little Limerick?" O'Harris leaned down and peered through the car window.

Andrew noticeably hesitated, one hand tightening on the steering wheel of his car protectively.

"Oh, well…"

"It is just for a short trip," Clara came forward to add. "We want to go to the newspaper office."

Andrew drummed his fingers on the steering wheel, considering what he could say without sounding rude.

"You really need to go there?" he said, trying to stall them.

"Look, old fellow, you have heard what has occurred at the dig?" O'Harris leaned into the car further.

"I haven't," Andrew admitted. "Is Susan all right?"

"Everyone is fine," Clara quickly said. "But they have dug up a body."

"They were meant to dig up a body, weren't they?" Andrew frowned.

"Yes, and no," Clara explained. "They have dug up a modern body. I am trying to discover who the poor man was. Professor Peabody is refusing to allow the police onto the dig site in case they spoil the excavation."

"And you are happy with that?" Andrew asked in surprise.

"No, not at all," Clara gave a soft snort as she spoke. "But I am stuck for the moment. I want to do all I can to try to find the man's identity."

"Come on, old boy, for a good cause," O'Harris coaxed him.

Andrew pouted, his mind on his precious car and the thought of relinquishing it to people who he had never seen driving. They could do anything to his car.

"Fine," he said at last. "But I'll drive you."

Clara wasn't going to argue further, she hurried to get into the back of the car and O'Harris joined her. Andrew reversed the car and turned around.

"You mean the landowner did not know there was a body in his meadow? Well, outside of the really old ones," Andrew said.

"Apparently not," Clara replied. "Else he would not have allowed the dig."

They sped along the road, the fields whipping by. Andrew was the sort of driver who likes to speed into corners and slam the brakes on at the last minute, before accelerating out of them again. It could not be described as a smooth driving style since Clara found herself being slung backwards and forwards every few moments.

"This body… the man has been murdered?"

"Looks like it," Clara said. It was hard to think of ways he could have ended up with such a stab wound accidentally, though it was possible.

"Nasty," Andrew whistled. "And with Susan working at the site too."

"I don't think any harm will come to the archaeologists," Clara hastened to add. "No one has been prowling around the site as if concerned the team might find something they should not."

Andrew did not seem impressed, though he said nothing.

They arrived in Little Limerick, which was a very pretty town just beginning to show the first signs of spring colour. The houses reminded Clara of scenes she had seen in paintings – handsome and quaint in an old-world way. She was not surprised when Andrew had to come to a sudden halt because a man was driving a flock of geese across the middle of the road.

They found the newspaper office close to the small school. It was in an old house with a sign on the wall indicating what it was. Clara thanked Andrew as she exited the car.

"Will you come back for us around four?" she asked him.

Andrew almost sighed at the inconvenience, then remembered himself. He was really trying hard to be less obnoxious and Clara appreciated the effort.

"Either father or I shall come back to collect you," he conceded, before he drove off.

"What are the chances we shall be walking home?" O'Harris said to Clara as the car vanished.

"Let's not think like that," Clara said firmly.

They entered the newspaper offices, which were much the same as the one back in Brighton. Various rooms on the ground floor had been turned over to the local journalists, so they could type up their articles. No one paid any heed to Clara's arrival. There was a small desk in the main hallway, sitting in the middle of the space and blocking the way past. There was no sign of the person who might man the desk, presumably a receptionist of some description who would deal with the general public who walked in wanting to place an advert in the paper or suggest an event or news item the reporters needed to know about.

Clara waited before the desk a while, to see if anyone turned up, then she poked her head around the nearest door.

"Hello, who do I need to speak to about looking at your newspaper archives?"

The room she had chosen happened to house two male journalists. They both had a desk, the two items of furniture facing one another, pushed together to make them one big desk. They seemed a little surprise by Clara's appearance.

One stopped prodding the tip of a pencil into his typewriter to adjust the ribbon. The other stared at them with his mouth open.

"You are English," this one said.

Clara widened her eyes, then made a pretence of looking

herself up and down.

"Goodness! So I am! I never would have guessed."

The second journalist started to chortle, until there was a soft snap and he realised he had lost his pencil lead into his typewriter.

"Why do you want the archives?" the first journalist asked, sounding disgruntled.

"Research," Clara replied, thinking fast. "About Edward Tennent."

This seemed to do the trick.

"Ah, Mr Tennent. Fine poet, very fine poet," said journalist number one.

"Lived in that big cottage," added his colleague. "Very popular in these parts."

"So I have gathered," Clara smiled. "He has been largely ignored by the English poetry community."

"It's a disgrace," Journalist one said sourly. "It's pure snobbery, of course. Just because he wrote about ordinary souls."

"You'll be writing a book about him then?" Journalist two asked.

Clara wasn't going to commit herself to anything so complicated, not when this was all a lie to get into the archives.

"I am considering it. But I need to see what material is available."

"I'll show you the archives," journalist two rose. "The receptionist is away, currently. She normally deals with everything, but her Chastity is pregnant."

"Chastity?" Clara considered the name which she could not imagine ever hearing in Brighton – the town had a certain reputation and a girl called Chastity within its confines was going to have to spend a lot of time explaining her name's origins. "Her daughter?"

"Her cat," the journalist stepped around the reception desk. "Been a bit of a shock, considering Chastity is a boy."

"You appreciate that if a supposed male cat becomes

pregnant that means only one thing," Clara said.

The journalist looked at her innocently.

"Oh yes, it's quite a miracle. We have had the priest out to see and everything."

"No, what I meant was…"

O'Harris nudged Clara and shook his head. She gave up, perhaps this was not the time to explain to the journalist that when a suspected boy cat falls pregnant, the most obvious logic is that he was actually a she all along.

They arrived in a room at the back of the house, the walls lined with shelves and each holding several large grey folio size books. The journalist pulled out the nearest one and laid it on the table. Inside each, carefully bound in place, were copies of the newspaper. There must have been hundreds of books, and thousands of newspaper articles. Clara felt her heart sink. With this much material she could be a long time searching for someone who went missing a decade ago.

"Everything is listed by year," the journalist explained. "And we have a card index with cross-referencing information."

He opened a cabinet with lots of small drawers and showed them the rows and rows of cards.

"You'll probably find things aren't as up-to-date as they used to be. We have been short-handed ever since the war."

He flicked his fingers over a bundle of cards.

"Well, best leave you to it. You shall find Mr Tennent filed under poet, the letter T and foreign. Since he was all three of those things."

The journalist slid the drawer back into place.

"I'll leave you to it, but will I get an acknowledgement in your book for helping you?"

He looked most anxious about this.

"I promise," Clara responded with complete sincerity, "that if I ever get this book published, you shall be the first person I mention in the acknowledgements."

The journalist beamed with delight and let them alone.

O'Harris raised an eyebrow once he was gone.

"Bit deceitful," he said.

"I believe every word was honest. Now, look for a card that says missing persons. We don't have long."

They started on the drawers and Clara soon had a collection of reference numbers for people who had disappeared after 1910. Presumably, most of them turned back up of their own accord, but some would have permanently vanished.

Somewhere among those files must be a clue to the bog man's identity. At least that was what Clara was hoping for.

Chapter Eleven

"You smell a little," Annie informed Tommy as they set about walking home.

Pip and Bramble had already paid undue attention to his trousers as a result of his escapade with the gutters. At least they were fully unblocked now, as an experiment with a watering can had demonstrated to a delighted Mrs Lynch.

Tommy pulled at the sleeve of his shirt and sniffed it though, to be honest, he had been so surrounded by pungent odours that day that his nose had rather given up the ghost.

"I shall make sure everything is washed thoroughly, but if you are determined to become a handyman for the duration of this holiday, I suggest you invest in some overalls," Annie continued. "We shall have to sneak you in the back door, to avoid the Campbells seeing or smelling you."

Talk of sneaking about reminded Tommy of what he had seen earlier. A frown crossed his face.

"Annie, if you had seen something that was not really hurting anyone, but which was morally wrong and could have the potential to hurt people if they knew about it, would you say something?"

Annie tried to revolve this sentence around in her head until it made sense.

"I think you need to explain that further."

Tommy gave a sigh, staring out across the fields they were passing. It was shaping into a pleasant spring evening and it felt awful to spoil it by discussing the disturbing adultery of Glorianna with her own stepson.

"I saw Andrew in town while I was doing the gutters," Tommy said. "He was with Glorianna."

The sentence sounded loaded to him, but Annie was oblivious to the implication.

"It is good they are getting along better, after what happened. Harmony is so important within a family," she said stoutly. "Hogarth must be relieved."

Tommy grimaced to himself. Hogarth didn't know the half of it.

"They seemed very friendly," Tommy added. "Quite a transformation."

"Sometimes it takes dramatic events to wake people up," Annie replied with her kitchen cupboard wisdom. To Annie, everyone would be a lot better off if they just tried to appreciate what others were going through and were nicer to them. Excluding, of course, certain baking rivals who deserved everything coming to them. But everyone else deserved compassion.

Tommy knew he was not making himself clear.

"I saw them holding hands, Annie," he said. "I saw them kiss."

Annie froze, quite literally, coming to a sharp stop so Tommy walked a couple of paces before his brain kicked in and he also stopped. He turned back toward her.

"Are you saying…"

"Andrew and Glorianna are lovers, I am sure of it," Tommy elaborated. "It makes me shudder to think about it."

Annie stood very still.

"Isn't that incest?"

"No, I don't think so. At least, well, I am not sure now you mention it. Perhaps legally speaking because of her being married to his father."

Annie whistled under her breath at the revelation.

"That is appalling."

"You see my dilemma? I never would have known a thing about it had I not happened to be behind Mrs Lynch's house. I was effectively spying on them. What do I do?"

"Confront them," Annie said staunchly.

"Then they shall know I was watching them," Tommy pulled a face. "That is not going to go down well."

"Would you prefer to ignore what you saw?" Annie demanded.

Tommy had considered that a perfect option. His silence told Annie all she needed to know. She sighed at him.

"Tommy, why did you even ask me?"

"I feel torn. I don't like that I know about them, even if it is none of my business," Tommy shrugged. "I keep feeling as though I have a duty to inform Hogarth, except I am not sure what good that would achieve, other than to cause further discord between father and son. I keep thinking that maybe he is simply better off not knowing."

Annie started to walk again, and they fell into step with one another.

"You would have thought Glorianna would have more sense," she said. "I have no faith in Andrew, not after his previous poor decisions, though you would have thought he would have learned something by now. How on earth did those two become lovers?"

"It does boggle the mind a little," Tommy agreed. "They were at each other's throats last time I saw them. I suppose time softened them to one another."

"Do you think it is serious?" Annie asked.

Tommy did not have an immediate answer.

"How do you mean?"

"Are they just, I don't know, passing the time?" Annie suggested. "Or are they intending for this to be a long-term arrangement, so Glorianna will need to obtain a divorce?"

"I could hardly tell that from what I saw," Tommy snorted. "Do people really consider things like that?"

"Not at first," Annie admitted. "But eventually there comes a point where a decision has to be made whether to take things further, or to accept that it shall always be some casual little fling. Almost always at least one of the lovers will want the situation to become more serious, it is rare for both to agree to keep things casual."

Tommy did not know what to say about this information coming from Annie. Anyone who knew her would have said she lived a pleasantly sheltered life unaware of such intricate human relationships.

"Where did you learn all that?"

"I read about it in my magazines," Annie explained. She was a fan of the many women's magazines now available on the market, especially the ones that included advice columns and stories about sensible young ladies facing grave dangers through no fault of their own. "You would be amazed how often the same scenario repeats itself. Someone gets involved with someone else they should not be with, and then one of them begins to fall in love, while the other is just out for a bit of fun. It never ends happily."

Tommy was flabbergasted, not so much by the information Annie had imparted, but by the fact she knew all about such things.

"Well, I don't know what to say," he confessed.

"There are very few outcomes to the situation that are going to end with everyone happy," Annie continued. "I really find it hard to see why Glorianna would want to destroy the family situation."

"What about Andrew?"

"Oh, he's a fool who does not see beyond his own nose. I told you, I have no faith in him. In fact, this is just the sort of thing he is liable to do," Annie shook her head. "But Glorianna ought to have more sense."

Tommy felt it a little unfair that Annie was holding Glorianna to a higher standard than Andrew, surely they were both equally culpable in this affair?

"That still leaves me wondering what to do," he said.

"Nothing," Annie said, contradicting her earlier statement.

"Nothing?"

"You said it yourself, you were not meant to have seen what you did and revealing your presence will only cause difficulties. It is best you leave them to it."

Tommy was not sure that was the answer he wanted to hear. He had told himself it was better not to get involved, but there was a part of him that felt guilty about such apathy. Surely he had a duty to do something? Or was he just going to make a bad situation worse?

"If you could get Andrew to confide in you, that would be different," Annie said after a moment.

Tommy glanced at her.

"What do you mean?"

"If Andrew was to speak to you about his affair and ask your advice, well, you could offer your opinion, couldn't you?"

Tommy had not considered that, but he dismissed the idea rapidly.

"He'll never talk to me about it. He doesn't like me that much."

"Maybe try to make him like you," Annie suggested.

They were nearing the house and Andrew's car was parked outside. Tommy felt a pang of guilt just at the sight of it. His already stricken conscience was made worse by the appearance of Hogarth from around the side of the house.

"Hello you two. What has happened to you Tommy?"

Tommy was glad of the distraction.

"I was helping an old lady out by cleaning her gutters."

Hogarth looked him up and down.

"Can't you hire people to do that sort of thing?" Hogarth had never lifted a finger to do a spot of repair work about his house. He had never even worked on his own car, as his son did. Getting his hands dirty, was not a phrase that entered his mind. You had people for that.

"I was available," Tommy shrugged. "I had nothing else to do, and it rather seems the poor woman has been neglected by her family."

"It was the least we could do, considering Mrs Lynch was kindly sharing her family recipes with me," Annie added. In her hands was a basket she had borrowed from the old woman and she now flicked back the cloth covering it to reveal a dark brown loaf of bread.

"It's called Barmbrack," she informed Hogarth Campbell. "Or sometimes Brack for short. It is a sweet bread especially baked around Halloween. You bake things inside it, a bit like Christmas pudding, and the items received reveal a person's fortune."

"Well," Hogarth said, a completely non-superstitious man, he found the whole idea of a fortune-telling bread entertaining. "I hope you have not baked anything into it, we wouldn't want to upset people at afternoon tea with bad news now."

He chuckled to himself.

"I always say Annie it is best not to know what is about to come, it only upsets a person. Ignorance is bliss."

Tommy felt the comment was almost directed at him and his misgivings about the sighting of Andrew and Glorianna, but it could not be, since Hogarth had no knowledge of the event. It was just his own guilty conscience twitching.

"You really need to change those clothes," Hogarth said, now becoming aware of the smell seeping off Tommy. "You smell worse than when we had a fellow come to the house to clean out an old water tank that had become blocked. It was pretty foul, you know, even the staff were complaining about the smell. Next time, don't allow an old lady to put upon you."

"Oh, I volunteered," Tommy said.

Hogarth gave him a strange look.

"Volunteered? Why ever would you do that?"

Tommy opened his mouth to explain, then

reconsidered. He did not think it was possible to convince Hogarth that it had simply been an act of human decency, a little bit of selflessness to make the world a better place. Mrs Lynch needed assistance and he had offered it. It had never occurred to him to hire someone to do the task.

"Never mind," Hogarth snorted. "You'll clean up quick enough. Though I dread to think what the housekeeper will make of your clothes. She is a regular tyrant, you know."

Hogarth chuckled to himself, amused at being so at the mercy of a servant.

"It quite reminds me of the staff we had at my old father's summer hunting lodge. You really felt you were imposing upon them when you asked them for anything. It was remarkable."

Still chuckling at this memory, and clearly a content and happy man, Hogarth wandered off to do whatever it was he was planning to do. Tommy felt more miserable than ever about his secret. How could he ruin Hogarth's good mood by speaking out about Andrew and Glorianna? Annie nudged his arm.

"Don't dwell on it," she said. "Ultimately, it is not a problem of your making. You are not responsible for your cousins."

"Why do people have to be so selfish?" Tommy complained as they headed around to the back of the house. "Andrew is just thinking about his own amusement, not how his actions will impact on his father."

Annie had no answer for him. They entered the kitchen and found themselves in the presence of Mrs Kelly, who they had vaguely hoped to avoid. She took one look at Tommy and her face coiled up into a grotesque appearance of abject horror.

"Did you fall in a ditch?"

"Near enough," Tommy responded, adding quickly. "I'll take my boots off."

It was as he was scrambling to remove his boots that Mrs Kelly's eyes fell onto the basket Annie was carrying.

"I know that wickerwork!" She declared in the sort of voice you could imagine an agent of the Spanish Inquisition using as they denounced someone. "That basket is from Mrs Lynch!"

Annie did not know what to say, she looked to Tommy for help, but he was stumped too.

"You have been speaking to Mrs Lynch?" Mrs Kelly demanded.

There seemed no option but to answer honestly.

"Yes, you see, she has been kind enough to teach me some traditional Irish recipes."

"All my days!" Mrs Kelly groaned to herself, she quickly drew a cross on her chest as if it would ward off the influence of Mrs Lynch. "Her and her old recipes! Is there bread in that basket?"

Annie, knowing a storm was coming and seeing no way to avoid it, winced as she said.

"It's Barmbrack."

"Barmbrack," Mrs Kelly braced herself against the side of the kitchen table. "Mrs Lynch's Barmbrack in my kitchen. I never thought I would see the day. Well, they say the Devil favours the English, so what should I expect."

Mrs Kelly was fanning herself with a big hand. Annie looked to Tommy for help. He dived in with both feet.

"What is precisely the problem with Mrs Lynch's cooking?" he asked.

"Oh, he asks what the problem is!" Mrs Kelly looked heavenwards as if expecting divine intervention.

Annie was tired of this game.

"Well, I only wanted to learn some Irish recipes and you were too busy to assist me," she said crossly.

"And you went to her instead?" Mrs Kelly threw up her hands. "That's it, I despair of the English! I won't stay another moment in this house with you laughing at me! I see how it is, I see it! Going to Mrs Lynch behind my back, I ask you!"

Muttering to herself, Mrs Kelly grabbed up her shawl and stormed out of the kitchen. They could hear her tirade continuing as she walked across the garden.

Annie met Tommy's eyes.

"What was that about?"

"I fear we stepped onto some old and timeless rivalry that we, apparently, should have known about despite never having been here before. Also, Mrs Kelly is short of a shilling or two."

Annie looked around the kitchen despondently, at the potatoes half-peeled and the meat sitting atop the stove.

"Oh Tommy, we have just ruined dinner!"

Chapter Twelve

The newspaper archives proved to have been organised in that gently chaotic way which is the prerequisite of all such places housed in rural towns where it is never really expected that anyone will ever look into the archives, anyway.

Once you worked out that the papers were filed by month first, followed by year, you started to get a grasp of the sort of mind behind the layout of the place. All the issues for December were filed in the same bookcase – all twenty years' worth. They were then subdivided, not, as might have been initially imagined, by year, but by day of publication. The newspaper came out on a Monday and a Friday, except on Bank Holidays, when the paper was delayed to the Tuesday. Thus, there was a shelf of all the issues that came out on a Monday, all those that came out on a Tuesday and so on. Only after this division was taken into account were the papers then filed by year, month and respective date.

But that was not the only way the archivist had conceived of arranging the collection. For special issues, such as the one commemorating the King's coronation, had been transferred to a completely separate section and then

A Body Out of Time

slotted away, not by date (which would be too easy) but by subject. There was a shelf devoted to Easter special editions, Christmas editions and miscellaneous unique occasions.

Not to mention that at one point the paper had gone through a period of experimenting with its format, with bigger sized pages that were fewer in number. These oversized versions were kept in a different area on taller shelves, though the filing of them ran along the same lines as the ordinary editions. In the face of such confusion, the card index seemed slightly laughable. It offered vague directions of where to look for certain items, but even it had its shortcomings. One card, for instance, that had the topic heading 'Festive Hat Festival' offered the location for this item simply as 'Christmas' and left it at that.

Clara aimed not to despair, even though it was tempting.

Between 1910 and 1920 they found five reports listed in the card index for missing men. Clara did not know how long it would take a body to become mummified in a bog, but she felt sure it took longer than a couple of years, so she didn't think it was worth going further than 1920. As for the earliest date, 1910 was probably being generous. O'Harris thought the watch looked like the sort he saw some of his fellow flying officers wearing during the war, such watches were just coming into fashion around 1915/1916. Their victim was unlikely to have had a watch earlier than that, but it didn't hurt to be cautious and go earlier rather than later.

Five reports should at least not be too hard to find. Three were definitely in the regular section. One was in the Easter subcategory and the fifth was in one of the extra-large editions. That also happened to be one of the earliest reports from 1910. Clara would look at that one last.

"How do we do this?" O'Harris asked as they headed for the 'regular' papers.

"First we find the report and see if the person involved

could be our man. Then we need to determine if they are still missing, which may mean either returning to the card index or trawling through the papers."

"Sounds like a lot of work," O'Harris frowned.

"In the normal scheme of things, I would have access to the police archives, and everything would be there on a missing person who had not been found. It would be a lot easier, but with having to keep the police in the dark, I don't have that opportunity."

Clara located the first missing persons' article.

"Too young," she said, reading the initial lines of text. "And a farmhand."

She moved onto the next one. This proved to be a gentleman of considerable age and was also dismissed. The third report seemed hopeful as it related to a man of the right age described as being a shopkeeper, thus someone who might own a nice watch as a luxury. Clara took the name and sent O'Harris back to the card index to see if there was another card relating to this individual.

"Got it!" O'Harris called back. "Look for the edition from 5 April 1915."

Clara found the issue and flicked through until she spied an article entitled 'Missing Man Found Drowned'.

"Well, that rules out him," she declared.

They headed to the Easter papers next. The missing man on this occasion was again of the right age, and a visitor to the region. Clara felt her concern rising as she read this. A visitor to the area, just passing through, would be hard to identify and it would be even harder to trace who might have been responsible for their demise. The article stated that the gentleman had only give his surname to the landlady of the boarding house he stayed in, and it was the worryingly dull title of Mr Brown. No one else knew the man or his business in the district. He had arrived with little luggage and what remained in his room contained such mundane things they were of no use in identifying him. Clara saw a dead end fast approaching. She showed O'Harris the article.

"Is it worth looked at further editions to see if he was found?"

Clara agreed this was worth a try and they explored several papers up to a year after the disappearance with no success. It was possible he had been found later on than that but trawling through the papers in the vain hope of finding reference to the man was simply not feasible. Clara carefully noted down all the details of the traveller, feeling almost certain they had their missing man.

She almost didn't bother with the final reference, but O'Harris was already pulling out the paper and digging through it.

"Clara," he called, "you should look at this."

Clara wandered over. O'Harris had the big paper spread out on the floor, it was virtually impossible to read it by holding it open, it was so inconveniently large. Splashed across the centre pages, the headline in an eye-catchingly large font was the blunt statement – Famous Poet Missing! Disappearance of Edward Tennent!

Clara stood beside O'Harris, trying to grasp what she was reading.

"Well, no one mentioned that before!"

The article was largely about the poet's life, his works and his time in the area. The information regarding his disappearance was consigned to three humble paragraphs. He had last been seen by his friends at the golf club, where he went at least three times a week. This was some distance from his cottage, and he was expected to be gone all day when he set out.

He left the golf club around seven in the evening to drive home. Since his car was later found in the wooden garage at his cottage, it was assumed he had arrived back. The housekeeper (Mrs Kelly) lived out and had gone home around four, being not required to cook dinner that day. No one would have been at home at the time the poet arrived. He had few family except for a niece who resided with him. She had been in Dublin at the time of his disappearance, visiting friends.

No one could say what had become of the poet after he arrived home. There were no obvious signs of foul play within the house, though it did seem the bed had been slept in. The clothes Mr Tennent had been wearing at the golf club were found discarded in his private bathroom. The back door to the property was unlocked and one theory was that someone had entered to kidnap the poet, hoping to ransom him. Another theory was that Mr Tennent had been overcome by a sudden depression and had left the house to do himself in. The sole evidence for this was that he was a poet and that was the sort of thing artistic people did.

Within the article, the niece made a moving appeal for information about her uncle and asked that if anyone was holding him captive they should release him at once.

O'Harris lifted his eyes to Clara, giving her an odd look. But it couldn't be, could it? The man in the bog the famous poet everyone in the area seemed devoted to? He would be around the right age and the cottage was not far from the site, walking distance, in fact. Clara glanced at her note concerning the unidentified traveller who had also disappeared. She had two missing men and only one body.

"Shall we look through more papers, see if he was ever found?" O'Harris asked.

"I think I know a quicker way," Clara replied.

She led the way back out to the front rooms of the property and popped her head back into the office where the two journalists were hammering out words diligently on their typewriters. The one who had been helpful before glanced up and smiled in her direction.

"Could I ask you a few questions?" Clara said.

The journalist looked only too glad to step away from his work. His colleague gave him a surly look, but he ignored it.

"Certainly," he smiled. "How can I help?"

They walked into the front hallway, which afforded an

element of privacy.

"I was unaware that Edward Tennent went missing," Clara began. "No one has mentioned it at all during my time here."

"People don't like to think of it," the journalist replied. "Brings a pall over all the good memories."

"Did they ever discover what became of him?" O'Harris asked.

The journalist shook his head.

"The niece made several appeals over the years. The story is always featured in our late summer edition around the time he vanished. We mark the anniversary. No one has ever come forward to explain where he went."

"And there are no suspicions? No theories?" Clara asked.

"There are plenty of those," the journalist chuckled. "Just none you can prove. Let's see, there was a suggestion he had run off with a mistress no one knew about. Another that the niece had done him in to be able to claim his inheritance. I even heard a story that Mrs Kelly killed him!"

"And do you have a theory?" Clara asked.

The journalist looked bashful suddenly.

"Not supposed to have a theory," he said. "It's a bit of a taboo topic."

"But a clever man like you, with access to so much information, must have some ideas," Clara cajoled him

The journalist brightened. If there was ever a way to appeal to a journalist, it was through his vanity and his belief in his own self-importance. Clara could not think of a journalist who did not have a high opinion of themselves and their ability to wheedle out the truth in any story. It came with the territory.

"Well, naturally I have considered it, we all have," he said. "Sometimes, at the New Years' party, we share our personal theories and people put forth any new evidence they have found. It is one of those things you can't just let go of."

"Must have been the biggest event ever to happen in

these parts," O'Harris nodded.

"Pretty much," the journalist agreed. "We don't get a lot of scandal around her, at least not the sort that doesn't involve husbands running off with other women. Aside from the great cattle plague that raced through the countryside back at the turn of the century, the thing everyone talks about when they want a good story to mull over is the disappearance of Tennent. It's the sort of thing you bring up when you are sat around the fire on a stormy night. I've heard the kids teasing each other that Tennent's ghost can be heard howling on the wind, forever trying to get back to his cottage."

"It's become part of the local folklore," Clara surmised. "No doubt there are various mistruths being happily repeated about the disappearance, but what do you think."

The journalist grinned at her.

"Me? I think Tennent upset someone and that night they came for him, dragged him out of his bed."

"The newspaper said there were no signs of violence," O'Harris remarked.

"Inside the house, there weren't," the journalist continued. "I figure they grabbed him and hauled him downstairs before he had time to think. What the articles don't mention are the footprints."

"Footprints?" Clara asked, curious.

"Outside the back door and going around the house, there were loads of them, all on top of one another. Had to have been two or three people at least. And there were prints made by bare feet too. They led in the direction of Murphy's meadow, then they disappeared as the ground became waterlogged."

Clara could feel that familiar sensation of pieces of a mental puzzle coming together.

"Anyway," the journalist continued. "No trace of Tennent was ever found. He was declared dead seven years later. I imagine we shall never know what became of him, or why someone took against him."

"You don't have a suspect in mind?" Clara nudged him.

"That is where I have always been a little stumped. Folks around these parts know how not to talk when they don't want to, and they never talk to journalists. They don't trust us."

"And the niece? Where is she now?"

The journalist had tipped his head on one side and was thinking carefully about Clara's questions. She could see he was contemplating just how much to say. The Tennent mystery had been every local journalists' baby for over a decade. Each had their own ideas and were secretly striving to prove their personal theory correct. The thought of an outsider (an Englishwoman of all things) coming in and perhaps solving the case right under their noses was difficult to consider. The journalist looked inclined to clam up.

"Tell you what," Clara said, deciding to offer some incentive. "You help me and if I learn anything new about Tennent's disappearance, you shall be the first person I let in on it."

"You know something, don't you?" the journalist narrowed his eyes.

"I don't know anything for certain, yet," Clara corrected. "But when I do, the information is yours."

The journalist grinned. What reporter would give up the chance of a scoop, especially on a case that was the biggest and most famous in the area. It was the sort of thing a journalist dreamed of.

"Exclusively?" he clarified.

"Absolutely," Clara lowered her voice. "Even before the police."

The grin broadened.

"All right then, what exactly do you want to know?"

Clara smiled.

"Let's start with you telling me how to find Tennent's niece."

Chapter Thirteen

Fortunately, for the sake of dinner, Mrs Kelly had the decency to return. She had considered that her desire to be paid for her work outweighed her wounded pride. She pointedly ignored Annie and Tommy any time she happened upon them, in a way that indicated she wanted nothing to do with them. As long as there was going to be no difficulty over food, the pair could live with her indignant silences and sharply turned back.

Andrew had fetched Clara and O'Harris, as he had promised, and they arrived just before dinner. Susan greeted them in the hallway looking rather flustered. She waited until Andrew was out of the way before speaking.

"You haven't mentioned the body to anyone, have you?"

"No one," Clara assured her. She had felt it prudent to keep the matter concealed, considering they were not involving the police just yet. "Well, except Andrew. We needed a lift."

Susan relaxed.

"Andrew will be no bother," she sighed. "It was father I was concerned about. He would get worked up over it, start saying archaeology is dangerous or something. And I don't even want to think what Glorianna will say."

Susan pulled a face at the thought.

"I have no intention of telling anyone else, other than Annie and Tommy," Clara promised her.

"Have you found out who he was?" she asked.

"Not precisely," Clara confessed. "We have two possible candidates."

"Oh, well that's good, isn't it?" Susan brightened up.

"Sort of," Clara replied. "You see, one of them is Edward Tennent."

Susan took a moment to grasp the implication, a whole display of emotions ran across her face, from confusion to recognition of the name, to surprise and then dismay.

"The poet fellow who had this cottage?"

"He disappeared one night," O'Harris explained. "Just utterly vanished. No one knows what became of him."

Susan's eyes had grown wide.

"I'm not sure Professor Peabody would like it if the victim turns out to be a famous poet. I think a lot of people would be upset."

Clara's mind swept back to the man with the donkey cart, how he could recite poem after poem by Tennent. Such a devoted follower would be most upset to discover his hero had met his end in a bog. Would he look kindly upon the people who found him?

"Not much we can do about that," O'Harris was explaining to Susan. "What we really need to do first is find out whether our victim is Tennent or not. Surprisingly, the newspaper archives did not have any photographs of the man."

Susan was thoughtful a moment.

"You know, up in the old attics there are boxes and boxes of stuff. Austin slipped away one day, and I found him up there. Most of this house is still furnished with the furniture Tennent used and I should say that all those boxes contain his personal possessions."

"How curious!" O'Harris said.

"Perhaps not," Clara added. "If no one could say what

became of Tennent, maybe his niece thought he might one day suddenly return and would want all his things. Better to keep them safe, at least for the moment, than to risk her uncle reappearing and finding all his property sold or thrown away."

"Mrs Kelly is always saying that one day Tennent's work will be as famous as Shakespeare," Susan interjected. "Perhaps the family are hanging onto his things in case one day they become valuable."

Clara thought her theory more logical, but there could be a grain of truth to Susan's too.

"What are you three doing in the hall?" Glorianna poked her head around the dining room door. "Come on, dinner is on the table. You look like you are conspiring about something."

"I was just telling them about the dig," Susan responded meekly. "I know you prefer me not to discuss it at dinner."

Glorianna grimaced.

"All that mud and talk of people being horribly killed. Definitely not conducive to the appetite."

She spun around and stalked back into the dining room. Susan gave Clara a despondent look.

"See what I mean? If she finds out about the murdered man, I shall never be allowed back to the dig."

"We shall not say a word," Clara reassured her.

Dinner proved to be Irish stew, with a good deal of potatoes and healthy portions of bread and butter. This was followed by porter cake, a mix of dried fruit and Guinness, that baked together into a dense cake. Mrs Kelly served hers with thick cream.

Food consumed, the party began to split up again, going about their respective interests. Andrew declared he was taking a walk to help the cake settle.

"Remember your coat," Glorianna called out to him as he left, then she turned to her husband. "What about we go for a walk Hogarth, it would be good for your constitution?"

"I have walked enough for one day," Hogarth said with

a contented sigh. He had had two servings of porter cake and cream. "You go if you want."

Glorianna hesitated.

"Would you not care for my company?"

"Go for a walk if you wish it. I am going to take a nap by the fire," Hogarth yawned to indicate he was close to falling asleep in his chair.

"I don't wish to go alone," Glorianna protested. "It's getting dark out there."

Hogarth grumbled to himself.

"Andrew!" he yelled.

Andrew reappeared at the dining room door. Surprisingly, he did not seem to have gotten far along in donning his coat considering how long he had been absent. You might have supposed he would have had the time to already have left the house.

"Andrew, take Glorianna with you on your walk," Hogarth commanded his son.

Andrew did a good impression of looking displeased with this idea.

"Really father."

"Just do it," Hogarth yawned. "I'm too tired to traipse out."

"Best be quick then, Glory," Andrew said to his stepmother, sounding as if he was dreadfully put upon. "I was just about to leave."

Glorianna rose, rolling her eyes at her stepson's apparent impatience, and headed out the room. Thus, it appeared that the pair were thrust into each other's company unwillingly. Tommy and Annie, who had witnessed the scene, had to admit that it was very cleverly done. You wouldn't have guessed the pair were really lovers.

Hogarth excused himself from the table next. Peg and Susan had already departed, that left just Clara's little company. Alone, she revealed to Annie and Tommy the saga of the bog body.

"Oh my!" Annie declared. Her eyes roamed about the

walls of the room and she gave a dramatic shudder. "To think the man who lived here could have died in that bog."

"And it's a regular mystery as to who would wish him harm," O'Harris added. "No one has ever offered a solution."

"Before we get carried away," Clara intervened, "we need to be certain it is Tennent we found. I suggest we investigate the attics Susan mentioned. Maybe there are some photographs that could assist us in identifying the body."

The revelation of the dead body put all thoughts about what Andrew and Glorianna might be getting up to in the dark out of Tommy and Annie's heads. They all headed upstairs to the attics which sprawled the length of the house. They were undivided and formed a massive open space, the only disadvantage to which was the sharply sloping ceilings. O'Harris banged his head twice on the way in, Tommy faired only slightly better, managing to just smack his head once.

There were a lot of boxes. Most were made of robust cardboard, but there were also big steamer trunks, the sort people used when travelling abroad and smaller suitcases and hat boxes. Clara bent down and opened the nearest box which proved to contain a typewriter. She presumed it was the one Tennent used to type up his poems. She could see some letter impressions on the old ribbon; the last words the poet wrote.

"There is a lot of stuff," Annie remarked.

"I should say every single thing Tennent owned that could not remain in the house when guests started renting it was brought up here," O'Harris opened a tall steamer trunk, revealing several suits.

"I don't like thumbing through someone else's things," Annie dragged a finger across the nearest box and looked alarmed at the dust that coated it.

"It's different when people are alive," Clara said to her. "But I think Tennent is dead and we are doing this to help him find justice, or rather his family. I don't suppose he

A Body Out of Time

cares much about things now."

"Well, there is that," Annie admitted with a sigh. She opened a box and discovered a fat spider sitting atop a straw boater hat. She shooed it away, being too practical to be scared and searched through the box which contained only shirts, neatly folded and packed away.

"A whole man's life is here, waiting for him," Tommy gazed around him. "What precisely are you looking for, Clara?"

"I would settle for a photograph of our poet," Clara said. "I want to try to identify this body."

Annie had opened another box.

"Whoever has this many pairs of pyjamas?" she said, amused at the extravagance of Tennent. "There are at least a dozen pairs and they all look rather new."

Clara came over and examined the night things. They were mostly made of cotton, though a pair of linen ones loitered at the bottom. Tennent seemed to favour a subtle strip in his pyjamas, though the colour varied from a pale blue to a light olive green. Unfortunately, the bog had eradicated the colour of the pyjamas worn by the murdered man. All that could be safely said was they were now an uninspiring deep brown colour. The best Clara could say was that Tennent appeared to own pyjamas similar to those on the body. It was something, but just how common were pyjamas such as these?

Tommy had found some boxes containing papers, he drew out a handful and glanced at the contents.

"Drafts for poems," he said. "Gosh this stuff is dire. 'How whimsical the sun shines, when down beneath the twisting pines, I never saw such pretty lines…'" Tommy moved to another poem. "'Love is like the horse in the meadow, he is such a dainty fellow, I try not to let him mellow, my heart ought to become yellow.' That doesn't even make sense."

"No poetry does," Annie sniffed. As homespun literary critics went, she was definitely more inclined towards prose. "At least it rhymes. I can't fathom a poem that doesn't rhyme."

"There are tonnes of these," Tommy groaned. "Oh, and now some short stories. Here is one 'Irish Gold, A Tale of Fortune'."

Tommy scanned through a paragraph or two.

"Flowery," he declared.

"He got published though," O'Harris had opened another box and this one contained magazines. Several of them had headlines on their front page such as 'New Short Story by Tennent'.

"There is no accounting for taste," Annie sniffed.

Clara felt they were being a little harsh on a man who could not defend himself, who was, in fact, very likely dead in a bog. It seemed rather disrespectful.

"My understanding is that Tennent's work conjured up nostalgia in those reading it, reminded them of a time that they remembered in that rose-tinted vague way that makes the past seem so much better than now. I think he tapped into a spirit of old Ireland, something that was being lost without anyone really realising it."

Tommy put back the papers he had grabbed out of the box.

"I can see that," he said. "But I am not a soul who thinks there is a point in looking back and saying things were better in the good old days. I think you have to concentrate on making things good now."

"Nostalgia is a funny thing," Clara replied. "Some people live on it, though that is probably not so wise."

They went back to their search, all a little more sombre after this interlude. They rather felt as if they had stepped through a doorway into the past, a bittersweet place where they did not belong. Annie started muttering about the dust and the spiders just to cheer herself up. She spotted an old wasp nest up a corner and her delight at finding something the temperamental Mrs Kelly had overlooked lifted her mood enormously.

O'Harris discovered a cricket bat and a set of golf clubs. He pulled a nine iron and examined it with what he hoped appeared to be a professional look.

"Expensive set," he said, though not certain this was true.

Clara was still working through box after box of papers. She discovered one was full of author copies of the last book of poems Tennent had published. He had signed them all but had obviously not had time to gift them to people. The letter from the publisher sat on top and informed Tennent brightly that they hoped to work with him again very soon. Little had they known.

It was Tommy who finally triumphed. Having given up on the cardboard boxes which contained more poems than any man deserved to have written, he had moved on to an old trunk plastered with labels from various countries. Tennent had been a keen traveller in his younger days. The trunk opened to reveal an array of personal items, including several diaries and notebooks. Tommy produced a photo album and called over Clara.

"This might be what you need."

He showed her the album, and they went through the pictures. There were several old sepia pictures on the first pages that were labelled as being of Tennent's parents. Then there were shots of children, presumable Tennent and his siblings.

"Go to the end," Clara said. "I need a recent picture."

Tommy opened the album from the back and there was a photo of a man holding a fish up and proudly beaming at the camera. It was titled as 'Big Catch 1909'.

"Is it him?" Tommy asked.

Clara stared and stared at the image. The trouble was it was grainy, and the man was smiling broadly which changed his face.

"I'm not sure," Clara admitted.

O'Harris peered over her shoulder.

"It could be him, then again, it might not," he said.

Tommy turned a couple of pages and revealed other photographs, but most were of Tennent at a distance from the camera, such as part of a group shot of a cricket team.

It was not helpful.

"Just when I thought we would have our answer," Clara sighed.

At that moment Annie appeared by her side. She glanced into the trunk.

"Is that a jewellery box?" she leaned down and lifted a round leather box from the trunk. Flicking it open she revealed it was empty but had once held a wristwatch.

O'Harris nudged Clara.

"Look at that," he said.

Clara was looking and thinking hard.

Chapter Fourteen

Clara had the address for Tennent's niece, which happened to be in Little Limerick, it was therefore agreed that they would all head for the town the next morning. Annie and Tommy would return to Mrs Lynch for further culinary lessons, while Clara and O'Harris would seek out the poet's only living relative. Tommy was keeping stum about what he had seen the day before and was doing a fine job of pretending it had never happened at all.

They borrowed Hogarth's car. He said he was going to have a quiet day, feeling rather jaded from all the walking and fishing he had done recently. He had found a book in the cottage library about Irish folklore and was going to spend the day reading. Clara could hardly blame him for opting to stay indoors, for the weather had turned and the spring showers April is famous for had struck. Heavy grey clouds were stalking the sky and Susan had headed off to the dig site dressed in a most impressive yellow hooded mackintosh and the sturdiest rubber galoshes Clara had ever seen on a woman. Susan was certainly taking her archaeology seriously. Clara felt a pang of pride to see her developing into an independent and educated woman. Was it wrong to think secretly to herself that she had had a hand in that?

They set off in the car with O'Harris driving. Tommy sat next to him and was given a spoken driving lesson as they went along. Tommy was desperate to learn to drive now he had the use of his legs back. He had also talked about getting a car. Annie had so far squashed the idea, as she had visions of Tommy suffering a terrible car accident. Clara was more concerned about the financial complications a car would bring.

They arrived in Little Limerick and looked upon a town that was not at its best in rain. Everything that looked quaint and rustic in sunlight, looked rundown and decayed in the greyness of a downpour. They dropped Tommy and Annie at the home of Mrs Lynch and headed off to find Tennent's niece.

According to the journalist Clara had pressed for information the day before, Tennent's niece, one Miss Heath, had never quite adjusted to the loss of her uncle. Before his death she had divided her time between the cottage and Dublin, where she acted as his informal agent, arranging new deals for books or magazine articles. Tennent, like many writers, made his living from a variety of literary sources. He reviewed books, wrote factual pieces on Irish life for popular magazines and short stories for others, and, of course, he occasionally published poems.

After her uncle's disappearance, Miss Heath had become reclusive. At first, she continued to fulfil those contracts he had undertaken that she could. Her uncle always had a wealth of articles and stories stashed away, so that was not such a challenge. His last book of poems went to press a month after he vanished and sold surprisingly well, better than any of his previous books. This was believed to be due to the press implying that some clue to the mystery of the poet's vanishing act might be found in the book, as well as the natural curiosity of the general public, stirred up by a string of newspaper articles concerning Tennent's disappearance and the theories about where he had gone. His mysterious departure and continued absence did more for book sales than any publicity tour might have achieved.

After a busy few months tying up loose ends, ensuring pieces were supplied where promised and trying to keep attention focused on her uncle's disappearance, Miss Heath found herself running out of steam. The press had lost interest, a grisly murder north of Dublin had grabbed their attention. With no new information about what had become of Tennent, the column inches given over to the story rapidly declined, until there was no mention at all. The police had met a dead end and the general consensus was that without any sudden new information there was nothing more to be done. It had to simply be hoped Tennent would reappear one day.

Miss Heath did not take the news well. She could no longer live in the cottage and moved to a smaller rented house on the outskirts of Little Limerick. She stopped going to Dublin, lost contact with her friends, and spent her days working on a biography about her uncle. It was rumoured that Tennent's publishers had given her an open contract on the project, allowing her all the time she needed to complete it. Some said she was waiting for an answer to her uncle's disappearance before she finished it, others, more cynically, said she was struggling to find worthy material to fill over three hundred pages. Tennent had not led a very dramatic life up until his disappearance, and there was only so much you could write about a man's literary style.

Miss Heath struggled for several years to get by. Having no income of her own she had relied on the wages her uncle had paid her for acting as his agent. After he was legally declared dead, she inherited his estate and the royalties from his books. She also was then free to rent out the cottage. She continued to live a frugal existence and, according to Clara's source, you were lucky to see her outside her house twice a week.

Clara was not sure what to expect in terms of a welcome from the woman. She imagined she would be deemed to be trespassing on her personal space. Miss Heath did not have visitors and despite being asked by several local societies to give talks about her uncle and his work, she had always refused. Clara was prepared to be sent away from the house with a flea in her ear.

They pulled up outside a grey stone house. It was a single storey old farm building, the sort of labourer's cottage once found across Ireland. Inside it would probably consist of no more than two rooms. It sat low to the ground, as if it had erupted from the earth, but given up halfway. A thin trickle of smoke was issuing from a chimney in the thatch.

Clara walked up a path to the front door. The curtains were drawn over the windows that faced the road. She knocked on the grey door and waited. O'Harris was just behind her, casting his eye over the front garden which was full of bits of rusted metal. He thought he could spy an old bicycle frame and a car fender, but he could not fathom what they were doing there.

It was a long time before the door was tentatively opened and a face peered around with big round eyes.

"Miss Heath?" Clara asked.

The woman stared at her as if she were a monster from another world. She was shorter than Clara and had large circular glasses that perched precariously on her nose. She was somewhere in her forties, a mousey, quiet looking woman, who it was difficult to fathom ever going about Dublin socialising with the literary world and securing work for her uncle. Stood in a long grey cardigan and dirty trousers, she did not look like someone dynamic enough to do anything like that.

"Yes?" Miss Heath asked with a strong hint of unease in her tone.

"I am sorry to disturb you," Clara said. "I am conducting some research on your uncle for a magazine in England. I hoped to be able to have a chat with you?"

Miss Heath looked at her as if she had just declared she was a cannibal looking for a victim.

"I don't think so," she said, starting to close the door.

"I say, isn't that the differential from a Rolls Royce?" O'Harris interjected before the door could shut. "What are you doing with it in your garden, if I might ask?"

Miss Heath stared at him for a long time, it was an unblinking stare that made your skin twitch.

"I'll show you," she said and much to Clara's amazement the door was swung open to welcome them in.

As Clara had surmised, the interior of the cottage was small to the point of being termed compact. The largest space was devoted to the kitchen area, which had a range and a table set in it. An armchair near the window created a seating area. A door on their left as they entered presumably led to the bedroom. There was nothing else.

The confined space was made even more claustrophobic, not just because of the drawn curtains, but due to a large muddle of rusting metal parts, clearly brought from the heap in the garden outside, standing on the kitchen table. They had been stacked up into a steep pile and set before them was an easel and a large canvas. Miss Heath was painting the metallic still life in oils, only on her canvas what had seemed random bits of metal had turned into a fantastical landscape. You could still see the spokes of an old bicycle wheel, and the twist of a metal pipe, but they had taken on the aspect of trees or rocks, even though they were painted in shades of rust red. Dancing among them were tiny figures. They were silhouettes, drawn with great care. The whole composition was both fairy-like and diabolical at the same time.

"You are an artist," O'Harris said, being quicker off the mark than Clara who was finding the painting too captivating, in the way disturbing things sometimes are.

"I don't like going outside much," Miss Heath explained. "But I found that by bringing bits of metal and other objects in here I could create my own fairy kingdom on my kitchen table. I use the rust too, in my paint, to get the colour."

"It's very good," Clara said, not sure if she meant it, but

knowing that it was impolite to suggest that a person's artwork was anything other than a masterpiece.

"It keeps me busy," Miss Heath shrugged.

"Do you exhibit it?" O'Harris asked.

Miss Heath pulled a face.

"Maybe one day," she tipped her head on one side and examined the painting critically. "My uncle wanted me to have an exhibition. It was a big passion for him. He was going to rent gallery space for me in Dublin."

She did not need to add why that had never happened.

"A lot of my paintings illustrate one or other of his poems," Miss Heath elaborated.

Clara found her eyes wandering from the canvas to the pile of metal and back again. She had read some of Tennent's poems. They had seemed insipid and sentimental to her. It was hard to see how they could relate to the strange forest of shapes Miss Heath had populated with the sinister dancing figures. Clara was starting to think she had not really understood Tennent's poems at all.

"What magazine is publishing an article on my uncle?" Miss Heath asked suddenly.

Clara hesitated a moment, her cover story knocked from her head by the sight of the bizarre painting.

"Oh, it's the Brighton Gazette," she lied, coming up with the first newspaper she could think of. "They are running a series on modern poets. When they heard I was going to be taking a trip to this part of Ireland, they asked me to make some enquiries regarding Edward Tennent."

Miss Heath nodded, seeming to believe the lie.

"It's nice my uncle is still remembered. It would be easy for people to just forget about him," she picked up a paintbrush and added a few strokes of paint to the canvas. "I don't normally allow visitors into my home, but I shall make an exception for you as you are intellectual and appreciate my work. I know the locals think I am quite crazy and don't like my paintings at all."

"I imagine they are rather down-to-earth souls," O'Harris sympathised. "The sort who like their paintings very practical. Nice landscapes with a well-drawn cow or two."

"That's exactly it!" Miss Heath agreed earnestly. "They look at my paintings and cannot understand the point of them. I sometimes think I would be better off in Dublin, but I can't stand all the people there and my uncle might one day return, you know? I feel I ought to be here if he does. They never found his body, you see, and he could have suffered some terrible amnesia."

O'Harris, who had endured just such an experience, nodded along.

"That could be it."

"He could walk into town one day, looking for me, unaware he has been gone so long," Miss Heath stared wistfully towards the drawn curtains on the front windows. "I should be here, just in case."

Clara shared a surreptitious look with O'Harris. They were both thinking of the body in the trench and their strong conviction that Edward Tennent had not gone far from home at all when he vanished.

Miss Heath had her eyes back on her painting. She was somewhere else in her mind, somewhere happier. Finally, she drew herself back to the real world with a sigh.

"What is it you want to know for the article?"

Clara drew out a notebook from her pocket (she always had one with her) and gave the impression she was about to take notes.

"I know the official bits about him," she said. "I am more interested in offering a personal angle on his motivation for writing his poems. Why did he come to Ireland, for instance?"

Miss Heath raised an eyebrow at her.

"And here I was thinking you were going to ask me about his disappearance."

Clara shuffled her feet.

"Well, now you mention it…"

Miss Heath smiled.

"Don't worry, it is the only thing anyone ever wants to

ask about. You know, my uncle once said that you only get to be truly famous as a poet if something unpleasant happens to you. Byron died abroad in mysterious circumstances. Shelley vanished from a boat, never to be seen again. Even Chaucer disappeared and no one knows what became of him. It seems to be the curse of poets."

"There must be lots of poets who did not vanish," O'Harris argued.

"Of course, but they don't get the same attention," Miss Heath gave him a sad smile. "To be truly famous, a poet ought to conclude his life either too young or in a way that causes people to speculate on what became of him."

"That's rather grim," Clara said, wondering just how far Tennent would be prepared to go to fulfil his own ideas of immortal fame.

"It is," Miss Heath said lightly. "Now, what is it you want to know about my uncle's disappearance?"

Chapter Fifteen

Tommy was on edge. Since there had been a break in the weather, he had decided to go out and begin clearing Mrs Lynch's garden so he would be able to see the walls of her house properly and determine where there might be further need for repairs. He was not worried about the work, though he suspected he was going to incur the wrath of a few large bramble bushes along the way, no, he was worried in case he saw Andrew and Glorianna again. It had been hard enough keeping a straight face the night before when they had gone through the charade of arranging to meet outside. He had to admit, it had been a very good performance; to all intents and purposes, it appeared that Glory and Andrew still detested each other's presence and would only endure it on sufferance.

What had changed between them to cause such a switch in their feelings?

Of course, it was not so much that Tommy was worried about seeing the pair, his anxiety was in case they failed to see him and so he might once again become witness to their complicated relationship. He would rather know nothing more about it.

At least tackling the brambles was highly distracting,

they put up a good fight, especially the ones that towered over his head.

"What be you doing, boy?"

Tommy turned at the voice which had an air of authority to it. He spied an older man, dressed in the clothes of a farm labourer, who was observing him with a mixture of curiosity and suspicion.

"Cutting down brambles," Tommy answered innocently. He was not impressed by being called 'boy'. He was sure the word had been used in a derogatory fashion.

The old man took a good look at the heap of already cut brambles.

"Why?"

Tommy let go of the recalcitrant stem he was grappling with and approached the man.

"Because it needs to be done and Mrs Lynch can't do it for herself," Tommy said honestly. He was feeling angered that no one else in this small community had taken the time to assist the old woman. "I think the better question is why has no one done this sooner?"

The man caught his implication and puffed himself up angrily.

"English, are ye? Come here with your ideas of right and wrong, stamping all over us Irish and suggesting we have failed in our duty to our own," he puttered. "Always the same, always."

"Well, haven't you failed Mrs Lynch?" Tommy retorted. "Who allows their aging neighbour to live in such a state when all it would take is a little work to make sure her home was watertight."

"You don't know a thing," the man snapped at him, pointing a finger at Tommy's chest. "I shall ne'er set foot beyond that gate, do you hear? Principles, that is what it is!"

"Principles?" Tommy nearly spat the word. "What principles make it acceptable to leave an old woman to suffer?"

"You know nothing! That's the truth!" the finger was

A Body Out of Time

wagging at Tommy again. "Bloody English, always think you know better!"

"If you mean do I know what Christian kindness is, well then you are right!" Tommy blustered back.

"Christian kindness? Hark at him!" the man cast his eyes heavenwards as if appealing to God, himself. "Don't talk to me about Christian kindness. There isn't a soul in this village who would see Mrs Lynch starve to death or freeze, but we shan't go further than that. If you knew the story…"

"You are holding a grudge, then?" Tommy interrupted him.

The man's eyes burned like fiery coals. He pulled himself up to his full height.

"You want to make it sound petty!"

"Isn't it?"

The man looked fit to burst.

"Ask yourself this, why is it Mrs Lynch's own children moved away and don't see her? When you have an answer to that, maybe you will appreciate why we keep our distance. Bloody English!"

The man hastily crossed himself, as if Tommy were some demon who had magically appeared in the front garden of Mrs Lynch's cottage, and then he departed, satisfied he had had the last word. Tommy let him go without challenging him further. He was curious, but he doubted he would get anything other than an argument from the old man.

"Causing trouble Tommy?"

Tommy looked left and saw that Andrew was wandering down the road towards him. He actually felt relieved to see him, as that meant Andrew knew he was there. Glorianna was not in sight, which was another blessing.

"What are you up to?" Andrew had an amused frown on his face.

"Gardening," Tommy shrugged out his hands. "Well, mostly clearing what was once a garden. We were directed to this house yesterday as Annie is looking for Irish recipes. The old lady inside seems to have been rather neglected by the community and is too frail to do this for herself. I thought I would try and help."

Andrew seemed bemused by this information and then his face lightened.

"What a kind gesture," he said, slightly stunned by the revelation. He glanced at the old cottage with its shabby windows and loose thatch. "It's more work than one man can handle."

"Well, yes," Tommy confessed. "But I shall do my best."

Andrew pursed his lips together, still assessing the condition of the roof thatch, then he came to a decision.

"I shall join you."

He rolled up his sleeves and fought his way through the sticky garden gate.

"Really?" Tommy said in surprise.

"I have been a selfish cad most of my life, cousin," Andrew explained. "I am trying to make amends. It was all that stuff with Susan a couple of years ago, and of course my disastrous second marriage. I saw myself in a new light and it was not a happy vision. I decided there and then I had to transform myself, strive to be a better man. It seems to me following your example would not be a bad way to achieve that."

Tommy was touched. Andrew was not someone who offered praise casually.

"Any help will be appreciated," Tommy agreed. "The locals seem to have an aversion to Mrs Lynch. Apart from making sure she has food and peat for the fire, they won't have anything to do with her. I haven't discovered the cause yet. Mrs Kelly blew her top when she learned Annie had visited her and learned to make Barmbrack bread."

"I find the locals a peculiar lot," Andrew said, some of his old dismissiveness returning. "Too close-knit. You ask me, there has been a lot of inbreeding over the years."

Tommy thought this rich coming from someone who was having an affair with their stepmother, but naturally

A Body Out of Time

he did not say that.

"I don't know about peculiar," he said, trying to be diplomatic. "Clearly there is some long-standing feud or disagreement concerning the lady. If I could get to the root of it, maybe something might be done."

"Now that sounds more like something Clara would say. She does like to be helping the world," Andrew said with familiar cynicism.

"It's not a bad way to be," Tommy replied, thinking that Clara was currently trying to solve a murder when she was meant to be on holiday. "If we all helped each other a little bit more, don't you suppose the world would be a better place?"

Andrew paused.

"I don't know, Tommy," he replied. "Helping one person could disadvantage and upset another. That's politics all over for you. If we could help everyone equally and everyone would be happy, yes, I suppose the world would be a better place. But mostly that does not happen. Look at just now. You are helping Mrs Lynch, you are not actively hurting anyone else in the process, but you have already offended two people that you know about by this innocent act. Who knows how many others are harbouring outrage over your attempts at home maintenance?"

Tommy lost some of his cheer. Despondently he looked around at the overgrown weeds. Andrew had a way of making what seemed a simple gesture of kindness, suddenly seem sinister. He had rather pelted Tommy's gentle dreams of making the world a kinder place by simple acts of generosity and selflessness.

"Don't take it to heart," Andrew said, seeing his face. "You are doing the right thing. Just don't think that you can make the world sound so easily. People are people. Complicated, selfish, judgemental."

Andrew sighed.

"Nothing is ever as straightforward as it seems."

He grabbed up a pair of rusty shears Tommy had cleaned and sharpened as best he could. They had been oiled and only stuck a fraction when you used them. Andrew started snipping at the nearest bush and tall branches and bramble creepers tumbled down. Tommy heaved them up into the pile he was making.

"We shall have to burn them," he said, sounding deflated. Yesterday he had felt he was doing something good and worthwhile. Today he felt as if he had unwittingly offended the entire village.

"Any thoughts of why Mrs Lynch is an outcast?" Andrew asked as more briars fell.

"Not really," Tommy answered. "She seems a nice old lady."

"In a place like this, it doesn't take much to become the despised one in the community," Andrew looked around the village with savage eyes. He had never fitted in and carried an air of resentment with him all the time. "Maybe she reads the tea leaves, or something, you know how Catholics are."

"I can't say I do," Tommy said, getting cross with Andrew's dismissive way of speaking about the locals.

"Catholics are very... fundamental. Doesn't take much to offend them," Andrew elaborated. "I knew some in the trenches. They made everyone edgy."

"I knew some too," Tommy countered. "I can't say they acted any different to the other fellows."

"You know what I mean. Say the slightest wrong thing about religion and you are some infidel going to cause God's wrath to come down on the entire regiment."

"I can't say that ever occurred to me," Tommy answered honestly.

"You clearly were lucky," Andrew snorted. "I always found my Catholic comrades to be quick to judge, yet also hypocritical. I bet Mrs Lynch feels the same."

Tommy did not respond. He had become snagged up in a large bramble creeper and was attempting to fight himself free without ripping his clothes. They continued their work in silence for a while. Andrew cutting, Tommy stacking. The cottage appeared from the greenery, the walls stained green and grey in places, but otherwise sound. It had been well-built in its day.

Around noon, the door of the cottage opened stiffly, and Mrs Lynch appeared shakily holding a metal tea tray in her hands. Annie was just behind her, watching her like a hawk in case the tray slipped, or the old woman collapsed.

"Why, there are two of you now," Mrs Lynch said. "Annie, dear, go back to the kitchen and fetch another cup and plate."

Annie departed reluctantly, as if she feared the old woman was just awaiting this moment to collapse on the doorstep.

"This is my cousin Andrew," Tommy made the introductions. "He was passing and saw me at work and offered to help."

"Nice to meet you," Andrew said politely to the old woman.

"My, oh my!" Mrs Lynch declared. "What good fortune has brought two such fine fellows to my door? And look what progress you have made! I can see the ground!"

Mrs Lynch cast watery eyes around her small front garden, for the first time in many years able to see the soil clearly. There was no grass, unfortunately, the weeds having suffocated the light from the ground for too long, but with everything cleared it was possible to see where a lawn might be restarted.

Mrs Lynch began to look overwhelmed. The tea tray rattled harder and Andrew nipped forward to gently take it from her.

"I don't come out the front much these days," Mrs Lynch said, clasping a hand to her heart. "I prefer not to see people."

Andrew met Tommy's eyes at this phrase, and they exchanged a look of mutual understanding and curiosity. Neither felt it was the right moment to ask for more.

Annie reappeared with the extra cup and plate.

"You must be both very hungry. There is freshly baked soda bread with lots of butter and cheese," she told them.

"I barely eat cheese these days," Mrs Lynch said with a wan smile. "It sits in my larder to serve the mice. I am delighted to have people to share it with. If only I had some jam, I would have made you a fine repast. Soda bread is delightful with butter and jam."

"It smells wonderful," Tommy smiled at her. "I am famished!"

The warm soda bread was sliced and passed around. Smeared with well churned butter, it tasted like the food of the gods after the hard work Tommy and Andrew had gone too. They washed it down with lots of tea and took chunks of cheese to complete their luncheon. All the while, Mrs Lynch sat in her doorway on a chair Annie had fetched, nibbling like a mouse on the smallest slither of soda bread and appearing to take great pleasure in watching her new friends eat.

"This is so nice," she said quietly to herself.

Tommy was not sure if she meant for them to hear her.

They were nearly finished when a woman with a child came along the road. She happened to look their way and, with a face like thunder, she crossed the road swiftly and marched along the other side. Mrs Lynch's good humour vanished.

"I shall be best getting inside now," she said, rising from her chair as quickly as she could and shuffling her way down the hall to her kitchen.

Annie watched her go with a sad face.

"I don't understand," she said. "She seems a dear old lady, but she tells me people avoid her and her family stay away. She is so glad to have someone to share her recipes with, but I cannot help thinking she should be passing them on to her daughters and granddaughters. Not a stranger."

Annie collected up the used plates and cups.

"I am starting to think we are the first people to show kindness to Mrs Lynch in a very long time."

She disappeared back inside. Andrew glanced at Tommy.

"Well?"

"Well what?"

"Are you, or are you not, going to get to the bottom of this mystery?" Andrew elaborated.

Tommy looked at the brambles, the stained walls, the loose thatch. Once he was back in England, the decay would return and who would next turn a helping hand in Mrs Lynch's direction? If he really wanted to help her, he needed to find a way to restore her into the hearts of the community.

"You know I am," he told Andrew. "Was there ever any doubt?"

Andrew smirked.

Chapter Sixteen

Miss Heath washed her brushes with turps in the big old porcelain sink. The sort of sink you could wash a couple of babies in both at the same time. It was so deep, she disappeared into it up to her elbows.

"I would prefer you call me Jemima, rather than Miss Heath," she said. "I feel that the 'miss' appellation at my age makes me sound like an old spinster. Of course, I am an old spinster, but that is hardly the point."

She arranged the brushes in a ceramic jar on the windowsill to dry. The curtains at the front of the cottage remained closed, presumably so passers-by could not see the display of ironwork on the kitchen table. The windows at the back of the cottage fortunately provided a reasonable amount of light to work by. Jemima glanced at her kitchen table and for a brief moment considered clearing it of its metal collection, then decided against it.

"I can offer you some tea?" she suggested.

This was warmly welcomed, as the day had a chill to it and the cottage a damp feeling that made the idea of a hot cup of tea very attractive. Jemima found them chairs from beneath a white sheet, dislodging a few unfinished canvases in the process. She ignored them as they tumbled into a heap on the floor.

"My uncle was always very supportive of my artistic endeavours. I am an orphan, you know. He raised me from the time I was eight years old," Jemima ransacked cupboards until she located a pretty teapot. "My parents died in a terrible accident involving their carriage and a train. It was the carriage driver's fault, everyone said so. But that doesn't make it any better, does it?"

She dispensed tealeaves into the pot.

"My Uncle Edward took me in, promised I should never be left alone as long as he was around. It was an awkward fit, at first, seeing as he was not used to having a child in his home, but we adjusted nicely."

"And when your uncle came to Ireland, you decided to come too?" Clara asked.

"Oh yes, by then I was acting as his agent. My uncle was a clever man, but not very practical. You should have seen the state of his correspondence and his accounts. His previous agent had been rather taking advantage," Jemima pulled a face, too polite to express her true feelings about said agent. "Anyway, I had finished university. I took English Literature, you know. And it seemed logical for me to take over and for uncle to pay me in return. We were living in London then, but uncle had always wanted to come to Ireland. He loved this particular area, so much of it features in his poetry. Have you read his books?"

"Excerpts," Clara confessed. "We discovered a lot of your uncle's papers and books up in the attic of his old cottage. We are staying there."

"Oh, so you are relations of the Campbells who are renting it?" Jemima asked.

"I am their cousin," Clara nodded. "When they invited me over and I realised where they were staying, well, I jumped at the chance."

Jemima appeared delighted by this.

"It is nice to think my uncle is being appreciated outside of Ireland. During his lifetime, his work was often criticised for being too colloquial, among other things."

"I don't think anyone ought to take the opinion of critics terribly seriously," O'Harris consoled her.

She handed him a teacup with rather stewed tea floating within. There were signs the milk was on the turn and Jemima had not used a strainer, so tealeaves floated across the brown surface like fallen leaves on a muddy pond.

"My uncle tried not to listen," Jemima said. "I told him to concentrate on his royalties, they were a far better indication of his popularity than the snide words of a critic. I really don't understand those people, you know. Why they have to be so mean and think it is terribly clever. I suppose that is why I have never had an exhibition. I couldn't face people saying harsh things about my work, not without my uncle there to back me up."

Jemima seemed to have shrunk into her cardigan a little bit. It was now more obvious why she had never left Ireland, or even Little Limerick. All her confidence had come from her uncle, he had been her safety net, her security. Without him, she was at a loss.

"Can I ask when you last saw your uncle?" Clara ventured.

Jemima shrugged her shoulders.

"It was the Thursday before he disappeared. I was heading to Dublin to see his publisher and take the final proofs back. He preferred to entrust them to my keeping rather than to send them by post. I promised I would see him on Sunday when I came back. I had arranged appointments with various people who might help with the publicity of the book."

"How did he seem?" Clara asked.

"No different to any other time I departed. Naturally, I have thought over those last hours time and time again. I try to think if there was some sign there, but honestly, I don't think there was. I really don't know what happened to him."

Clara sensed they were running into a dead end already.

She decided to try a different approach.

"Your uncle was involved in the community around here?"

"Oh, heavily," Jemima nodded. "He didn't want to be one of those Englishmen who stand aloof from the locals. He loved Irish culture, that is why it features so heavily in his work. If there was a society, charity, or philanthropic endeavour about, he was involved with it."

Jemima was proud of this, but her face fell the next moment.

"I rather feel I have let the side down in contrast," she sighed. "I hide away from the world. That was not how my uncle was at all."

"Don't be too hard on yourself," O'Harris spoke. "We are all different."

Jemima nodded, but didn't seem convinced.

"It seems quite a peaceful place to live hereabouts," Clara was trying to draw out some useful information. "Not a lot of trouble?"

"No, not really. Mostly everyone knows everyone else. There are a few rough elements about, but they are no bother to me."

"The sort of rough elements who might rob an older man living alone in his cottage?" Clara said.

Jemima met her eyes, a hint of understanding crossing her face.

"You man, could my uncle have disappeared during a robbery? It is one theory that has been popular around these parts. Someone broke into the house and disturbed my uncle who maybe chased them away, only for something to happen to him," Jemima shook her head. "I don't know, it seems unlikely."

"Your uncle sounds like the sort who got on with everyone," O'Harris observed. "Hard to imagine anyone wishing him harm."

Jemima did not answer at once, and there was a darkness to her tone when she did.

"Uncle had no time for trouble-makers. He became a

local magistrate not long before he vanished. He could be hard on people he felt had harmed the community."

Clara pricked her ears. This was the first indication of someone having a potential grudge against the man.

"Magistrates are sometimes targeted by those they have brought before the law," Clara hinted.

Jemima gave a small nod.

"It has crossed my mind that perhaps someone was after revenge on my uncle. The thing is, he had only overseen a handful of cases before then. Nothing big, either."

"What sort of cases?" O'Harris asked.

Jemima frowned as she made the effort to remember.

"There were a couple of cases of people being drunk and disrupting the peace. Oh, and some of the local lads broke into the church and stole the plate. They were caught before they could sell it on. My uncle oversaw their case and insisted on the toughest sentence for them. They would have been in prison at the time he vanished, however."

Clara was not sure if that was something or nothing. She filed it away in her memory, nonetheless.

"What did the police make of his disappearance?" she asked.

"I think they initially thought he had been kidnapped and were expecting a ransom," Jemima replied. "At the time he vanished there had just been that dramatic kidnapping in County Clare. A businessman was snatched, and his family were asked for money to see him safely returned. The police wondered if some local boys had cottoned on to the idea."

"Which local boys?" O'Harris asked.

"Specifically?" Jemima thought for a moment. "The Lynch brothers were top of the list. They were always getting into trouble and being Protestant, they rather stirred up resentment. If anything went missing, you first blamed the Lynch boys."

"You said 'were'?" Clara pointed out.

"They moved away after my uncle vanished. They had

A Body Out of Time

been hounded by the police without anything being found and I think they had enough. They were tired of this place and thought they could find better work elsewhere."

"Any reason, apart from local prejudice, that it might have been supposed they harmed your uncle?" O'Harris asked.

"They had done some work for my uncle, through one of his charitable endeavours. He was trying to improve the lives of local lads, especially those with troubled pasts. The police thought this might have given the Lynch boys an opportunity to learn that my uncle was relatively wealthy. Then again, he was really the only important person around these parts, so if you were going to target someone for kidnapping, he was the obvious choice," Jemima drained her cup. "More tea?"

Clara and O'Harris politely refused. The milk had definitely been off, and Clara was a little queasy just at the thought of it.

"I'm sorry, but I don't want this article of yours becoming fixated on my uncle's disappearance," Jemima added. "His literary work ought to be the focus."

"Of course," Clara smiled. "And it will be. Perhaps we could discuss some of his local poems? Did he, for instance, write much about the bog that was close to his cottage?"

"You mean the old meadow where that dig is now happening?" Jemima was helping herself to more tea. "My uncle believed that had once been a sacred area. The peat diggers would find odd things that suggested people had thrown offerings into the waters and there is a suspected Bronze Age fort in the hills beyond the cottage. There are all sorts of legends too, my uncle collected them. He thought it was important to record folklore because he believed it reflected folk memory, the stories often being allegorical."

"Then he was fascinated by the bog? Did he know it well?"

"If you mean did he go poking around there, then no," Jemima shook her head. "Bogs are dangerous places and even once the area was drained for the peat digging, my uncle through it prudent to stay away. The mud is so deep in places you can sink in and disappear."

Jemima suddenly seem to have heard what she said, and her eyes grew wide again. Clara pretended not to notice; she didn't want to seem to have led the discussion back around to Tennent's disappearance.

"I can imagine your uncle being intrigued by this Lethbridge fellow who believes there was a horse carved into the bog," O'Harris spoke.

"Intrigued, but he would not have believed it," Jemima said. "No one believes Lethbridge, that is why he has never been allowed to dig anything up."

"You have heard about him, then?" Clara asked.

"He came here," Jemima said, seeming to find the notion incredulous. "He made some vague compliments on my painting I did not take seriously and tried to persuade me to help him get permission to dig. I explained it had nothing to do with me."

"He is certainly very determined," Clara noted.

"Obsessive," Jemima corrected with a snort. "My uncle would not have had time for him."

She was done with her tea and becoming restless, she laid a hand on the pile of scrap on her table and seemed to be lost in thought.

"Do you have any other questions about my uncle?"

Clara tried to think of something to say, but nothing sprang to mind. She had wanted to know what Jemima thought about her uncle's disappearance and she had that. There seemed no reason to dally further.

"Thank you for your time, Jemima," Clara rose. "I think we should have enough material for my article."

"If you need some nice quotes from his work, you know where the boxes are kept in the attic," Jemima rose too and showed them towards the door. "Please, if you could avoid discussing his disappearance in the article, I would greatly appreciate it."

"I promise," Clara reassured her. "Not a word about his

disappearance shall feature."

Easy lies when she had no intention of producing an article.

"I wish I knew what became of him," Jemima sighed as they left the house. She stood on the doorstep and stared into the distance, vaguely in the direction of the cottage. "I feel I have been waiting for an answer for too long. It is like it has trapped me here."

Jemima glanced back at her work.

"My life has been on hold, ever since."

"Maybe now is the time to change that," O'Harris suggested.

Jemima's eyes widened at the suggestion.

"Oh no, I don't think so. You never know, my uncle might still be alive and could come wandering back," she looked wistfully down the road as if he might suddenly appear. "I have to be here for him."

Clara and O'Harris said their goodbyes and walked away down the road.

"A little crazy that one," O'Harris said. "She still thinks her uncle is alive."

"I'm not sure I would classify hope as craziness," Clara replied.

"It is when it stops you living your life."

"What do you think? Did we get anything useful from that?" Clara changed the subject.

"I'm not sure," O'Harris admitted.

"Shame we can't see the police files," Clara said, annoyed. "Well, we have further work to do."

"What next?"

"I am not really sure, but something shall come to mind, it always does."

O'Harris offered her his arm and she took it. They walked side-by-side, comfortable to just be in one another's company until they reached the car.

"Shall we see how do-it-yourself Tommy is getting along?" O'Harris said. "He is probably desperate to be rescued by now."

Clara chuckled to herself, thinking of Tommy waist-deep in brambles and looking like a live scarecrow.

"Yes, we better rescue him. Who knows what trouble he might have got himself into by now!"

Chapter Seventeen

Seeing Andrew working with Tommy was certainly a surprise. The pair had made good work of the front garden and it was now a bare patch of earth. They were discussing buying grass seed to finish the job when Clara and O'Harris turned up in the car.

"You have been busy," Clara remarked.

"It went rather well with the two of us," Tommy remarked. "We had a fair few observers too. People pretending to casually walk past but taking a good look nonetheless."

"They were probably surprised Englishmen knew how to get their hands dirty," Andrew said, forever cynical.

Annie emerged from the cottage with her latest bundle of cooking.

"Scones," she said. "Cooked in a pan, rather than the oven. They ought to be eaten immediately, but Mrs Lynch says they shall taste almost as good cold."

"Mrs Lynch?" Clara noted the name, but now was not the right time to talk further and she swiftly moved on. "I'm glad you have had a good day. We best get the boys home to wash up. I can't remember the last time I saw Tommy this filthy."

A Body Out of Time

Tommy made a performance of looking himself up and down, as if he had only just noticed the dirt upon him.

"Do you suppose Mr Campbell will mind them in the car?" O'Harris glanced at the shiny vehicle.

"My father shall not suffer us to walk home," Andrew said with indignation and made haste to clamber inside.

Tommy grinned at them and followed suit. Annie frowned.

"Have I got to sit with them two?" she said despondently.

Clara glanced at the car which did not offer many other options.

"You could sit in the front?" she suggested.

Annie had particular views on driving, one of which was it was better not to be able to see where you were going or how fast the person behind the wheel was taking the corners. After considering her choices, she decided to make the best of a bad deal and clambered into the back, poking Tommy in the ribs to get him to shove up.

They headed home as a new rainstorm brewed overhead, talking about everything other than Edward Tennent, as Andrew was in the car.

Susan and Professor Peabody were standing on the doorstep when they drove up to the cottage. The looks on their faces did not inspire hope. Peabody seemed beside himself over something. For one terrible moment Clara envisioned he had found a second body of the modern murdered variety. Her mind sparked back to the missing visitor who she had almost completely dismissed after satisfying herself that the man in the bog was Tennent. What if he too had ended up in the muddy water?

She could hardly wait for the car to stop to get out, but she controlled herself with thoughts that Andrew was watching and was so far unaware of anything amiss at the dig. Once the car had drawn to a halt, she exited with as much calm reserve as she could muster. Brightly smiling at Peabody and Susan, she pretended she had never heard about a stabbing in the bog.

"Hello you two," she said.

"Miss Fitzgerald," Peabody almost spat her name, but she didn't think it was personal. He seemed agitated about something.

"Mr Lethbridge has started his rod tests," Susan elaborated. "He thinks he has found the outline of a horse already and he says it goes right through our trenches."

"I never should have agreed to let him stick his stupid iron rods in the ground," Peabody puttered. "Natural geological anomalies are just as likely to cause some to go deeper than others!"

"You didn't give yourself much choice," Clara reminded him, just a little satisfied that his insistence not to call the police had landed him in this position.

"I never had a choice!" Peabody snapped. "Well, he isn't messing up my trench system, blackmail all he wants! I can play that game too. If he makes a fuss, he'll never be allowed to work on that site."

"I suggested the professor come to dinner, to cheer him up," Susan said, moving out of the way to allow her brother and Tommy into the house.

She glanced curiously at Andrew's appearance.

"He has been gardening," Clara explained.

"Andrew?" Susan said in amazement.

"The very same."

"And what have you been doing, Miss Fitzgerald?" Peabody asked, sounding surly.

Clara didn't like his tone and thought he could be a lot nicer to her, considering she was helping him out of a difficult situation.

"I have been identifying your corpse, Professor Peabody," she said clearly.

"Shush! Keep your voice down!" Peabody cringed and glanced over his shoulder into the house. Fortunately, there was no one around, Clara had checked before she had spoken. "Does that mean you know who he was?"

"Yes. I think it very likely your corpse is the one and only Edward Tennent, poet and former resident of this very house. He disappeared mysteriously in 1910 and was never heard of again."

"Goodness!" Peabody gasped and slapped a hand to his face. "That is the worst news I could have."

"Do you think?" Clara said. "I think it is better I have been able to identify him before we speak to the police, than to have to give them just an anonymous corpse."

"But the publicity!" Peabody shrieked and then remembered himself. He dropped his voice. "There will be press trampling all over my excavation if we are not careful. The Tennent disappearance is one of the most dramatic things that ever happened around here. I have been visiting this area for a few years now, to research the site and make arrangements, the negotiations took forever, and every summer the same story appears in the papers – what became of Edward Tennent? I'm amazed they haven't put up a sign somewhere stating, 'this was where Edward Tennent vanished from'. They are obsessed by it and sell it to all the tourists who come through. They'll want to turn the bog into some sort of shrine to him, or something."

Peabody looked utterly bleak.

"Never mind, Professor, if we can get the dig finished before anyone learns about this it shall not be a problem," Susan said softly.

"Finished?" Peabody spluttered. "This is just the first season! I intended to come back again next year to do the east quadrant. I have in mind a five-year plan for completing the whole site. How can I do that if people are traipsing across the place to see where the famous Tennent died?"

Clara did not know what to say, there was nothing she could do, nothing anyone could do. They had found Edward Tennent and that was that.

"Are you any closer to knowing what happened to him?" Susan asked Clara. "At least if we can answer that, we shan't have the police poking around too much."

"Honestly, I don't have an answer," Clara replied. "We have spoken to Tennent's niece and she has not been able

A Body Out of Time

to suggest anyone who wished her uncle harm."

"You didn't tell her about the body?" Peabody said in horror.

"No," Clara said, annoyed he asked. "I indicated I was researching an article on her uncle."

Peabody relaxed.

"We think we found something important," Susan interjected.

She glanced behind her and all around, before slipping her hand in her pocket and withdrawing a handkerchief. The handkerchief was rather muddy. She unfolded it to reveal a tarnished object.

"We think it's a pocketknife," Susan explained. "The workings are so caked up we haven't been able to do much with it. We surmised it fell out of the pocket of the person who stabbed Mr Tennent."

Clara took the oblong object. It did look like a folded-up pocketknife, the casing being made of polished wood, and gaps along the edges suggesting where various tools or a blade could be pulled out. However, it was dense with black mud and it would take a lot of work to free any of the components from their sheath. Clara rubbed her finger over the wood, trying to see if there were any markings on it, initials perhaps. It had been stained so dark by the mud it was hard to see anything.

"Of course, it might have fallen from a peat digger's pocket," Peabody snorted, dismissive of the importance of the find.

Susan ignored him.

"This might be the murder weapon," she said.

"I think the blade would be too small, but possibly," Clara nodded. "I shall try to get it cleaned up, if the professor isn't concerned, I may be compromising important historical evidence, that is."

Peabody gave another snort. He had folded his arms over his chest and looked fed up with the whole affair. Clara turned the pocketknife over in her fingers a few more times and then slipped it into her jacket pocket.

"Did you say Tennent disappeared from this house?" Susan said, giving a shudder. "I don't like the thought of that. Was he murdered here?"

"Really, Susan, don't be so emotional," Peabody grumbled. "I thought you better than that."

"That's enough," Clara told him firmly. "Recent events have been a shock for us all. No one expected to find a recently deceased poet in the bog."

"That is for certain," Peabody groaned. "I still can't fathom it. Why put a body there? It was bound to be discovered sooner rather than later. They began cutting the peat in that area in 1909. It was why I have pushed so hard to do this excavation. They were digging up bits and pieces at random, sometimes just discarding them back into the bog. I dread to think the archaeology we have lost."

"It has also crossed my mind that it is the wrong place to bury a body, unless, of course, you want it to be found swiftly," Clara agreed.

Peabody gave her a hard look.

"What are you suggesting?"

"Nothing, actually, just speculating," Clara assured him. "No one, except the killers, knows what happened that night."

Peabody glowered out towards the setting sun.

"I'm going off to smoke my pipe," he muttered and wandered off.

Susan turned to Clara and her earlier worry was replaced by a slight smile. She spoke in a confidential voice.

"Jason has asked me to go for a walk with him after dinner. There is to be a full moon tonight and we are going up on the hill to see it. He thinks, if the sky is clear, we might be able to see Venus or Mars too. And he is going to teach me the constellations."

"As long as that is all he teaches you," Clara smiled at her.

"Whatever do you mean?" Susan frowned anxiously.

A Body Out of Time

"Nothing," Clara quickly added. "Just remember Venus was the goddess of love and symbolic of women, and Mars was the god of war and symbolic of men. And full moons are supposed to bring out the passionate side in people."

"Really?" Susan said, her eyes widening with a hint of excitement.

"Or madness," Clara added. "Depending on your perspective."

"I shall be perfectly proper, Clara," Susan grinned at her, finally catching her meaning. "Jason is a gentleman."

"Aren't they all," Clara sighed as Susan walked off, head held high and a skip in her step.

Putting aside her thoughts about Susan going for a night-time ramble with her American friend, Clara searched out Annie and Tommy. She found them in Tommy's bedroom, where he was complaining that he was lacking in pairs of socks.

"I was sure I packed enough for the week, where are they?"

"Don't ask me," Annie grumbled, watching him with her hands on her hips as he ransacked a drawer. "You refused to let me help you pack."

"I was in the army, Annie, I can pack my own luggage."

"Can you now?" Annie raised an eyebrow. "So, where precisely are these socks?"

Clara stepped between them, determined to stop another typical Annie and Tommy domestic argument. The two bickered as if there was no tomorrow, she was certain they really rather enjoyed it.

"Clara, I am going to have to ask your O'Harris for fresh socks!" Tommy remarked to his sister.

"Oh, for heavens' sake!" Annie declared and stalked out of the room, a few moments later she returned and threw a pair of men's socks at him.

"You stole my socks?"

"No, I packed extra because I knew you would forget," Annie said triumphantly.

There was a moment where Tommy debated going

barefoot just so he would not have to admit she had been right, then he conceded defeat. It was easier, and he liked warm feet.

Now they were settled, Clara closed the bedroom door and held out the muddy pocketknife she had been given by Susan.

"They found it in trench two," she explained as Tommy took it. "Since our victim was in his pyjamas, I doubt he dropped it. Possibly it belonged to the killer."

Tommy tried to pull out a blade.

"It is pretty caked up."

"Exactly," Clara said. "Maybe you could get it clean? If we could find something on it that identified its owner, that might be a lead."

"I can try," Tommy agreed.

"The other thing I wanted to mention concerns your new friend, Mrs Lynch."

"What about her?" asked Annie, looking just a little defensive. She liked Mrs Lynch a lot.

"Miss Heath, the niece of Edward Tennent, told us that when her uncle first vanished, among the suspects the police considered were the Lynch brothers, who were prone to trouble. They have now moved away. I wondered if they were related to Mrs Lynch?"

"She does not much mention her family," Annie said. "I rather feel they abandoned her."

"Something happened," Tommy said. "We don't know what, but the village will have nothing more to do with her than utterly necessary. It is very sad, as she seems such a nice lady."

"Perhaps it has something to do with the Lynch brothers?" Clara suggested. "Maybe their actions have tarnished her if they are related. Not that I have any real evidence to indicate they harmed Mr Tennent."

"I was going to make some enquiries, anyway," Tommy said. "I wanted to find out what had caused the rift between Mrs Lynch and the village, in the hopes it might somehow be mended."

Clara smiled at her brother.

"What is that look for?"

"Neither of us can stop being detectives, even for a moment, can we?"

"It's not about being detectives," Annie interrupted. "It's about helping people, and you ought to never stop helping people."

"You are quite right Annie," Tommy nodded at her. "It's just sometimes the people we help are, well, dead."

"Then again, they often have relatives who are very alive," Clara said. "Such as Miss Heath."

"Then we are doing the right thing," Annie concluded. "And that is that."

Chapter Eighteen

"Where are we going today?" O'Harris asked Clara the following morning. "Back to the niece? Or do you have a suspect to interview?"

"Actually," Clara said, smiling at him. "I was thinking of examining the crime scene in greater detail."

O'Harris frowned as he adjusted his thinking to what she meant.

"That means this house?"

"Yes," Clara confirmed. "We are going to search it from top to bottom and see if we can find some clue to this mystery."

"Not to sound defeatist, but Mr Tennent died over a decade ago and since then this house has been rented out to various guests."

"That is true, but there remains much of Tennent about the place. This is all his furniture after all, and in the attic are all his belongings. Somewhere among them, perhaps we shall find a motive."

O'Harris obviously thought that farfetched.

"Supposing it was just a burglary gone wrong? Some local thugs thought Tennent was out and tried to rob his house, he disturbed them, and they killed him in a panic."

"There was no sign of that according to his niece. If Tennent was stabbed within the house, there ought to be some blood, at least. The stab wound was deep, it would have bled heavily. I don't think it was made by a pocketknife, I think someone used a damn big knife to dispatch him, and you don't usually bring a weapon like that to an ordinary house burglary."

O'Harris' whistled.

"You think Tennent was deliberately murdered? That that was always the intention?"

"I do," Clara agreed, melancholy at the thought. There was something disturbing about the idea that in a small, intimate place such as this there were those who could plot the death of a neighbour. "Looking at the facts as we know them, and the limited evidence we are aware of, it does not suggest to me a burglary gone wrong. For a start, nothing had been taken and there was no sign that any attempts had been made to take anything."

"What do you mean?"

"Think about it, the burglars entered through an unlocked back door. That, in itself, is not suspicious as I doubt many people around here worry about locking their doors. The thieves, therefore, had easy access to the ground floor and would not have made much noise entering. Logically, they would have ransacked this floor for anything valuable before heading upstairs. There ought to have been signs of things missing, for instance. Instead, they appear to have headed straight up the stairs to Tennent's bedroom, touching nothing along the way."

"I see your point," O'Harris was glancing around the sitting room they were in. "There are plenty of valuable things around here to attract a thief's attention."

"That brings us to the second reason I am unconvinced robbery was the motive. They dumped Tennent's body while he was still wearing an expensive watch. We might argue that they were in shock about what they had done, the watch slipped their attention, I think it more likely it did not interest them."

O'Harris thought about this for a while.

"The lack of a blood stain from the killing does seem to suggest Tennent was killed elsewhere. But it could be the thieves got lucky and he bled onto a rug or sheet they were able to remove."

"That journalist told us there was a muddle of footprints outside the back door and leading around the house, and that among them appeared to be sets of bare feet. That tells us Mr Tennent walked out of this house."

"Ah, I forgot about that," O'Harris groaned to himself at this slip of memory. "And it wasn't a kidnapping because they murdered him straight away."

"And they never asked for a ransom," Clara added. "Kidnappers sometimes kill their victims and still ask for a ransom. There was never anything like that. In fact, the killers seem to have been happy that everyone assumed Tennent had just wandered off. The only complication to this theory is that the body was hidden in a place it was bound to be found sooner rather than later."

"The bog," O'Harris gave a shudder at the thought. Bogs were a little too much like the mud-filled shell holes soldiers had drowned in during the war. He kept allowing his mind to wander to the possibility that Tennent was not quite dead when he was plunged into the murky waters. "Perhaps it was symbolic, and they were not worried about him being found. Maybe they didn't intend to be here when he was."

"Symbolic," Clara considered. "The bog was an ancient site for sacrifice and possibly execution, depending on your interpretation. Yes, there could be more to the killers' reasons for hiding the corpse there than just that they wished him to be out of sight."

"Doesn't get us much further forward, does it though?" O'Harris sounded despondent.

Clara had to admit there seemed a strong possibility they would never truly resolve this case. Too much time had passed, and it was not as though there had been much to go on when Tennent originally disappeared. The only difference now was that they had a body and a pocketknife which might, or might not, have been dropped by the killers.

"I want to talk to Mrs Kelly, see what she thinks about all this," Clara said to O'Harris.

O'Harris pulled a face.

"You are brave. I thought she was going to bite my head off when I asked her if she had moved my wellington boots yesterday. You might have thought I had accused her of stealing them."

"I don't deny it shall be a challenging interview," Clara concurred seriously. "But there is one thing to remember about the Mrs Kellys of this world."

"What is that?"

"They want to feel important and needed. If you can convince them that they are the key to resolving a situation, you would be amazed at what you can achieve."

"Are you sure?"

Clara hesitated.

"Mostly sure."

They headed for the kitchen, noting the house seemed to have fallen quiet with the departure of most of the family. Susan was at the dig; Clara had not had a chance to ask her how her walk with Jason had gone, but she had seemed very cheery at breakfast. Clara was hopeful that the American had restricted himself to just showing her the constellations as he had promised.

Andrew had vanished somewhere in his car. The absence of Glorianna and Hogarth, along with young Austin, suggested they too had ventured out somewhere. Peg had last been seen moping about near the footpath leading up into the hills. She was not adapting to Irish life well, even if it was just for a holiday.

Annie and Tommy had gone into Little Limerick. Clara had a vague idea they had bagged a lift off Andrew, and it was just possible he had decided to continue his sudden helpfulness from the day before and was joining them in their attendance on Mrs Lynch, but she wouldn't hold her breath. Clara's opinion of her cousin vacillated between thinking there was no hope for him, and a tentative delight he might actually improve one day and become a considerate human being.

The good news in all this was that Clara and O'Harris had the house to themselves and could therefore pursue Clara's theory that some clue might remain within its walls without fear of being disturbed. After all, the family were still largely unaware of the discovery of the body and Clara would like to keep it that way for as long as possible.

Mrs Kelly was humming to herself as she made dumplings for her Irish stew. This seemed to be Mrs Kelly's standard dish, and no one dared ask her if an alternative supper might be on the cards at some point. Clara felt as if she was crossing an invisible line as she stepped into the kitchen. Mrs Kelly looked up and her fearsome gaze furthered this apprehension.

"I don't have your wellingtons," Mrs Kelly informed O'Harris fiercely.

"I know, I discovered them in the hall cupboard, where Mrs Campbell had put them," O'Harris said with forced cheer. He had had a squadron commander who was rather like Mrs Kelly, though he had not such a fine moustache. "I am quite happy to have them back."

Mrs Kelly narrowed her eyes at him, as if she suspected he was trying to make fun of her.

"Mrs Kelly, might I ask if you were housekeeper here when Mr Tennent was resident?" Clara said, deciding it was better to dive in with both feet than to paddle at the edge waiting for the crocodile to bite.

"What is it to you?"

"I was just curious," Clara said. "Mr Tennent was rather famous. It must have been quite an important job looking after him."

Mrs Kelly's face did not change at the intense flattery, she was still eyeing Clara as if she had crawled out of the bog and was dripping mud over the floor.

"Mr Tennent was a fine man," she said at last.

"I only discovered yesterday that he disappeared," Clara added. "I always just assumed he passed away, not that he vanished and left quite the mystery behind him."

"What is it to you?" Mrs Kelly said suspiciously.

"Just idle curiosity, really," Clara said. "It seems such a shame the police never were able to locate him."

Mrs Kelly gave a snort at this.

"You were not impressed by the police's efforts?" Clara jumped on the sound.

"The police around here are more like beanpoles in uniform. I wouldn't rely on them to find a lost cat," Mrs Kelly pounded her dumpling mix unnecessarily. "I remember them about this house, making a mess, traipsing in mud and being of no use whatsoever."

"I suspected as much," Clara nodded sadly. "I said to Captain O'Harris, I suppose the police were a fat lot of good, didn't I say that John?"

"You did," O'Harris agreed keenly.

"You see it all the time," Clara continued. "And I would bet my life, Mrs Kelly, that they were dismissive of what you had to say on the matter?"

Mrs Kelly huffed.

"You aren't wrong there."

"I thought as much," Clara sighed. "People never pay heed to what the housekeeper has to say. It is criminal. I hope they were not rude to you."

"They wouldn't dare," Mrs Kelly wagged a doughy finger in the air. "They just didn't listen. Didn't want to know. I could have told them a thing or two."

"If they had listened, perhaps they would have found Mr Tennent?" O'Harris interjected.

Mrs Kelly did not immediately reply. Clara wondered if they had gone too far, then the older woman lifted her head and there was no mistaking the tears in her eyes.

"You ask me, that poor old man was dead afore we all knew it," she said to them. "Never did anyone any harm, but that is how it is sometimes. The ruffians of this world live to a ripe old age, no one bothering them, and the good souls, they get cut down."

"Are you saying Mr Tennent was murdered?" Clara asked, dropping her voice to a conspiratorial whisper.

"I don't know…" Mrs Kelly began, Clara quickly spoke.

"I am sure you have a better idea of what went on here than anyone. Maybe you had even been concerned for Mr Tennent's wellbeing?"

"No one would listen to me," Mrs Kelly said, sniffing sorrowfully. "If they had, maybe he would not have gone."

"What were you worried about, Mrs Kelly?" Clara asked.

Mrs Kelly stared at her dumplings, then she wiped at her eye with the back of her wrist.

"No one ever listens to me. I am just a woman who makes the dinner. What do I know?"

"I'm listening," Clara said softly.

Mrs Kelly drew in a shaky breath and some of her indomitableness seemed to have faded.

"There is lots goes on around here people don't take heed of. They think it better that way. The problem with Mr Tennent was that he was always looking and listening. He saw things you were best off not seeing."

"Such as?" Clara encouraged her.

"Back in those days, when Mr Tennent disappeared, we had a problem with the smuggling of certain items into this area. Items that could be used by those who thought Ireland should be free of the English yoke."

O'Harris had gone very still, as an army man he knew the troubles that had occurred during and shortly after the war. Irish independence had been a brewing situation for a long time, but it had all really kicked off in 1916 when the Irish Republicans had started the Easter Rising. It had boiled over into a civil war in 1919 when the Irish Republican Army started gathering arms and began attacks on the British Army barracks and the Royal Irish Constabulary. Ultimately, the conflict had led to the Anglo-Irish Treaty in 1921 which provided for the establishment of the Irish Free State within a year, but also

A Body Out of Time

agreed that Northern Ireland could opt out of the agreement and remain British territory. There had been lots of turmoil during those short years of war and it had been a dangerous time to be English in some places. But surely such danger had not spilled over into Little Limerick?

"What sort of items?" O'Harris asked.

Mrs Kelly was beating her dumpling mix in a way that would do nothing for its consistency, but which was assisting her to keep her emotions under control.

"The usual sort. Guns. Stuff for bombs," she sniffed. "Those damn Lynch brothers were at the bottom of it all. They always had republican tendencies, encouraged by their grandmother."

"Is that why Mrs Lynch is avoided by everyone?" Clara asked.

"We didn't want any trouble here. We always did well from the English visitors coming to see us," Mrs Kelly sniffed. "What does independence mean to us anyway? I don't see how anything is any better now we are a republic. You ask me it was more about men getting to play at soldiers, and after all that bother in France and Belgium too. You would think they would be sick of it, wouldn't you?"

Mrs Kelly retrieved a handkerchief from her pocket and wiped her eyes.

"I never was one for violence, never," she said. "And poor Mr Tennent, he was so blind to it all."

"What are you saying, Mrs Kelly?" Clara asked her gently.

"I can't say for sure, no one except them who knows, can say for sure, but I think Mr Tennent saw something he ought not to have done and that is why the Lynch brothers killed him."

Mrs Kelly drew herself up and her voice shook as she contemplated everything.

"And they damn well got away with it, didn't they?"

Chapter Nineteen

Andrew pulled the car up alongside Mrs Lynch's cottage and stared at the quietly decaying façade. The cottage had the appearance that it was settling into the ground and if it kept up the way it was going it would sag right down into the earth, like a candle left out in the sun.

"What are you planning on fixing today?" he asked Tommy idly.

Tommy looked at the cottage, at the now obvious holes in the thatch, the mould on the walls and the rotting wooden eaves and window frames.

"That is a good question," he responded.

"The chimney needs a good sweep," Annie said. "I am sure there is an old bird's nest up there. It smokes terribly."

"That thatch needs looking at too," Andrew pointed to the corner of the roof where a large bundle of reed thatch had clearly fallen down overnight. "That needs to be a priority."

"Know anything about thatching?" Tommy asked him.

Andrew pulled a face.

"That's what I thought. There are some tasks that might be beyond us."

"It can't be that hard," Annie said staunchly. There were

A Body Out of Time

few tasks Annie would shirk from, even if they did require a degree of specialist knowledge. Annie was of the opinion that if you went at something with enough determination there was nothing you could not do. "You could patch it."

Tommy decided not to argue with this, it was never worth getting into a debate with Annie about such things, she always seemed to win.

"Looks like you could do with a hand," Andrew said casually. "Maybe I'll stick around for a bit."

Tommy exchanged a discreet look with Annie. This new, helpful Andrew was not only unexpected, but slightly alarming.

"You haven't anything better to do?" Tommy asked lightly. He wanted to add, you are not meeting Glorianna today then?

"Not really," Andrew answered. "Besides, I rather enjoyed myself yesterday."

Annie gave Tommy a small shrug. Never look a gift horse in the mouth.

"All right Andrew let's see what we make of that thatch," Tommy said.

Annie left the boys to work on the thatch. Things did not look promising when Andrew picked up the bundle that had slipped off and it disintegrated in his hands. She knocked on the front door and waited to be admitted. She waited and waited.

When too much time had passed, Annie tried the door which was, as she had expected, unlocked. She stepped into the dark narrow front hall and called out for Mrs Lynch, her heart firmly in her throat. The woman was very old, she told herself, and there was a frailness beneath her exterior of robustness. Old people died suddenly. She thought of her dear old grandmother who had dropped down dead churning butter, it had been a shock. Every time they had some of that season's butter, they could not help but think of nan. Everyone said, out of respect, it was the nicest butter they had ever tasted.

Annie crept through the house, really not wanting to

find Mrs Lynch dead and yet knowing that if she did not look, then who would? She stepped towards the bedroom and peered around the door, heart pounding as she looked towards the cramped bed where the old lady slept. She was infinitely relieved to see the bed was made up, and the pretty quilted counterpane (Mrs Lynch had sewn it during her last pregnancy) was perfectly in place.

Annie's relief evaporated as quickly as it came. What if the old lady had never made it to bed last night? Perhaps she had died in her sitting room or the kitchen? Annie was almost trembling at the thought when she heard a soft sob.

She jumped, her nerves being that on edge by now, but the next moment she realised a sob meant Mrs Lynch was still alive somewhere and she sent a silent prayer heavenwards for that. She traced the sound to the kitchen, where Mrs Lynch was sitting at her well-worn table her head in her hands, crying gentle tears.

"Mrs Lynch?" Annie asked.

The poor old woman nearly jumped out of her own skin and had she a weaker heart that might have been the end of her. She stared at Annie.

"Oh Annie, you gave me a start."

"Sorry," Annie said. "When you didn't answer the door, I was worried."

Mrs Lynch glanced in a dazed way towards the hallway.

"I didn't hear you. I have been so wrapped in my thoughts."

"What has happened?" Annie asked softly.

"Nothing that was not to be expected," Mrs Lynch gave a sad smile. "I don't know why I break my heart so. My daughter, Siobhan, has passed away."

"I am very sorry to hear that," Annie said sympathetically.

She noticed there was a letter on the table before Mrs Lynch.

"I don't know why I get myself in a dither about it," Mrs Lynch sighed. "She was a good age, you know, not like my poor Mary who died in childbirth so many years past."

Annie frowned.

"How old was Siobhan?" she asked, trying to get her head around things.

"Let's see," Mrs Lynch considered. "She was my middle girl, yes, she would have been seventy-six next birthday."

Annie nearly staggered at the news.

"Seventy-six?" she gasped.

Mrs Lynch gave her a mischievous look.

"How old do you think I am, Annie?"

Annie hesitated. She hadn't really given the question any thought. Old people reached a stage where their age became unreadable, at least to the young.

"I don't know," Annie said, not sure there was a good answer to give.

Mrs Lynch was smiling.

"I shall be one hundred at my next birthday," Mrs Lynch grinned. "Now, what do you say to that?"

Annie opened her mouth, but words failed to come out. She looked around the neat and tidy kitchen, the precious domain of the elderly woman who seemed at once so strong and yet so fragile. She fell back on her usual standby in the face of uncertainty.

"I think I shall make a cup of tea. Tea is good for shock."

"Who is more shocked, you or me?" Mrs Lynch asked her, amused.

"I've never met anyone…" Annie began and then stopped herself.

"Anyone so old?" Mrs Lynch finished for her. "Well, if it is any consolation neither have I and I never ever contemplated living this long. Honestly, longevity is not what it is cracked up to be. I had ten children, you know, and now only four are still alive. To outlive not only your children, but several of your grandchildren is chilling. I think I would rather have perished in my seventies."

"Don't say that," Annie was shaking as she filled the kettle. "Let's not talk about death."

"Sorry, Annie," Mrs Lynch sighed. "But death is as much a part of life as, well, living."

"Do all your family live away from you?" Annie asked, thinking that it had been bad enough when she had just thought Mrs Lynch was a relatively old lady neglected by the community, now she knew she was close to being a centenarian it seemed criminal.

"Yes, all of them. There was never enough work in these parts. Over the years some of my children and grandchildren opted to leave Ireland altogether to seek better lives. They went to Canada, America, even England," she smiled at her weak joke. "My eldest daughter married a local man and remained here. She passed a few years back. She had no children, much to her sadness, so I found myself alone. For a time, my grandsons were about these parts, but they left before the war. They were a bit of bother, if I am honest, and I was glad they were gone."

Annie turned around to face the old lady, she desperately wanted to ask the question that had been nagging her these last days, she wanted to know how the seemingly innocuous Mrs Lynch had ended up an outsider in her own village, but the words died on her tongue as she looked at the old lady's kindly face.

"Could you not go live with some of your grandchildren?" Annie asked instead.

"I've never been invited," Mrs Lynch replied without anger. "I suppose they forget I exist. You see, they live their lives far away from me, several I have never even met as they were born in other countries. Even the ones in Ireland barely remember me. We were always very independent souls, my family, that does tend to make us a little self-absorbed."

Mrs Lynch took it all with such understanding. She did not resent that her family had forgotten her, she did not even seem to mind that her neighbours had abandoned her. She just accepted it. Annie slowly realised this was a sort of resignation to the situation. Mrs Lynch had lost hope some time ago, and with that she had also lost her anger. Now she was just apathetic to her fate.

A Body Out of Time

Annie wanted to say she could not go on like this, but was it her place to say such a thing? She fidgeted about making the tea instead.

"You have been very kind to me," Mrs Lynch said. "I do appreciate it."

"You have been generous in teaching me your recipes," Annie replied honestly. "I feel we are only returning that generosity."

"Not everyone would think that way."

"Well, more fool them," Annie was finding her resolve again, she sat down at the table, remembering what she had discussed recently with Clara. "Mrs Lynch, do you know we are staying at the cottage Mr Tennent used to have?"

"I guessed as much," Mrs Lynch nodded. "Is it still furnished with all his things?"

"It is."

"Must be like stepping into a mausoleum," the old woman snorted. "I always said Miss Heath was a bit wet about these things."

"It just seems like a furnished cottage to us," Annie answered honestly. "We didn't know it was Mr Tennent's stuff until the other day. You know, all his papers and things are up in the attic?"

Mrs Lynch gave an appropriate shudder at the thought.

"Of course, we only just learned that Mr Tennent actually disappeared into thin air."

"No one disappears into thin air," Mrs Lynch said solemnly.

"Well, no," Annie conceded. "But we had all assumed he had passed away, like most people do. Then we discover he vanished one night and was never seen again. It makes more sense now why all his things are still there. Miss Heath expects him to return one day."

"I did say she was wet in the head," Mrs Lynch wrinkled her nose in distaste for it all.

"What do you make of it? His disappearance?" Annie pressed on.

"I really haven't given it thought," Mrs Lynch replied

haughtily.

Annie did not believe that for a moment, who would not spend a lot of time considering the disappearance of a famous neighbour? There wasn't much else to think about in this quiet district after all.

"It must have been quite the tragedy," Annie continued. "Miss Heath has clearly never recovered."

"He probably wandered off into the hills," Mrs Lynch said, tiring of the conversation. "Old men do that sometimes. They go for a walk and get into trouble. Maybe his heart gave out and he fell into one of the old crevices up there. He would be nothing but bones by now."

"That's a grim thought."

"It's how we all end up Annie. Now, what shall I teach you today? I have gifted you quite a collection of recipes already, but I have many more. Let me think."

Mrs Lynch rose from her table and moved around her kitchen, checking to see what ingredients she had available to her and muttering as she came across each.

"Yes, we could do that. Ah, but I would have liked some raisins. What is this? Ginger, hm, and a tin of treacle."

Annie let her distract herself, knowing she had obtained all she was going to for the time being. Mrs Lynch had been coy, and it was the first time Annie had known her to not want to talk about something that had happened in the village. Over the last couple of days, Annie had come to know Mrs Lynch as a woman who talked voraciously and freely about everything and anything that came to mind. There had been no subject she would not voice an opinion on, and yet suddenly she was reticent. What was it about Mr Tennent that seemed to have this effect on people? Any time his name came up, people looked askance and tried to change the subject. It was as if he was a bogeyman you might conjure up if you spoke about him.

Mrs Lynch had turned back from her examination of the cupboards and was staring at Annie.

"What is it?" she demanded.

Annie had not realised she had become lost in her

A Body Out of Time

thoughts. She startled out of them guiltily.

"Sorry Mrs Lynch, I was thinking about Mr Tennent again. I can't help it. Being in his old house, it rather feels like his ghost is all around you. Not literally, of course, I don't think he haunts, but there is this atmosphere as if he hasn't quite left the place."

"Well he hasn't, what with Miss Heath keeping the place like a shrine to him," Mrs Lynch huffed. "You know, when my husband died, I was heartbroken, but once the funeral was over and done with, I packed up everything that was personal to him and put it in the coal shed and then I gave bits away or sold them as it took me. People called me hard, thought it showed I didn't care for him. It was not that. I knew I had to move on, that having those things around me would only remind me of him and bring back the hurt of losing him. Perhaps I was hasty, but I see far too often women heading the other way and never getting over the loss of their husband. Imagine if I had been like that? I would have been mourning him these last thirty years."

"I do agree," Annie said. "But it is a bit different with Mr Tennent because no one knew what became of him. That makes things harder for Miss Heath."

Mrs Lynch softened.

"There is that," she admitted.

Annie came to a decision. She had promised to say nothing about the body in the bog lest talk spread through the village, but if there was one person who would not have the opportunity to tell anyone about the discovery it was surely Mrs Lynch? And they needed information, information that might only come if they offered an incentive or two.

"Mrs Lynch," Annie said, resolved to her course of action. She would justify it to Clara later. "There is something I ought to tell you about."

Chapter Twenty

Mrs Kelly got herself into such a dither that they had to help her sit down in a chair and hastened to make her a cup of tea to calm her. The dumplings were long forgotten, and the poor woman looked like she might have to go home and lie down for a while. When Clara's frantic searches for the tea failed, she turned instead to a bottle of sherry she found in the back of a cupboard and poured out a small glass for the fraught housekeeper. At another time, Mrs Kelly would never consider taking a drink of alcohol so early in the day. That she gulped down the glass in one, indicated how upset she truly was.

"Those Lynch boys," she said, the empty glass trembling dangerously in her hand. Clara retrieved it before it slipped and smashed on the floor. "They were trouble from the day they could walk. Their grandmother never could see it, always excusing their actions. We all gave a sigh of relief when their father decided to up and move the family to Cork, but if they didn't come back when they were all grown to live with their grandma! They said it was to keep an eye on the old woman, you ask me they had got themselves into some serious trouble in Cork and needed to keep out of sight a while. Well, it wasn't long before they were up to mischief here too."

Mrs Kelly shook her head sadly.

"Never saw it, their grandmother, never saw the problem they were. But then she had her opinions too. Ireland ought to be a Free State, she would say, my boys are only making their point, no harm in it," Mrs Kelly snorted crossly. "I can't see how being a Free State has changed anything about these parts, except we don't get as many visitors in the summer since the troubles and that is a problem for a lot of folks who rely on visitors for their income."

"Politics aside," Clara said. "What does this have to do with Mr Tennent?"

"But you can't put the politics aside," Mrs Kelly snapped at her. "It's all intertwined. Mr Tennent was English when all was said and done. Oh, he loved this place more than some Irish do. He saw it with eyes of wonder. Everything was fresh to him. When you read one of his poems it brought alive the things you saw every day and took for granted. It could make a person feel quite guilty for showing such disregard to the magic of the place they lived in.

"Some people don't take kindly to it being pointed out by an Englishman how wonderful their home is and how they have forgotten that."

"You are saying people resented him?" Clara asked. "I thought he was beloved by everyone?"

"He was, or rather his work was, but sometimes people found it hard to tally up how much they loved his poems, which seemed to capture the true Irish spirit, with the fact they were written by an Englishman," Mrs Kelly sighed. "But that wasn't my point. Mr Tennent was oblivious to what was going on around him in terms of modern politics. He lived in the past. It was where he was happiest. He took no heed of the troubles, said it would never touch us here. I liked to think he was right, except there was those damn Lynch brothers.

"Hotheads, the pair of them. They wanted to make a

statement and their grandmother encouraged them. Mrs Lynch had always been something of a political activist. In her younger days, if there was a protest march or a petition to sign, she would be there. Behind her back we called her a blue-stocking and laughed. Well, she raised her children in the same frame of mind and look where it led? Half of them left to go abroad, saying Ireland was a dying place and there was no sense staying. And she approved of that."

Mrs Kelly seemed to almost vibrate with outrage as she considered how the Lynch family had up and left, abandoning their ancestry and their homeland. It was not the sort of thing she would ever contemplate doing.

"You stick things out," she said. "Through the good and the bad. Your country is like your family, you stand by it, support it and you wish the best for it. The Lynches never understood that."

O'Harris gave Clara a knowing look. She was thinking the same as him. How quickly Mrs Kelly had become hypocritical, at one moment condemning the Lynch brothers for wanting to fight for their country's independence and the next condemning their relatives who had left Ireland rather than get caught up in its problems.

"Maybe the Lynch brothers did understand that, in a misguided way?" Clara suggested.

Mrs Kelly huffed haughtily.

"Don't be ridiculous. All they wanted was a good fight," Mrs Kelly folded her arms over her chest. She was looking much more composed now and formidable with it. "The Lynch boys were always that way."

"I am not sure I understand what this has to do with Mr Tennent," O'Harris spoke. "Did he have a disagreement with the Lynch brothers?"

"Mr Tennent didn't disagree with anyone," Mrs Kelly said fiercely as if to imply otherwise was a slur on her former employer. "The problem was the Lynch brothers were using the bog to hide things. Weapons and so forth. We didn't know about that until later, of course, had I been aware I should have summoned the police and poor Mr

Tennent would never have been involved."

Clara was gradually joining together the disjointed segments of Mrs Kelly's explanation. She thought she understood.

"You think Mr Tennent saw them hiding the guns, or discovered the secret caches, and the Lynch brothers decided to get rid of him before he could report it?" she said.

"The day before he disappeared, Mr Tennent said to me he had thought he had seen people at the bog at night. He told me I ought not to go past that way when I walked home. You see? He knew all right, he knew what was going on."

"But he didn't tell the police," O'Harris pointed out.

"Mr Tennent didn't like to get involved," Mrs Kelly dabbed at her nose with a handkerchief that had been starched to within an inch of its life. "If only he had said something. Told the police."

"Weren't the peat diggers working the bog back then?" Clara said. "Surely it was a dangerous place to hide things?"

"The bog is vast," Mrs Kelly shook her head. "And the Lynch boys knew where the peat diggers were working. You ask me, at least one of the diggers was working with them and could tell them the best spot to hide things."

"Still, to get rid of Mr Tennent..." O'Harris began.

"Hah! They would not have given it a thought!" Mrs Kelly barked, her ire stoked. "Maybe they caught sight of him, I don't know, but they feared he would reveal them and so they got rid of him. The police suspected them. They were tipped off about the weapons not long after Mr Tennent vanished. The Lynch brothers bolted and haven't been back. Guilty hearts, can't you see it?"

"They might have bolted just because they feared being arrested over the weapons stash," Clara pointed out. "That does not immediately make them guilty of harming Mr Tennent."

"It does in my mind," Mrs Kelly said with the sort of

expression that suggested, given her own way, she would see the Lynch brothers hanged from the nearest tree without the preamble of a trial. "Who else could it have been?"

"Makes you wonder who tipped off the police," O'Harris said, thinking aloud.

"Perhaps their accomplice peat digger?" Clara suggested. "Or someone else spotted them. They might not have been very discreet."

"I wish we could find them," Mrs Kelly sniffed again, the tears not quite all dried up. "Then we could make them say where Mr Tennent's poor body is. He deserves a proper funeral, a real Irish one with all the trimmings."

"You sound confident he is dead," Clara said, she knew it was the logical conclusion, but since Miss Heath had been reluctant to admit to it, she wondered if Mrs Kelly might be the same.

"He is dead. I knew he was dead the day I found this house empty," Mrs Kelly rested a hand on her heart. "I felt it. It was like a light had gone out of the world."

"Tell me about the morning you found he was gone?" Clara perched herself on the edge of the table, settling in for a good story.

Mrs Kelly was in a vocal mood now, her usual barriers to conversation broken through by the sherry and the opportunity to 'say her piece' to Clara. She felt as if she had someone who would understand her and would be open to listening. Over the years Mrs Kelly had told her story to everyone in the village, her husband had heard it multiple times, and no one wanted to hear it again. It was good to have someone new to explain it to and Mrs Kelly was finding the temptation too great.

She would never normally speak of this to a visitor, for fear it would upset them, but Clara seemed a robust sort of person, mentally speaking, not one to get the heebie-jeebies easily. Mrs Kelly actually rather liked her. She couldn't be dealing with girls who wailed and screeched at the slightest provocation. In a way, Mrs Kelly had found a kindred spirit, albeit one who had chosen a very different path in life from that of a housekeeper.

"That morning I walked up the drive as always. It was a cold start to the day, but it felt as if things would brighten up and get quite sunny. I had plans to get all the white linen done. Miss Heath was due back from Dublin later in the day and I was going to make sure she had new sheets on her bed and the room was aired. I walked around the back of the house and the first thing I saw was this patch of footprints all around the kitchen door. Someone had stomped about in the flowerbeds and had mushed up the grass where it was wettest.

"That caused me to pause, especially when I saw that the kitchen door was open. My first thought was that an intruder had gotten in. I hastened into the kitchen, seeing there was more mud over my nice clean floor. I had this flutter in my chest, like a bird trying to fly out and I think already, in that moment, I knew something had happened to Mr Tennent.

"He wrote this poem once about an abandoned house, where the magic had all gone from it because no one lived there anymore. I never understood that poem better than in that moment. Something had gone. I could feel it. The magic had fled.

"Naturally, I went upstairs to Mr Tennent's room and I saw his bed as if he had been disturbed in his sleep. My heart was pounding like crazy by then. I called and called, hoping he would answer me. I checked his study and the library. I even went up to the attic. By then I knew he was gone, but I didn't want to admit it.

"Finally, I had no choice but to ring the police and tell them he was missing. They came over and peered at the footprints and the mud in the kitchen and were about as much use as a fork is for eating soup."

Mrs Kelly pursed her lips at the word 'police'. They had clearly failed her deeply, that look said.

"There were no signs of a struggle?" Clara asked. "You know, things disturbed or broken?"

A Body Out of Time

"Nothing," Mrs Kelly answered. "Just the ruffled bed sheets. The police suggested Mr Tennent had wandered off in the night, sleepwalking, perhaps. I was never so furious as when I heard that suggestion. I told them, Mr Tennent does not sleepwalk, and if he did, he would most certainly have worn his slippers. I found his slippers, you know, under his bed, and it upset me greatly to think he had left the house without them. His feet must have been so cold."

It was this last little detail, the thought of a man about to be murdered being forced to walk out of his own house barefoot, that seemed to make the situation all the more real and tragic. Clara found herself thinking of Mr Tennent feeling cold and scared, wondering what was about to come, being walked to the bog and then being stabbed. It was all rather horrid.

"I would wring their necks," Mrs Kelly said. "I would, if I could get my hands on them."

They knew she was referring to the Lynch boys.

"What a terrible thing to happen," Clara said softly. "I am very sorry, Mrs Kelly."

"It's one of those things you can never get over," Mrs Kelly shuddered to herself. "I'll never forgive them, I don't care if it is not a very Christian thing to say, I shall never forgive them. Mr Tennent was a lovely man. He was kind and gentle. He made you see the world in a better way. They destroyed something inside me when they stole him away. I shan't ever forget that."

Mrs Kelly had finally finished feeling sorry for herself. She glanced at her neglected dumplings and pulled herself together like a general about to march his men into war.

"Dinner won't cook itself, more's the pity," she declared. "Thank you for the sherry, but I must be getting on."

It was the politest Mrs Kelly had ever been to Clara, or for that matter to anyone in the house, and she decided not to push her luck. She and O'Harris left the kitchen with more food for thought.

"Supposing Mrs Kelly is correct and there was a peat

digger involved in the gun smuggling," O'Harris said as soon as they were outside earshot. "He might know of the murder, too?"

"A guilty conscience caused him to reveal the Lynch brothers? Possible. But how would we find him?"

They paused in the hallway, thinking hard.

"How many peat diggers could there be around here?" O'Harris said. "And how many would be likely to work with the Lynch brothers?"

"Well, it's the best lead we have for the moment. But if this peat digger was involved in the murder, he shall never confess to it."

O'Harris looked so glum, Clara took his hand.

"It's a good idea, though," she told him.

Chapter Twenty-One

"Well, well," Mrs Lynch sat back in her chair and considered what Annie had just revealed to her. "Poor old Mr Tennent. He didn't deserve that, even if his poetry was diabolical."

"You are the first around here to criticise his work," Annie said.

"Everyone else is too caught up in the past. All they see is this fake nostalgia Tennent conjured up in his work."

"It's terrible to think he was murdered," Annie toyed with the handle of her teacup. "And lying in that bog all these years."

"I always wondered what became of him," Mrs Lynch became thoughtful. "When he first disappeared, I thought it was some sort of stunt for his new book. Despite what folks around these parts might tell you, his last book of poems was badly received and didn't sell well. It seemed quite possible he staged a disappearance to raise publicity for his newest endeavour. You know, add a little flair of mystery to the thing. Of course, as the weeks went by, I began to think otherwise."

"We haven't told Miss Heath or anyone else. Professor Peabody is worried if the police hear about it, they will force him to shut down his excavation."

"And that is more important than a murdered man?" Mrs Lynch raised an eyebrow and Annie blushed under the implication. "Don't worry, I ne'er talk to the police."

"I did hear a little something," Annie said uneasily.

"What was that, then?"

Annie twitched the handle of her cup to the front and then the back of her saucer as she crept around what she wanted to say, what Clara had asked her to investigate. How did Clara find it so easy to talk about difficult things with people? Annie felt so awkward.

"You have something you want to spit out," Mrs Lynch said, her insight had not weakened with age. Now her tears for her daughter had eased, she was alert and intrigued by what Annie had told her.

Annie gave a sigh.

"I heard the police were after your grandsons, Mrs Lynch, that they chased them from Little Limerick, as a result."

"Was that Mrs Kelly telling you things?" Mrs Lynch asked.

When Annie gave no response, she assumed, as it happened incorrectly, this was the case.

"That woman has had it in for me since her son Duncan went off to America with my granddaughter Erin. It broke her heart, and she blames my family, but mainly me. She considers me a bad influence. She doesn't see that the young have to fly free, and that it was her clinging to poor Duncan that made him so desperate to get away."

"I did notice Mrs Kelly had a sharpness about her when your name was mentioned," Annie admitted, deciding she would allow Mrs Lynch to think it was the cottage housekeeper who had revealed her secrets rather than mention that Clara had spoken to Miss Heath while investigating the matter.

"That woman is all sharpness," Mrs Lynch said, with a hint of sadness. "So, she thinks my boys were involved in Tennent's disappearance? I can't say I am surprised.

Everyone thinks that around here."

"Is that why..." Annie stopped herself. For a moment she had felt prepared to ask Mrs Lynch about her isolation, then her nerve had left her. It was the gentle smile Mrs Lynch had on her face. She looked too sweet and inoffensive. Annie didn't feel as if she wanted to upset her.

"You are wondering why no one comes to see me? Why none of my neighbours help me out and people walk by my house as fast as they can without running?" Mrs Lynch was not offended. She had spent a lifetime being the odd one out and had learned how not to be upset by it. You either let such a thing destroy you or you rose above it.

"It is a lot of things, Annie. Over the course of near enough a century of living, I have done a few things that the folks around here can't forgive. None of them wrong, mind you, just outside what people felt was respectable or proper. Folks around here don't raise their heads above the parapet and are horrified by anyone who does."

"What sorts of things?" Annie asked, despite not being sure she wanted to know.

"Let's see," Mrs Lynch became thoughtful. "I involved myself in several marches to Dublin concerning the rights of workers. I was seen as very wild for that. And then I involved myself in the Irish Suffrage for Women movement. I would try to rally the young women, convince them they had other options than to just get married and produce children. I offended a lot of mothers and fathers that way and when Mrs Bell's Kiera fell pregnant and declared she would not marry the father because she was an independent woman, well, the blame came straight back to me."

Mrs Lynch was chuckling to herself as the memories poured forth.

"Back when my girls were young, the local schoolmaster declared he was only going to teach the sciences to the boys in his class, because girls did not need to know it. I was so furious when I heard I went to the schoolhouse and threw stones at the windows until they broke. Then the next day when my girls went to school, I marched into the classroom with them and I refused to leave, and when the sciences came up, and the schoolmaster told the girls to go to another room to practice their sewing, I wouldn't let them leave. I demanded to know what right he had to consider my girls less intelligent than the boys in his class and less worthy of an education.

"We argued over that for months, you know. And every day I went to that school and I wouldn't let the girls leave when the sciences were being taught. I was called names by the other parents. I even had the police called to arrest me, but they knew better than to tackle me. Finally, the schoolmaster gave his notice and left. The next one along was more agreeable to my way of thinking."

Annie was smiling as she listened. She found herself picturing Mrs Lynch as Clara, stood defiantly in a schoolroom, demanding to know why the girls were being taught differently to the boys.

"I suppose the final nail in my coffin, so to speak Annie," Mrs Lynch hastily added when she saw Annie's face, "was the trouble my grandsons tended to get into. You see, they inherited my temper, but not my common sense. I only got fired up over things that were important, they got fired up about everything. As boys they got into fights all the time, no amount of hidings from their father stopped them. It was like they could not control themselves. Their father finally got work in Cork. He was tired of the folks casting him the evil eye as they walked past. He felt moving away was the only option. I don't know much of what the boys got up to in Cork, but one day they were suddenly back on my doorstep, the fear of God in their eyes. 'Please, nana, we has to stay with you,' they said to me and perhaps rather foolishly I let them. I don't know what they were running from, I didn't want to know.

"At first, they were good as gold, then they started to relax, and the old ways slipped back. They heard about the movement for an Irish Free State, something I heartily agreed with, mind you. However, I was not going to start using violence to achieve it and I would never have encouraged anyone in that. I think Ireland needs to be free to make its own damn mistakes, and I hold to that. The boys took things too far, though.

"They always did get fired up and they loved a fight. Ah, Annie, that was just their nature. I don't think anything could have changed them. I don't know how they came into contact with the boys who were arming themselves to put action behind their words, but that was what they did. They didn't tell me a thing, of course, not that I could have done much about anything. I didn't leave the house even then. I have this terrible fear of falling. I feel safe inside my home, I can lean against a wall if I feel weak. I never thought I would be a one to never leave my house, but that is how it is. I guess the next trip out of here will be for my own funeral."

Annie winced at this. Mrs Lynch reached out and patted her hand.

"That is nothing to fret about. I am quite ready for it, you know. I am looking forward to catching up with everyone who has gone before. Did I mention I am the only Protestant in this entire village? My darling husband was from Northern Ireland and he was a Protestant. I had never been quite taken with Catholicism and when he talked about his faith it quite took my fancy. I don't think I have ever been forgiven for that either."

Mrs Lynch was amused by this, and even chuckled to herself.

"Where was I? Oh, yes, my boys were up to no good, but I never knew about the guns in the bog until after Mr Tennent went missing."

"Guns in the bog?" Annie gasped, her mind whirring to the dig and visions of the innocent archaeologists accidentally setting off a gun that had been hidden in the mud.

"That was where they were hiding the illegal arms they were being sent by others. They would pass them on to whoever needed them," Mrs Lynch shrugged. "The police found them all, don't worry. Anyway, the rumour spread that Mr Tennent must have seen what they were doing, and my boys had kidnapped him to stop him from talking. The problem was, the night Mr Tennent vanished, my boys were here with me."

"All night?" Annie asked.

"All night," Mrs Lynch said firmly. "I had a terrible earache. I was in so much pain, and so dizzy I just kept throwing up. I was weak and couldn't keep a thing down. The boys thought it was the end of me and didn't leave my side. I never slept a wink that night, I couldn't. They read to me and kept me company. Gareth kept warming cloths by the fire and resting them against my head to draw out the pain. Eoin made up one of my old pain recipes and helped me to drink it. Honestly, without those two I doubt I would have survived that night. I think I would have just given up."

"Then they could not have touched Mr Tennent," Annie said with a nod. "They were innocent."

"I told the police that and everyone thought I was making up the story to protect my grandsons. Annie, I hope you appreciate that I would never do such a thing? I am loyal to my family, but I also think we have to take responsibility for our actions. If they had been out that night, I would not have lied for them."

Annie did believe her.

"Anyway, things became very difficult for my boys after that and the gun smuggling looked likely to land them in prison, so I told them to leave. They were reluctant to go, didn't want to see me on my own, but I said to them 'if you are in prison, I shall be on my own anyway.' I wanted to know they were safe. They were foolish, of course, and I told them I wanted no more of this gun smuggling, but I didn't want them in prison either."

"Where are they now?" Annie asked.

"I honestly don't know," Mrs Lynch sighed, the first hint of sadness entering her face. "I told them not to write to me, it was too risky if the letters were intercepted. They could be dead for all I know."

Mrs Lynch became sombre.

"You know, I think the thing that really turned folks against me was the suspicion that my boys had killed Mr Tennent and I had helped them escape justice. I don't regret anything I did, but I can see how others would interpret it as me protecting a pair of murderers. Nothing has been the same since then."

"I am very sorry to hear that," Annie frowned.

"It has been good to be able to tell someone my side of things," Mrs Lynch smiled at her. "I do think you coming along has been a godsend. I would have hated to leave this world without someone knowing the truth."

Annie was thinking hard.

"But what did happen to Mr Tennent?" she said. "Someone took him from his house and murdered him, and there seems no reason for it."

"I don't suppose I am much help with that," Mrs Lynch agreed. "I never even set eyes on the man. He was like some legendary figure around here, if you listened to people talk. I was always rather inclined to just think of him as a second-rate wordsmith who happened to have found a gullible audience. But each to their own."

"It is so curious," Annie's brows drew together sharply as she turned the matter over and over in her mind.

"I don't suppose it shall ever be solved," Mrs Lynch said with her own sadness. "I don't much like that idea, but as a Christian I must believe in divine justice and just because a person does not face punishment in this life, does not mean they escape it in the next. Truthfully, I think that is worse than any earthly punishment we can deal out."

As much as Annie might like to subscribe to this point of view, she knew Clara would not accept it. Earthly justice was not just about punishing the wicked, as Clara would say, it was also about protecting the innocent and helping people to continue on with their lives. The mystery of Mr Tennent was going to haunt this small corner of Ireland if it was never resolved and that was probably not a good thing. Besides, if they could find the real culprit and exonerate the Lynch brothers, then surely that would also cause people to see Mrs Lynch in a new light? They would realise how wrong they had been in the way they had treated her and maybe they would act better in the future. That had to be worth the effort, didn't it?

"If this isn't about guns, or things," Mrs Lynch said. "Then I can only think Mr Tennent was killed because of something closer to home."

"His family?" Annie said, stunned.

"Or someone in his household," Mrs Lynch sniffed, a slight devilment in her gaze. "It is said that Mrs Kelly is rather good with a carving knife."

Chapter Twenty-Two

Clara was feeling that she had lost her way with the investigation. There was simply nothing concrete to go on. No real suspect with the Lynch brothers being only vaguely connected to the crime, and through suspicion rather than real evidence. The problem was over a decade had passed since the crime and there had not been many clues when it first occurred, let alone all these years later.

Clara was frustrated. It was almost as if someone had randomly decided to kill Mr Tennent for no reason at all. But there had to be a reason, didn't there?

Brain feeling full of cotton wool with the mystery of it all, Clara suggested to O'Harris they take a walk in the direction of the bog dig site. She hoped the fresh air might spark some ideas.

O'Harris was toying with the mud caked pocketknife which Tommy had left behind when he went out. He was working a thumbnail into the gaps, trying to loosen the blade.

"You know what I think when someone dies and people say they had no enemies?" he remarked, a look of concentration on his face.

"Tell me," Clara said.

"I think they are either lying or didn't know the person as well as they thought they did."

Clara considered his statement.

"You are right. When you delve into something, there is always more to the matter. People have enemies even when they are the nicest souls in the world. People think if they say someone had enemies it implies the person was unpleasant, but that need not be the case. For instance, a younger brother might hate his older brother not because they have ever argued, but because the older brother is destined to inherit the family fortune. Jealousy makes powerful enemies."

"Yes, and from what Mrs Lynch was saying, albeit in a roundabout way, Mr Tennent was a little resented for being an Englishman in Ireland, writing about Irish folklore."

"Jealousy over his success," Clara nodded. "But I have not heard of anything serious enough to prove that a motive for murder."

They were nearing the road and trotting along it was a familiar donkey pulling an equally familiar cart.

"Mornin'," the cart driver said, touching the brim of his hat. "Good ta see ya have sorted your shoes."

Clara lifted up one foot, encased securely in a rubber wellington boot.

"I learned my lesson," she smiled at the old man.

"People usually do," he agreed companionably. "Do ya need a lift ta town?"

"No, we are fine, thank you. Just walking to the bog."

"Ah."

The old man looked in the direction of the bog, a strange expression on his face.

"I don't go near ta place. Too much death abouts."

"I don't believe we caught your name, last time we met?" O'Harris said.

"Mr Cork," the old man grinned, revealing tobacco brown teeth. "And this is Ned."

He patted the donkey's rump. The creature had come to

a contented halt and seemed uninclined to move for some time.

"Have ya had a chance ta read some o' Mr Tennent's poems yet?" Mr Cork asked them.

"We have," Clara agreed.

"What did ya think?"

Clara picked her words with care.

"They evoked a sense of nostalgia, even for us who were unacquainted with this place. They seemed to speak of another time and place that was just out of reach."

"They made me a little sad," O'Harris concurred. "I felt I had lost something I never even had."

Mr Cork nodded his head, pleased to hear their assessment.

"Mr Tennent had that way about him," he sighed. "His words speak ta my heart and bring a tear ta ma eye."

"Did you know him? In person, I mean?" Clara asked.

"I did," Mr Cork said sadly. "I sometimes gave him lifts in my cart."

"We didn't know about his disappearance until recently," Clara said. "It came as a shock to us. Poor man."

Mr Cork looked forlorn.

"Poor man, indeed. One day here, ta other gone. And no one ta say where he went."

"No one seems to know who was responsible either," Clara added, hoping it sounded suitably sinister.

Mr Cork took the bait.

"Everyone always looked the wrong way about it all," he said. "They thought it was them Lynch boys, that was the easy option because they were known to be trouble and later on it was found they were hiding guns in the bog. But I ask ya, if they thought Mr Tennent saw something, why not just move the guns? Making tha man disappear instantly made them look suspect."

"You are right," Clara said, wondering why she had not thought of that before. As soon as Tennent was found missing, the hue and cry was raised, making the bog unviable as a hiding place for guns. Better to have just moved them and kept the matter as quiet as possible.

"It was a peat digger who suggested the Lynch brothers as suspects, wasn't it?" O'Harris said.

"Ay, that was Jimmy McLear," Mr Cork said. "A nasty bit of work, too. Would rather find myself in trouble with the Lynch brothers than him."

"Does Jimmy still live in the area?" Clara asked, thinking he was someone she needed to talk to.

"He does, over on Finney's Farm. His wife's father runs the place. Jimmy is good for nothing much, since the accident."

"Accident?" O'Harris asked, feeling he was expected to. Mr Cork had that look on his face of a person who wants to tell you more but doesn't feel they quite can unless you ask for the information first.

"He had an accident in the bog," Mr Cork said. "Jimmy has never made sense when speaking of it. He says someone reached up and dragged him into the mud. When they found him, he was ha' drowned and he has been a nervous wreck ever since. Can't go near ta bog. Can't go near a muddy puddle, for that matter."

"Was this before or after Mr Tennent died?" Clara asked, exchanging a subtle look with O'Harris. She wondered if he was thinking the same as her.

Mr Cork thought for a moment.

"After," he said at last. "Yes, yes, he had the accident, then a few days later he was chirping to the police, like a choirboy."

Mr Cork mused on this a bit longer and then added.

"I always thought the Lynch brothers had fallen out with him and tried to drown him, or at least there had been a fight, and that was why he tattled to the police about them."

"You don't think it was a guilty conscience, then?" O'Harris suggested. "Considering he might have been involved himself?"

"Nah," Mr Cork shook his head. "Jimmy doesn't have a conscience."

A Body Out of Time

He grimaced.

"Ya know, the folks about here are always going on about the Lynch brothers, how bad they were, but Jimmy McLear could be just as bad. Get some beer into him and he was a devil. Trouble was, the lassies all adored him because he was good looking and could charm the angels from heaven," Mr Cork snorted at the fickle nature of women. "We were quite surprised when he actually married. And she a plain little thing. Though it was just as well, for he han't worked a day since that strange do in the bog, and his little wife and her family support him."

"You think he married her for her money?" Clara elaborated.

"Well, he had his pick, didn't he? Even that Miss Heath was bellyaching over him."

Mr Cork vaguely waved in the direction of the cottage.

"Not that her uncle approved. He saw Jimmy for what he was, all right."

There was a knowing look in Mr Cork's eye. The implication was that Jimmy had been after all he could get from Miss Heath, namely her uncle's fortune, and outside of that his interest in her was limited. Clara thought of the mousey woman they had met in her tiny cottage, shut away from the world while she painted. She was not a person who could be imagined having a dangerous love affair, she had seemed too quiet, too humble. Obviously, they had been wrong.

"What do you think happened to Mr Tennent?" O'Harris repeated his earlier question. "If you don't consider the Lynch brothers responsible, you must have another theory."

Mr Cork sucked in his lower lip and his brow lowered as he went into deep thought over this question. No doubt he had spent many hours contemplating who had snatched away his favourite poet. Every time he read a piece by Mr Tennent, so the question would stir up once more. After a long time, when he seemed to have drifted off to another place, Mr Cork roused himself to give an answer.

"I think someone wanted him dead," he said. "And that was all there is to it. It weren't about robbing the house. It weren't about his poems. It weren't about guns in the mud. It was vengeance, for a grievance none of us know about."

That was not terribly helpful, Clara felt.

"You ask me, that Mr Tennent had big thoughts on his mind, big troubles. Sometimes he sat in ta cart and he was solemn as the priest at a graveside," Mr Cork glanced at the cart as if he might see the dead poet sitting there. "He ne'er spoke on it, though. And I asked him. I asked what troubled him so? He said it was nothin', nothin' at all."

Clara could not help also looking at the back of the cart. In her mind she was conjuring up an image of Mr Tennent, sitting despondently. What had been troubling him?

"He left ta world behind to come here," Mr Cork continued. "A man don't do that unless he has a lot he wants ta forget about."

"You think he came to Ireland to get away from something?" Clara said. "Some terrible problem?"

Mr Cork shrugged.

"That was my impression. He loved this place, that I know for sure, but he also had something that was eating at him. He never went back to England, never. It spoiled this place for him, not being able to go back."

It was the first time anyone had mentioned that Mr Tennent had a past he was trying to leave behind. Clara reflected that this new information actually made the poet feel more real. It also added a new insight to her appreciation of his poems. When you knew that he was a man trying to leave behind his past, and unable to return to the place he was born, you read his poems with fresh eyes and saw a man who was truly, desperately hankering for a place he could never have. The verses took on a new aura of melancholy. Tennent had known what it was to lose something he loved and to feel there was never any going back, and no way to heal the wounds. His poems had been a window into his breaking heart.

"That makes sense," Clara said, with sudden

understanding. "It changes the way you read his poems."

"That it does," Cork agreed. "You know, if I had been a wiser man, I might have thought of a way to get him to talk about his problems. But all I am good at it is driving this donkey cart."

"I think you sell yourself short," O'Harris replied with a smile. "I think you have more wisdom than you realise."

"Hm," the old man huffed. "Hasn't done me much good."

He chuckled and patted the donkey's shaggy coat.

"Still, it isn't a bad life and at least I am free to live it."

He glanced up at the sun, judging time.

"I must be going, there is a market to get to. Ya sure you don't want a lift?"

"No," Clara promised him. "We are sure. But it has been good to talk."

"You are determined ta go ta the bog then?" Mr Cork added.

"We are, I'm afraid," Clara smiled at him.

His cheer disappeared and he cast a wary eye in the direction of the dig.

"You mark my words, the dead don't care ta be disturbed," he said. "That there was once a sacred place and it should ta remained a sacred place. They never should ta dug the peat there. I told 'em so. But I am one old man, and people say ta old ways are gone. 'We believe in God and Jesus, Mr Cork, not some silly old heathen gods.' I say it int about what we believe, but about what once was believed. The earth remembers, see? Ah, but I don't suppose I make any sense ta you modern folks."

"On the contrary, I understand," Clara assured him. "It makes very good sense to me."

Mr Cork stared at her a while. He seemed to be contemplating if she was serious or was just saying things to please him. Ultimately, he decided she was genuine, and a small smile graced his lips.

"I see you aren't such English fools after all," he said, shyly. "I rather thought you were like all the rest when you arrived with no rubber galoshes and looking as if ta dust of town was still in your hair."

"Well, it probably was," Clara confessed. "But we are certainly not like the other tourists you get. I go so far as saying we are somewhat unique."

O'Harris cast her a sidelong look of amusement.

"That you are," Mr Cork grinned. "You be taking care now."

He nodded to them, then flicked the reins and made a clicking noise. The donkey, which had appeared almost asleep, or possibly comatose, it was hard to tell, now roused, cocked one ear backwards and after a suitable length of time when Mr Cork swore at it and made idle threats of violence if it failed to move, it shook its soft head and clattered forward. The cart bounced over the road and Mr Cork waved them farewell.

"That was interesting," O'Harris said.

"Very," Clara nodded. "I think we shall need to speak to Mr McLear."

"I'm sure I saw a map that showed Finney's Farm a few miles in that direction," O'Harris pointed past Clara. "We could walk it."

Clara was about to suggest they set off at once, when she was distracted by a cry from the dig site. She and O'Harris walked to the far wall that lined the road and looked across the meadow to the bog in time to see Professor Peabody gallop across the mud, fling himself at Mr Lethbridge (who was stood watching him in astonishment) and grapple him to the ground. There they began to wrestle.

"Oh dear," Clara sighed as she started over the wall. "What has happened now?"

Chapter Twenty-Three

Lethbridge was down on the ground with Professor Peabody attempting to grapple him into a headlock. The eccentric academic was too dazed by the situation to react, fortunately the professor was not much of a fighter himself. Before Clara and O'Harris could reach the scene, Jason and Rufus were hauling the enraged archaeologist off his victim. Lethbridge sat up on the muddy earth and stared at his assailant as if he had no clue as to what had just occurred.

"You third rate nincompoop!" Peabody yelled. "We agreed, you hear! Agreed!"

Clara reached Lethbridge who was making no attempt to get up from where he was sat.

"Mr Lethbridge?"

He looked up at her as if waking from a dream.

"Yes, my dear?"

"He couldn't resist! Just couldn't resist!" Professor Peabody was screaming. "After all I had agreed to! He has done himself no favours!"

Rufus and Jason had managed to manhandle Peabody into the finds tent. His shrill voice could still be heard crying out his fury. Clara crouched down by Lethbridge.

"I think you ought to get up."

Lethbridge seemed to remember where he was at last. He looked at his muddy clothes with distaste and then levered himself up into a standing position. He brushed his hands together, though all that did was move the mud around.

"What happened?" O'Harris asked.

Lethbridge looked forlornly at his shirt sleeves, which were now beyond redemption. He had lost a button which had, admittedly, already been coming loose, during the scuffle. He plucked at the barren strands of thread where once it had been and glanced at the ground in the vain hope he might spot the button, then he sighed.

"I'm not really sure. I was just putting in my latest rods – I have had some exciting findings already you know! I am positive we have a horse carving here – and then Peabody launched himself at me. Called me a traitor and an imbecile. I don't know what that was about and, quite frankly, it was positively rude. I should give him a piece of my mind."

Lethbridge started towards the tent and O'Harris hastily grabbed his arm.

"Perhaps not just now," he said.

The fight had returned to Lethbridge and he was almost trembling with outrage at the thought of what had just occurred. The delayed reaction was quite impressive.

"There must be a reason Professor Peabody snapped," Clara said, trying to work out what had happened along with defusing the situation. "Had you put any of your iron rods too close to his dig site?"

"No fear of that, he has all his team watching me like hawks," Lethbridge snorted.

"Then what could possibly have happened?"

"I don't know," Lethbridge said in exasperation. "I was just getting on with my own work, minding my own business."

"Hang on," O'Harris interrupted, he had spotted something at the far side of the meadow. "The police are here."

They all looked up and saw a trio of policemen walking towards the dig site. They were in the uniform of the Civic Guard and would have looked very smart and serious, except they kept getting their boots stuck in the mud and had to yank themselves free, which spoiled the impression.

"Oh," Lethbridge said idly. "I wonder if they are to do with the fellow who came earlier."

"What fellow?" Clara asked.

Lethbridge blew out his cheeks as if this was an incredibly taxing question.

"I don't know his name, but he was in a dark brown suit and he forgot to wear wellingtons, so his trousers were thick with mud. He didn't look like a peat digger and he certainly wasn't an archaeologist."

O'Harris glanced at Clara.

"Are you thinking what I am thinking?" he asked.

"Someone has told the police about the body," Clara nodded. "The man in the suit was likely the inspector, or whatever the equivalent rank is in Ireland. No wonder Peabody is furious. It looks like his dig site is about to be shut down."

Understanding dawned for Lethbridge, you could actually see the moment realisation hit on his face. His expression of confusion lifted to one of indignation.

"And he thought I had called them?"

"I'm guessing you didn't?" O'Harris replied.

"Of course not, that would spoil my investigation of the site," Lethbridge looked hurt that O'Harris had to ask. "This is terrible."

The police had marched through the dig site, watched anxiously by the archaeologists in their various trenches. The uniformed men disappeared inside the finds tent and a new wail of outrage flooded over the site in the next moment. Peabody was having the worst day of his life.

"Well, that is that," Clara said, feeling relieved someone had had the courage to summon the police, and a little ashamed it had not been her. She had allowed her concerns for Susan to overrule what she had known was the right thing to do.

"Ought we to return the pocketknife?" O'Harris whispered to her.

She was about to answer when a bluff man exited the tent, his face red as beetroot and a hard look in his eyes.

"That's the man," Lethbridge mumbled. "I think I best go collect my rods."

He departed as surreptitiously as he could. The red-faced man looked around him, scowling.

"Damn it, why are you all just stood there? Get out of those trenches!" he barked at the archaeologists.

The diggers looked flustered as they scurried out of their trenches, one was clutching a small object he had just excavated.

"What is that? Evidence you are removing?" the burly man snapped at him.

"No. This is a Bronze Age brooch, probably put into the bog as an offering to the gods…"

The police detective, as Clara assumed he was, snatched the object off the digger.

"Could be this was put in with the murdered man, hey?" he demanded.

"Well, n…no. He was found in that trench and I was digging this one over here…"

"Then this isn't important to my case," the detective snapped, and with that threw the brooch over his shoulder and back into the mud.

The digger made an anguished noise at the back of his throat and had to be held back by one of his friends.

"Listen up!" the policeman addressed them. "As of now you all have to leave this site and not return. It is a crime scene and until we resolve this matter you can do nothing here. So, go back to your lodging houses, or even better, go back to England."

The man strutted about the site looking like the king of the castle. The diggers reluctantly walked away, some having to be forced to leave by their friends. Peabody emerged from the finds tent with Susan at his side.

"You should know I shall be making a formal complaint concerning all this," the professor declared fiercely.

"You're just lucky I am not arresting you for concealing a crime!" the detective retorted.

Peabody deflated, but his defiance still burned strong.

"I shall come back!" he declared before leaving with Susan.

Clara watched him leave then walked over to the man in the dark brown suit. He was middle-aged and looked like he had carried a lot of muscle in his prime, but this was now turning to fat. He had an arrogant expression on his face which Clara felt did not bode well.

"Good morning," she said to attract his attention.

"Everyone must leave the site. This is the scene of a murder," he said to her the second his head swung her way.

Clara was undeterred.

"Yes. I heard you earlier. Might I ask your name?"

"Inspector O'Connor of The Civic Guard," he declared.

"Well, I'm confused, I thought the Royal Irish Constabulary was the police force in Ireland?" O'Harris said.

He received a surly glare from O'Connor for that observation.

"They were, until 1921. But being agents of a foreign power, they were disbanded, and a new independent force was established. The Civic Guard."

"Were you in the Royal Irish Constabulary?" Clara asked innocently, feeling the need to push the man's buttons.

"Certainly not!" O'Connor declared with expected ferocity. "I would not sully myself! my mother would have rolled in her grave!"

"I was just wondering how a person gains enough experience to become an inspector in a little under two years."

"Are you implying I am not fit for the job?" O'Connor growled nastily.

O'Harris took a protective step towards Clara. She was not intimidated, she had met men like O'Connor before, puffed up on their own sense of self-importance.

"I don't believe I said that," Clara said calmly. "I was merely curious how you came by your policing experience."

"I served alongside Michael Collins in the fight for Irish independence. Had I been with him that fateful day he died, I should have prevented the assassination," O'Connor said with staunch conviction. "Since then, I have played my part bringing peace to the new Ireland."

None of which answered Clara's question.

"About the murdered man..." she began.

"Are you still here?" O'Connor hissed at her. "I said everyone is to leave, that includes nosy Englishwomen!"

"Steady on!" O'Harris cried.

Clara was not fazed. She had approached O'Connor to take his measure, to know if he was the sort of policeman she could work with and to decide just how competent he was to solve the murder of Mr Tennent. She had seen enough.

"We should leave John," she said to O'Harris, tugging slyly at his jacket to indicate she had something else to say.

O'Harris still glowered at O'Connor but walked away with Clara. As they were leaving, Clara spotted an object on the ground and bent to pick it up. It had caught a glimmer of the sun as they went past. It was the brooch O'Connor had so disrespectfully flung aside.

Behind them, O'Connor had walked into the finds tent. They heard a sudden bang and crash.

"Sorry, Sir! I bumped into it!" cried a mortified voice.

"Who cares?" O'Connor rumbled back. "It's only old things."

There was a crunch as someone stood on something and crushed it beneath their feet. Clara flinched at the sound.

"Let's hope it was nothing important," O'Harris said, his face also indicating how appalled he was at the behaviour of the police.

"I don't like admitting this, considering I am usually an

advocate for involving the police and doing things by the book," Clara said as they made their muddy way up the meadow. "But I completely understand now why Peabody did not want the police involved until he could secure all the items from the dig site. And I find myself agreeing with him."

"Inspector Park-Coombs would never behave that way," O'Harris said stoutly and with an air of pride as he thought of Brighton's constabulary. "We can't let them destroy the dig site, Clara, we just can't. I don't hold out much hope of that O'Connor fellow being able to solve the case, either. Seems to me he hasn't the first clue about detective work."

Clara thought she heard another crash from the tent and winced. She knew he was right. As important as it was to find justice for Mr Tennent, the destruction of irreplaceable Irish archaeology could not be allowed. And, if there were any more clues lying in the trench where Tennent was buried, they had to find them before the heavy-handed methods of O'Connor caused them to disappear for good.

They joined the forlorn archaeologists on the road running along the top of the meadow.

"Look what he has done," Peabody pointed down to the dig site. "I hope you are happy, Miss Fitzgerald, seeing as you wanted the police summoned too."

"Professor, my opinion on the matter has been completely reversed," Clara informed him. "I now fully appreciate why you were so concerned about the police being involved in this matter and I wish to offer you my full assistance in rectifying the situation."

Peabody frowned at her.

"What does that mean?"

"It means that I wish to assist you in recovering your archaeological finds. We can't do much about the trenches, but we can rescue all the finds from the tent before they are irretrievably destroyed," Clara held out the brooch she had retrieved to him.

Peabody gave a deep sigh at the sight of it.

"What do you propose?" he asked.

"A night-time operation to transport everything from the tent. I have a hunch that our detective friend will do very little to secure the scene and probably won't even leave a guard. We should be able to retrieve everything easily."

Peabody was not the only one listening now, behind him the other diggers were curious.

"I hadn't finished up in my trench," one said. "I had just exposed what I think was the tip of a sword."

"Ever dug by lamplight?" Peabody asked him.

The man shook his head.

"It isn't easy, but in an emergency you do the best you can. We'll salvage what we can from the trenches tonight too."

Everyone was nodding their agreement as the operation formed in their minds.

"Damn Lethbridge!" Peabody said suddenly, clenching his fists.

"Lethbridge did not speak to the police," Clara responded. "Of that I am sure. He was as surprised as everyone else when they turned up."

Peabody frowned.

"Well, who else? Only those at the dig knew of the body," Peabody paused ominously. "And you!"

He pointed a shaky finger at Clara. She pushed away his hand.

"I certainly did not speak to the police. I made a promise to Susan I wouldn't, remember?"

"Clara is trustworthy," Susan interjected. "I am positive of that."

Peabody still had a sceptical look on his face, and he seemed ready to accuse Clara of anything in that moment. She spoke before he could reach a decision.

"Would I offer to help if it really was me?"

Peabody opened and shut his mouth uselessly.

"I have been doing exactly as I promised you I would,

investigating the matter of this body discreetly. I have told no one of its discovery, that I can assure you," Clara continued.

Peabody still looked twitchy, but he seemed to accept her explanation.

"Then we have a traitor in our midst!" he said loud enough that everyone heard. "Someone from the dig reported this to the police. Well, I hope they are satisfied as they watch all that rare and irreplaceable Irish archaeology being trampled on. Fifty years from now, no one will remember the name of Tennent, but if we had done our job properly, they would have remembered this place. This place and the people who once used it would have become immortal."

"All is not lost," Susan told him gently. "As Clara says, we shall come back tonight and rescue what we can."

Peabody clamped his lips together in a thin line.

"But will that be enough? I ask myself."

Chapter Twenty-Four

Working alongside Andrew had produced a new understanding between him and Tommy. Or so Tommy thought. As they worked and the dogs played among the debris of the garden, there seemed to be a bond forming. Andrew had even gone up in Tommy's estimation when he helped out Pip, who suddenly came bumbling over on three paws, the fourth held up pathetically. Andrew happened to be nearest her. He crouched down at her side and tenderly inspected the offending paw. A thorn proved to be the source of the drama and with this removed Pip was restored to her usual playful self. She wagged her tail, jumped up at Andrew to express her gratitude, then barrelled off to torment Bramble some more.

Tommy saw a smile on Andrew's face, and he warmed to him further. Dogs saw the truth in a person, he would always say, and Pip had found kindness in his cousin.

All this newfound friendship started to loosen Tommy's reserve about the recent tryst he had witnessed between Andrew and Glorianna. He found himself considering the unthinkable – mentioning what he had seen to Andrew.

"I say, things seem a little better between you and Glorianna," he said to open the topic. "That must make things easier in the house."

"Glorianna isn't precisely going anywhere, it makes sense to get along with her," Andrew sounded gruff again and Tommy lost some of his nerve.

He became distracted trying to force some of the old thatch back into place, which only resulted in it falling apart in his hands.

"Bother," Tommy sighed.

"Do you need a hand?" Andrew came over to assist him, his mood had lightened again.

Tommy took another perilous step towards revealing what he had seen.

"I thought I saw you and Glorianna in town together the other day."

"Did you?" Andrew said noncommittally. "I probably gave her a lift to do some shopping."

"I was here, at this cottage," Tommy edged his way along. "It was a couple of days ago. I was cleaning out the gutters at the back."

"You have been productive," Andrew said, not taking the bait.

Some of his familiar sarcasm had returned. Tommy pegged down some mouldy thatch that was not going to last another winter and decided to dive in feet first. What was the worst that could happen?

No, actually, best not to consider that.

"I saw you and Glorianna stood outside this cottage. You appeared very close."

Andrew tensed; his fingers moved slower as he tied up a bundle of thatch.

"What precisely did you see?" he asked, with a threat of aggression in his tone.

He sounded just like his father right then.

"I think we both know what I saw. It was… unexpected."

"Have you told anyone?"

Andrew's tone was definitely fierce now. Tommy decided to modify the truth.

"I didn't see it as any of my business to tell anyone."
Excluding Annie and Clara.
Andrew relaxed.
"That's... thanks, Tommy. Some people would not be so considerate."
"Is it serious, you two?"
Andrew shrugged.
"I don't really know. It all happened so suddenly. After my disastrous wedding escapade, Glorianna was colder towards me than ever. I was close to leaving the house, except I had no idea where to go. You have probably grasped that out of me, Peg and Susan, only Susan has made a path for herself away from the family. I've been drifting for so long, I couldn't tell you what it is like to do anything productive," Andrew paused. "Until this, that is. Helping this old lady, it feels rather good, actually. I feel I am doing something worthwhile at last."

Andrew handed up the bundle of thatch.

"Maybe I need to become some sort of odd job man," he laughed to himself, but beneath the laugh was a thread of misery. "It began at Christmas. The affair. My father had to go to London for some business and he became unwell and could not return. Glorianna was very worried for him and was not coping with the house and so forth. One day I came across her crying. She looked so pathetic. I could have walked away, maybe I should have. Instead, I went up to her and tried to comfort her.

"That was when things changed. I don't know, it was like I saw her in a new light. We didn't immediately take things further. We were just friendly. Without father around she felt very lonely and I was feeling low over my failed future, so it seemed natural for us to come together and keep each other company.

"Then, on New Year's, we both got rather drunk and things took another direction. Since then, we seem unable to keep out of each other's company."

Andrew paused. Tommy thumped a bundle of thatch into place, a means of letting his thoughts come together before he spoke.

"Do you love her?"

"No, I don't think so," Andrew answered. "Though I am not sure I know what love is. I thought I loved my first wife, and that did not end so well."

He handed Tommy more thatch.

"It's just, if you don't love her, you are playing a dangerous game having this affair," Tommy said. "If someone finds out, someone other than me, your father is going to be furious and heartbroken. You will lose him, you know."

"I have considered that Tommy. I lay in bed and think about it. In truth, I don't want to hurt him, and I keep telling myself I must stop, but then I find myself with Glorianna and I lose all my senses again."

Tommy thought about this, about Andrew's propensity for self-destructive behaviour.

"This is not going to end well," he said.

"Father need never know," Andrew said firmly.

"These things have a way of being discovered. The longer it goes on, the more likely Hogarth will learn of it. I can't tell you what to do, it's not my place, but I think you are fooling yourself if you really believe you can keep this a secret."

Andrew was silent, tying up another bundle of thatch. Tommy was about to change the subject, his point made, when Andrew spoke.

"You are right. I need to make a decision. If this is about lust, then I am being stupid risking my father's trust. If it is about love..."

Tommy looked up sharply as Andrew tailed off.

"I thought you said you didn't love her?"

"I don't think I do, but I am not sure," Andrew sighed. "I need to consider that a possibility."

"What will you do in that case?"

Andrew was quiet a long time.

"Glorianna could divorce my father and be with me," he said, finally.

"If she wishes to," Tommy said darkly. "She might not want to give up Hogarth's money. She might also care for your father."

Andrew's face darkened.

"She does not just think about money," he snapped.

And in that moment, Tommy was convinced Andrew did love her. Only a man in love would react so sharply to such a comment. A sense of doom came over Tommy as he saw the possible way things might go. He was fairly certain Glorianna married Hogarth for his fortune and if she divorced him and went off with Andrew, she would lose all that. She might be behaving foolishly and risking everything, but ultimately Glorianna was prudent and cold. She would not forsake Hogarth and his bank account for his son, who would be penniless without his father's good graces.

"As you say," Tommy deflected the outburst. "Perhaps it would be wise to talk to Glorianna and decide which way things should go, before there is no turning back?"

Andrew was tired of the conversation. He yanked the knot on the thatch bundle hard and then passed it to Tommy.

"We must be nearly done?" he said.

Tommy was not sure if he was referring to the thatch or their conversation about his affair. He decided to opt for the safer topic.

"I think we have done our best. With any luck it will keep the rain out."

Tommy patted the thatch, taking a little pride in his work.

"Tomorrow, if the weather holds, we ought to paint the walls."

He descended the ladder to join Andrew.

"I can see how people can take pleasure in doing things like this," he observed. "It gives you a sense of satisfaction."

"Poor old Mrs Lynch," Andrew replied. "Being neglected so. Makes you feel furious towards the rest of these folks."

A Body Out of Time

Andrew cast a dark look around him, happening to catch the eye of a passing woman, who flinched at the ferocity of his gaze. Tommy was relieved that Annie appeared at the door in that moment.

"You have been busy," she said, proud of their endeavours. "Mrs Lynch is feeling quite tired and has gone to lay down. I think we ought to leave her in peace."

"Sounds like a good idea, looking at that sky," Andrew pointed a finger at the gathering thick grey clouds. "I'll get the car ready."

They gathered up the dogs and brushed the dirt off them before they bundled into Andrew's car. They had finished the roof just in time, for no sooner were they driving off, then the clouds opened and pelted them with heavy rain.

They were glad to get back to the house, though a little surprised when they discovered the entire dig party crowded into the dining room and holding a council of war. Tommy was not astonished to see that Clara was chairing it.

"What ho? What is this all about?" he asked as they wandered in.

"The Civic Guard have taken over my dig site," Peabody wailed, a look of desperation in his eyes. "They are damaging the finds as we speak. There could be nothing left when we return."

He hid his head in his hands and shocked everyone by beginning to sob. Susan glanced around the table, and when no one offered assistance, she reached out and gingerly patted his shoulder.

"We are going to conduct a night raid of the site and rescue everything," Clara explained. "We are preparing as we speak."

"Oh dear," Annie sighed. "Well, if that is the case, would you care for some apple tarts I made today with Mrs Lynch? They are her own recipe."

She placed a covered basket on the table and whipped off the tea towel that was hiding its contents. Keen eyes fell on the baked goods within and it was not long before everyone was helping themselves. Except for Professor Peabody.

"How can anyone eat at a time like this?" he demanded, his face red from crying. "This is a national calamity! Thousands of years of history are at risk of being destroyed by those thugs."

His words, though emotive and powerful, only paused the sounds of eating for a brief moment. Annie's cooking had that effect on people. The world might be ending, but you would still finish whatever it was she had baked that day.

"We are going to resolve this situation," Clara promised Peabody. "But we can do nothing until nightfall."

"Why are you getting involved in all this?" Andrew asked abruptly.

He sounded very much like the Andrew Clara remembered, the one who had referred to her as a busybody.

"The Civic Guard are a rather new force, and I am not convinced their inspector has much notion of how to go about investigating a murder," she informed Andrew. "He also has no regard for the importance of the dig site and the finds there. We have to protect the archaeology."

"What about solving the murder?" Andrew asked, looking directly at Clara.

"I'll do my best," Clara said. "Now I see that the police are not to be relied upon."

"Clara thinks the murdered man is Mr Tennent, the man who had this house and who disappeared," Susan added. "It makes sense."

Andrew had a new look on his face, he was intrigued.

"I think you can count me in, then. If Susan needs help saving her archaeology, who am I to refuse?"

"Good," declared Clara. "We shall set out as soon as it is dark. We need all the time we can get. With any luck the Civic Guard won't place anyone to watch over the site, but if there is someone there, we shall deal with them. In the meantime, everyone needs to eat and prepare themselves. I have told Mrs Kelly we have extra guests for dinner."

Clara came around the table, helping herself to the last of Annie's apple tarts as she went past.

"How was your day?"

"Tiring, but productive," Tommy grinned. "I'm going to take a bath, if you'll excuse me."

"Me too," Andrew sniffed at his shirt. "I smell like a pond."

The two men wandered off, leaving Annie with Clara.

"They seem to be getting on well," Clara said, slightly surprised.

"They are," Annie nodded. "Clara, I have some information for you."

She directed Clara to the hallway where they could not be overheard.

"Mrs Lynch has told me, and I utterly believe her, that her grandsons were with her the whole night Mr Tennent disappeared."

"Ah," Clara said thoughtfully. "That is curious."

"It means they could not have caused his disappearance."

"And the peat digger who claimed they had been responsible was lying, or else had got the wrong end of the stick," Clara tapped a finger against her chin. "The Lynch brothers did leave soon after, however."

"Mrs Lynch says that was because she told them to. She was scared they would be falsely arrested, with all the village against them, and the discovery of the guns."

"They certainly were not clever about what they were doing. But it seems they were not murderers. But who else could it be?"

Annie flicked her eyes up and down the hallway to see who was around, then dropped her voice to a whisper.

"Mrs Lynch suggested someone. She said we should look closer to home and at Mrs Kelly."

Clara nearly laughed at the suggestion.

"Mrs Kelly?" she hissed. "But she was so distressed at

this disappearance."

"I can only say what I was told," Annie said stoically. "Mrs Lynch says Mrs Kelly is good with a carving knife. Those were her exact words."

"And Mr Tennent was stabbed," Clara nodded, feeling a pang of horror at the very idea.

Chapter Twenty-Five

"It's rather like a night operation during the war," Tommy remarked to O'Harris as they donned their wellingtons. "Except without the machine guns and a bombardment."

He paused for a moment.

"Nor the barbed wire, the gas or people dying."

"In short, it's nothing like it at all then?" O'Harris suggested.

"Well, it is at night, and we are doing this surreptitiously," Tommy defended his statement. "And there is a lot of mud."

"On that I agree," O'Harris groaned. "I wanted to leave mud behind in peacetime."

Annie was fussing around them. She had made it quite plain she was not going to participate. The thought of traversing a wet, boggy meadow in the dark was just not her cup of tea, even for the sake of archaeology. She had, however, snuck into the kitchen once Mrs Kelly had departed and made flasks of hot tea and lots of sandwiches. There were enough sandwiches to feed an army.

She distributed them among the group in various bags and baskets.

"There will be a hot meal waiting for you when you

return," she informed them, and though no one knew exactly when that return might be, every one of them was certain Annie would have food awaiting them, no matter the hour. It would be just ready the second they walked through the door. That was Annie's magic.

Susan pulled a woolly hat down over her head, making sure all her hair was tucked in. She was dressed all in black and looked like some military assassin, ready for action. Clara was surprised at how seriously everyone was taking things.

Even Peg had formed part of the brigade, though that was more out of boredom than any real sense of outrage over the damaged historical finds. In Peg's case, the night raid was a good enough reason to take her out of the fugue she had been suffering since reaching Ireland. Clara had barely had a chance to speak to her during their stay, but she sensed her despondency. Even if she had been able to talk with her, she had no idea what she could say to make her feel better.

"Ready?" Professor Peabody demanded of his troops.

He was wearing a waxed jacket and a deer stalker Sherlock Holmes would have been proud of. He had loosened the ear flaps and tied them under his chin, so he had the appearance of some sort of pointer dog.

His motley crew made murmurs of agreement and he set forth into the night, a general ahead of his army. They walked from the house, crossed the road, and were soon stood behind the wall of the meadow. There was a crescent moon in the sky casting a silvery sheen on the damp grass. Where water had pooled, it glimmered in the light.

There was no sign of anyone about. As Clara had suspected, Inspector O'Connor had not deemed it important to leave someone guarding the crime scene. Presumably, the body had been removed and now the inspector had lost interest in the place. Whether that meant he would allow the archaeologists to continue their work was questionable. He seemed like a man who was inclined neither towards history, nor the English. He

A Body Out of Time

might refuse to allow them to dig for the reason of their nationality alone. He had seemed the sort of petty, pumped up man inclined to such mindless acts of authority.

They clambered over the wall and crossed the meadow as quietly as was possible. Which was not all that quiet, since their boots kept getting stuck in the mud and there would be a frantic squelch as a leg was wrenched free.

As they neared the dig site Tommy, who was out ahead, held up a hand to stop everyone.

"Listen!" he hissed.

They listened. Now their squelching march had ended they could hear a new sound cutting across the night. It was the steady sound of snoring.

Peabody flinched.

"It's coming from the finds tent!"

It seemed a guard had been left and he was taking his duty none too seriously. Well, he could not be blamed for thinking a muddy meadow would attract few trespassers. If only he had realised how determined archaeologists could be when their discoveries were in danger.

Tommy waved to O'Harris.

"We've got this," he whispered to the others and then he started to quietly progress towards the tent, O'Harris at his heels.

"Told you it was like a night raid during the war," Tommy reminded O'Harris. "Sneaking up on an enemy sentry."

"We are not going to bayonet him, are we?" O'Harris said.

Tommy gave him an unamused look, which was utterly lost in the dark. He realised this a moment later.

"No," he said, which failed to convey what he thought of the jest.

They reached the tent flap and peered around it. The snoring guard was sitting in a chair in one corner, a blanket wrapped around him and his head nestled on a bundled-up coat. It was not the most comfortable sleeping position, but it was clearly serving him well. He was deep in the land of nod, his snores so loud that it was obvious why he had not heard the approaching diggers.

"We'll tie him up and blindfold him," Tommy suggested.

O'Harris looked around him and noticed some old sacks near the tent flap. They had been used for shifting clumps of mud thought to contain precious small items. The sort of delicate things it was too risky to try to uncover in a trench. O'Harris picked up the nearest bag, which smelt of earth, but was otherwise dry.

They walked carefully into the tent. It was going well until Tommy caught his foot on something in the darkness and nearly overturned the big table in the middle. He made a terrible racket, and the guard was stunned from his sleep. As he opened his eyes and tried to grasp what was happening, O'Harris lunged forward and threw the bag over his head.

The guard reacted as was to be expected – attacking O'Harris and trying to wrestle free the bag. Tommy regained his footing and ran forward to assist him. He grabbed one of the man's arms and received a slap from his free hand. O'Harris was still holding the bag down as tight as he could, to prevent them from being recognised. This also had the effect of slowly stifling the man, who began to gasp desperately for air. He stopped flailing at them, and Tommy was able to grab both his hands and bind them at the wrist with a length of cord he wrenched from one of the tables.

O'Harris loosened his grip on the sack, so the guard could breathe, and they stepped back.

"That should do," Tommy whispered.

O'Harris went to the tent flap and waved in the rest of the party.

"What's going on?" the guard demanded, having recovered enough to speak.

No one answered him. The dig team was in the tent and Peabody was passing out instructions.

"We'll take everything out in crates. The finds should

be in trays, stack them in those if you can. Smaller things might be best in pockets."

Jason gave a sharp moan. He had discovered that the item that had been accidentally destroyed by the police was a delicate clay figurine of a man on a horse. It was now in several pieces and some parts had been ground to dust.

"It was unique," he groaned forlornly.

Peabody's outrage could be sensed by everyone, but he managed to keep his cool and concentrate on organising the rescue of everything else. They cleared out the finds tent by lamplight, packing things as fast as they could, while taking due care. The guard was surrounded by people but blind to them also. He kept turning his hooded head from side to side, trying to work out what was going on.

"That's the property of the Civic Guard!" he said defiantly. "It's illegal to remove it!"

No one was listening.

"You have assaulted an officer of the law! This will go badly for you!"

"We should have gagged him too," Tommy mentioned to O'Harris.

"Too late now," O'Harris shrugged.

Once the tent clearance was well underway, some of the diggers departed for the trenches to recover the artefacts they had been unearthing when the Civic Guard arrived. Peabody was busy taking a crude inventory of everything. He seemed satisfied that despite his worst fears nothing was missing. They started to form a convoy back up to the house, each taking a section of the longer journey and passing the crates and sacks to each other. This way the salvaged finds made a rapid progression from the site.

"It is an imperfect solution," Peabody sighed to Clara as they both paused in their tasks.

He was making sure nothing had been left behind in the finds tent, while she was keeping an eye on both the guard and the progress of the team conveying the finds away.

"It is better than nothing," Clara reminded him.

A Body Out of Time

Peabody nodded, but she knew what he was thinking. He had spent years investigating this site and persuading the relevant people to allow him to dig here. Now, in the span of just a few hours, all that work had gone to waste. It was unlikely the temperamental landowner would let them dig here again after they had discovered a murdered man in his meadow – the famous missing poet, no less. It could be decades before archaeologists were allowed to explore this bog once more. In the meantime, the peat diggers would continue their work and who knew what they would uncover and destroy in the process? A whole segment of Irish history could simply vanish and there was nothing Peabody could do about it.

The bound guard started to fuss again. Every once in a while, he would try to loosen his bonds.

"Now stop that," Clara told him. "We have caused you no harm, just be patient."

"You'll never get away with this, you English thugs!" snapped the guard.

"Fine words from a man who was complicit in the destruction of his own history," Peabody retorted. "If it wasn't for us you would never know the skill and sophistication of your own ancestors. We are trying to save that, to give Ireland a future through its past. Culture, my friend, culture is the mark of a strong society!"

The guard was unprepared for this outburst and obviously did not know what to say. He fell back on his favourite tried and tested statement.

"You'll never get away with it!"

Peabody grunted at the man's single-minded ignorance and went back to checking under the tables. Clara was looking out of the tent and gave a start. Peabody heard and banged his head on the underneath of the table as he stood up.

"What is it?"

"I thought it was that inspector coming," Clara said. "But it is only Lethbridge."

Peabody probably would have scowled less if it was the

inspector. Lethbridge was marching across the meadow as fast as it was possible with the ground sucking at his feet. He was waving a hand and calling out.

"Hey, what are you doing?"

"Be quiet, you stupid man!" Peabody hissed under his breath.

"I suppose we could have told him," Clara said.

"I'll have nothing to do with the idiot."

Lethbridge was just cupping his hands about his mouth to aid his shouts when he abruptly vanished. Peabody and Clara froze.

"Did you see that?" Peabody said, sudden realisation dawning. "He has sunk in the bog!"

They heard a faint cry for help and raced outside in the direction of where Lethbridge had last been seen. Jason and Rufus were clambering out of a trench to join them. O'Harris and Tommy were not far behind, but it was Peg who reached him first, having been assisting in the trench nearest to where Lethbridge had vanished.

"He's gone right under!" she shouted at them, arms up to her elbows in water.

Peabody fell to his knees beside her and rummaged in the water.

"I think I've got his arm!"

They had all gathered by now and between them they wrestled Lethbridge out of the deep water of the bog. He spluttered muddy water and groaned, but at least he was alive. They dragged him out and rested him on the ground, where he gasped and whimpered.

"Something stabbed my side," he mumbled.

Clara brought her lamp closer and what she thought had been a mud stain on his shirt proved to be blood. She lifted his shirt and saw there was a small gash in his flesh.

"Best get him to the house," she said.

O'Harris and Rufus helped Lethbridge to his feet.

"Take it careful," Susan said anxiously. "There could be more watery holes like that one."

Lethbridge was coughing and shivering as they helped

him slowly across the meadow.

"That man is a walking disaster," Peabody sighed, flicking brown water off his hands. He saw that Clara was crouched by the water. "What are you doing?"

"Something stabbed Lethbridge in the side," Clara said. She was moving her lamp along the edge of the mud, where grass became water. Something caught her eye and she reached down and dislodged it from the earth.

Peabody stepped a bit closer to see what she had found.

"It's a peat cutting blade," he said.

It looked like the blade of a very large carving knife, only it was partially broken. The point had been sticking out of the soil by several inches.

"We have found a couple of them so far," Peabody shrugged. "If they snap, the peat diggers just abandon them in the water."

"Rather dangerous," Clara said. "Lethbridge could have been killed if he landed on this the wrong way."

"I don't suppose the peat diggers think people will be wandering about here much," Peabody shrugged. "Or they don't really care."

Clara splashed the broken blade in the muddy water and watched as it glistened in the moonlight. Its handle had snapped, making it useless to the peat diggers, yet it was still a sharp and deadly blade.

It was as the moonlight spun across the tarnished old metal that a fresh idea came to Clara, a thought of how a man with no enemies could end up dying in a bog, apparently stabbed by attackers.

But why? Why had he been here at all?

Peabody was walking back to the tent. Clara rose and followed him, her mind racing. She was thinking about how Lethbridge had suddenly disappeared in the bog and if they had not seen him go down, how he could have drowned without anyone knowing.

And slowly things began to make sense.

Chapter Twenty-Six

It had been expected there would be trouble the next day after the night-time operation. An irate Inspector O'Connor knocked hard on the door of Mr Tennent's cottage early in the morning, while most of the household were still trying to recover from their adventures of the night before. Only Hogarth, Glorianna and the ever awake Austin were up and about. Fortunately, Mrs Kelly opened the door to the inspector, and no more fearsome an individual could be envisioned to take the wind out of the puffed-up policeman.

Annie had felt it prudent to give Mrs Kelly a carefully crafted account of what had happened at the dig. The discovery of the body, the suspicion it was that of Mr Tennent, the trampling of the police over the dig site and what that could mean to the precious Irish archaeology – the archaeology that was part of the lost world Tennent wrote about and adored. It was this final, choice suggestion that settled things in the mind of Mrs Kelly. Anyone who would work against her dear Mr Tennent was her enemy. Annie had surreptitiously added that Clara was working on discovering what had happened in the bog and was liable to do a far better job than the police – just think how useless they were when Mr Tennent disappeared in the first place, after all – and that sealed the deal. When Inspector O'Connor arrived at the house, he found himself confronting a woman who considered him the spawn of the Devil and was going to have no truck with his nonsense.

"I need to speak to the household," O'Connor told Mrs Kelly.

She folded her arms across her ample bosom, an indication that war had been declared.

"You shall talk to no one under this roof without a good reason."

O'Connor was not a local man, he therefore had no idea of the dangerous territory he was about to stumble into.

"Madam, this is a Civic Guard matter. A crime scene has been interfered with. A member of our force was trussed up."

"Crime scene?" Mrs Kelly asked him nastily. "Crime scene? What crime scene can there be in a bog? In the mud and the water? The crime scene was here, thirteen years ago, and your predecessors didn't do a thing about it!"

"That was the Royal Irish Constabulary," O'Connor countered. "That was nothing to do with the Civic Guard."

"And that makes it better?" Mrs Kelly demanded. "Exactly how long has the Civic Guard been in existence, Inspector?"

O'Connor blinked. No one had ever defied him like this. No one had ever asked such questions.

"Madam, as you well know, we were founded last year by the Provisional Government, to replace those foreign controlled scum of the Royal Irish..."

"My nephew was in the Royal Irish Constabulary," Mrs Kelly said with a hint of pride in her voice. "He looked very smart in his uniform."

O'Connor changed tack.

"Of course, there were many good Irishmen in the RIC. Natural to want to bring law and order to their country."

"And now there is you," Mrs Kelly said with an unpleasant edge to her tone that suggested O'Connor was something soft and smelly she had just stood in.

O'Connor brazened out this insult on his dignity.

"I am an Inspector, Madam, in the Civic Guard. You ought to show a little respect."

"Ay, as you did our fine and noble history? I can understand 'foreign scum' smashing up Irish historical artefacts, you almost expect it. But I thought a native-born man would have a bit more heart."

O'Connor was thrown again by this change of direction, and he impulsively replied by saying exactly the wrong thing.

"It was only some old bits and pieces."

"And that is precisely what makes me ashamed to be considered of the same nation as you!" Mrs Kelly snapped; a thick finger pointed at the inspector. "Mr Tennent understood how things were. He understood how precious the past was to the future of Ireland and he was English!"

"Madam! The future does not come from little bits of pot and broken swords!"

"And that is where you are wrong!" Mrs Kelly said stoutly. "And I'll have you know something. Not a single soul left this house last night."

"How can you know that?" O'Connor barked.

"Are you calling me a liar? Holy Mother of God! I have never been so insulted! I shall tell the village! I shall tell Father Oakes! Calling me a liar!"

"That is not what I meant!" O'Connor said, aware he was fighting a losing battle and not sure how that had happened.

In O'Connor's experience of power, which had been brief and had occurred because of the Civil War, all you had to do was say a few magic words (usually, 'you are either working with us or against us') and people did exactly as you asked. Of course, he had used to carry a gun, but now he was not a freedom fighter, but a respectable policeman. It suddenly dawned on O'Connor that this was the problem, followed by the equally sound realisation that if he tried to strong-arm Mrs Kelly, perhaps at the point of a gun, he would be liable to end up with a cracked skull.

A little notch had been chipped out of O'Connor's shell of self-importance, and it was going to begin a crack of destruction that would prove unstoppable. Arrogance occasionally meets its match.

"Madam…"

"If you call me madam one more time, I shall box your ears!" Mrs Kelly informed him and O'Connor unconsciously winced. He seemed to have regressed to boyhood before her.

"You have to appreciate that a crime has been committed!" O'Connor tried one last effort.

"Yes," Mrs Kelly said coldly. "It was criminal when they allowed rebel goons to become police inspectors, when good, honest lads who had done all their proper training and passed their exams find themselves without work."

O'Connor attempted to keep up with the conversation, which seemed to be diving off in different directions every moment.

"Now we are referring to your nephew again?"

"How long have you been a policeman, Mr O'Connor," Mrs Kelly said coldly.

O'Connor was so rattled, he failed to notice she had dropped his title.

"I was one of the first taken into the new Civic Guard," he said proudly, finding some of his old pluck.

"And before that?"

"Before that?"

"What did you do, Mr O'Connor?"

This time he noticed the loss of his title.

"Inspector O'Connor and I have you know I was a proud volunteer in the freedom movement."

"But what did you do?" Mrs Kelly demanded. "Freedom fighting does not pay the bills."

O'Connor shuffled his feet. This should not be happening to him. He had his brown suit on, he had his title, he had the back-up of the men under his command and yet here he was being cowed by an old woman with a hint of facial hair.

O'Connor was rapidly regretting not bringing any men with him, but then again, if they had been here, they would have seen his humiliation and there was still strife among the Civic Guards, tension and internal disputes that could see a man an inspector one minute, and a nobody on the street the next. Better they did not see O'Connor being berated here on a doorstep, not when a couple of his inferiors were already contemplating how they could have his job for themselves.

"Well?" Mrs Kelly asked, and her tone meant there was no way to avoid answering.

"I was a milkman," O'Connor said in a very small voice. "I don't see what that has to do with anything."

Mrs Kelly looked satisfied.

"I don't want any milk today," she told him, and then she slammed the door in his face.

O'Connor stood on the doorstep, dazed by the whole thing. He raised his fist to knock again, but his bluster had been kicked out of him and his knuckles did not connect with the wood. He took a step back and then turned around. He was certain that Miss Fitzgerald was involved in all this, but if he was unable to get past Mrs Kelly, he would have to settle for someone more accessible. Professor Peabody would be his next target. That man did not have a housekeeper to guard him.

What Inspector O'Connor could not know was that the landlady of the boarding house where Peabody was staying was a good friend of Mrs Kelly's and had been speaking on the telephone to her that very morning (the Tennent cottage had all mod cons) and was now fully briefed as to how to respond to the arrival of the inspector on her doorstep. It was going to be a very bad morning for O'Connor.

It was close to eleven when Clara headed downstairs, still yawning from her adventures and oblivious to the confrontation between Mrs Kelly and Inspector O'Connor. Her first port of call was the long living room where she discovered Mr Lethbridge sitting in a flimsy ray of sunshine coming through the window. He had his eyes shut and seemed quite content. He opened them when he heard Clara enter.

Last night, having helped Mr Lethbridge to the house, there had been a debate about getting him to the local hospital which was several miles away. Lethbridge had not wanted to go; in fact, he was itching to get back to the dig site. Clara knew that sometimes patients who had suffered an accident were living on a surge of adrenaline and would attempt to keep going rather than be sensible and rest. It seemed to be a coping mechanism for some.

As it turned out, Lethbridge's wounds were not deep and were cleaned up by Clara who insisted on using a splash of alcohol on the cut to try to deter the bacteria there must have been in the mud. Lethbridge screeched when she did this, but if it stopped an infection setting in, it was worth it.

Cold and wet, Lethbridge had been assisted to the bathroom where he could bathe and warm up, while Clara explained to a trembling Glorianna that no one was being murdered in the house, despite a scream waking her from her sleep.

Finally, warm and dry, Lethbridge's injury did not look in desperate need of hospital attention and it was agreed he could stay at the cottage for the night. His surge of energy had worn off and he was dead on his feet. He was almost asleep before they laid him on a bed.

"Good morning, Mr Lethbridge, how is your side?"

Mr Lethbridge placed a hand protectively over his wound.

"I feel I was rather lucky. I have seen the blade that stabbed me and if it had not been lying at such a shallow angle, I think it would have killed me."

Clara nodded. She had been thinking the same. Funny how luck could be good or bad, depending on your perspective, wasn't it bad luck Lethbridge fell onto the peat blade at all?

A Body Out of Time

"Did you rescue everything?" Lethbridge asked.

"We believe so. Some of the items had been badly damaged."

"Scoundrels," Lethbridge scowled. "And it's their own cultural heritage too."

"Not everyone thinks like that, unfortunately," Clara sighed. "Still, we have salvaged what we could, and the dig has not been completely ruined."

"What about the body?" Lethbridge said. "Do we know what happened to that fellow?"

"Ah, well that's quite interesting," Clara smiled. "Your fall last night actually gave me an idea of what might have happened to the poor chap."

"It did?" Lethbridge frowned. "How curious. Then who killed him?"

"I have a couple of people to speak to first before I reach a conclusion, but I think it was more a case of 'what' than 'who'."

Lethbridge was puzzled.

"I don't think I understand."

"All will become clear, hopefully. But first, I need to visit someone."

After a hearty brunch, courtesy of Mrs Kelly and Annie who had suddenly developed a deep camaraderie overnight, Clara, O'Harris and Tommy set off towards Little Limerick and to the home of Miss Heath. Clara had not said a lot about her suspicions, she just promised all would become plain as the day progressed – hopefully.

Tommy yawned and dozed in the passenger seat as O'Harris drove. They reached the humble little cottage with its stack of iron in the garden and its eerie appearance of being semi-abandoned. Smoke was creeping out of the chimney, which indicated Miss Heath was present.

"I'm relieved to see the inspector is not here," Clara said as they left the car.

"Do you think he has worked out who the body is, or rather, was?" O'Harris asked.

"I don't know. It seems likely that whoever told him

about the discovery would not have been aware of who the victim was. We have kept that very much to ourselves."

"In which case, he may not even be aware he should speak to Miss Heath," Tommy said, masking another yawn behind his hand.

"Possibly," Clara nodded. "Though, considering he has full access to the police files, it should not take him long to work out that the man who lived right next to the bog went missing back in 1910."

"One would like to think," O'Harris said with sarcasm.

Clara could not blame him for his grim opinion of the inspector, though she liked to think that even such a man was capable of discovering the identity of the body in his charge. If not, it was a pretty sorry state of affairs for everyone.

Clara led the way to Miss Heath's door and knocked lightly. It was not long before the mousey woman with glasses opened it and peered at them. She looked to be wearing the same grey cardigan they had seen her in the other day.

"Oh, hello," she said. There was a hint of anxiety in her tone. "Are you back to hear more about my uncle?"

"It is a little more complicated than that," Clara explained. "Could we come in?"

Miss Heath looked like she might refuse, a mix of emotions crossed her face, then she decided to let them into her private domain. They entered the kitchen and found themselves looking at a new construction of metal parts on the table, dominated by an old bicycle frame. Tommy, who had not been present the other day, looked on in astonishment.

"Well?" Miss Heath asked, glancing at a picture that was half-completed and was clearly calling to her.

"Have you been visited by Inspector O'Connor, at all?" Clara asked her.

Miss Heath shook her head.

"Who?"

"He is an inspector in the Civic Guard."

"Oh, a policeman," Miss Heath screwed up her nose. "Why would he come here?"

Clara sighed, there was no easy way to say this.

"Miss Heath, we believe we have found your uncle's body in the bog."

Chapter Twenty-Seven

Miss Heath sat down heavily in a chair. She stared in a lost fashion at the floor, her mouth hanging open just a fraction, then she ran a hand through her hair, pulling it behind one ear.

"You found him," she said.

"Yes," Clara replied. "The police have been informed, however, I do not believe they are aware of whose body they have. That is something I have kept to myself, mainly as they have not asked me."

Clara glanced at Tommy.

"We found a pocketknife by the corpse."

Tommy held out the knife to his sister. Clara took it.

"It is pretty caked in mud and, despite our best efforts, we have not been able to open it. That being said, I think it would still be possible to identify it as belonging to Jimmy McLear."

Clara held the knife out to Miss Heath. She stared at it.

"Jimmy," she mumbled, then added. "That isn't his knife."

She didn't take the knife.

"Jimmy lied to the police when he said the Lynch brothers had been at the bog that night," Clara soldiered on with her accusation, even though the knife was no longer evidence. "He knew they would be the obvious suspects, what with the guns they had been hiding there, with his assistance. The question I wondered was why he told that lie, what motivated him? Then it occurred to me. Jimmy knew what happened to Mr Tennent, he witnessed it, he was involved and to avoid blame falling upon him, he distracted the police by telling a lie about the Lynch brothers."

Miss Heath had gone grey, her skin taking on a similar hue to her old cardigan.

"I intend to go to see Mr McLear today and learn the truth. I would like you to come too."

"Jimmy didn't kill my uncle," Miss Heath said weakly.

"No, but he knows what happened and he has kept it a secret all these years, as have you. Secrets have a way of destroying you slowly. As I said, I have not offered my information to the police. I am doing this so your uncle can be at peace and so that you and Jimmy can be free of your burden."

Tommy and O'Harris were looking at Clara curiously. They had not been informed of her hunch.

Miss Heath clasped her hands together and paid rivetted attention to the floor.

"Well?" asked Clara. "Aren't you tired of all this?"

"Very tired," Miss Heath admitted. "I have hidden myself away from the world all these years, as a punishment and because I was so afraid. I am done with all that."

"Come with me, then. We shall speak to Jimmy and clear the air. It's time this secret was put to bed."

Miss Heath did not move at once, then slowly, like a doll being pulled up by invisible strings, she stood and nodded at Clara.

"I'll come," she said.

They showed her to the car and settled her in the back, then O'Harris pulled out a map of the area he had bought for 3d and located the farm where Jimmy now resided.

A Body Out of Time

Clara sat beside Miss Heath.

"Who told you about me and Jimmy?" Miss Heath asked.

Tommy answered.

"An old man with a donkey cart."

"Mr Cork," Miss Heath sighed. "He goes past the cottage most days. I thought no one knew."

"Such things don't tend to remain private," Clara said. "Something always slips out. Someone sees something they weren't meant to. Was it such a bad thing that you had to keep it hidden?"

"Jimmy was a cad," Miss Heath allowed a smile to creep onto her lips. "I had no illusions about him. My uncle was horrified by our association and forbid it."

"I suspected as much," Clara replied.

"We were going to be married," Miss Heath sighed. "I believed he loved me, but I imagine I was wrong. All these years on, things look different. Nothing was ever the same after my uncle vanished."

They travelled up a slight hill and then came down into a valley were a stone farmhouse nestled at the base. Smoke plumed gently from the chimney and cows called mournfully as they wandered outside. O'Harris slowed the car down and moved along at a crawl as the cows gathered around the car curiously. Eventually he had to come to a stop.

"Ahem, not sure what you want to do chaps?" he said, a grin on his face as various chestnut brown bovine heads nudged at the car and peered in the windows.

"I don't like cows," Miss Heath winced.

"They are just curious," Clara assured her.

She carefully opened her door, which encouraged one of the cows to slip its head inside the car and nuzzle her, hopeful for food. Clara nearly lost her hat and Miss Heath made a strange squeaking noise that appeared to be a suppressed scream. Gently but forcefully, Clara pushed back the cow and exited the car.

"Now, off you go," she informed the herd. "Go find some

clover to munch on. Shoo! Shoo!"

The cows stared at her with big soft eyes and waited patiently to see if she provided them with food.

"That worked," Tommy chuckled.

Clara glared at him as her hat was almost knocked off again by a cow.

"Hey there!" a voice came from behind the herd. "What are you folks about?"

A man limped through the cows, squeezing between the animals. The cattle kindly moved out of his way, occasionally giving him an affectionate lick on the ear.

"Hello Jimmy," Miss Heath said from the car.

Jimmy glanced into the vehicle and the colour seeped from his face. The years had not been kind to Jimmy. He had once been rakishly handsome, with a charm to match, now he looked haggard and worn. Big bags sagged under his eyes and there was a looseness to his skin that made it seem to be a size too big for him. He was incredibly thin, the sort of person who naturally tends towards a slight frame. He had a nasty limp on his right leg.

He stared and stared at Miss Heath, as if he thought he was dreaming her.

"They've found my uncle, Jimmy," Miss Heath told him. "It's over."

Jimmy swallowed, the noise audible, and looked at the car and the people within.

"What do you want, then?"

"Just to talk and hear the truth," Clara said. "Not so much for our benefit, but for yours. You have been living under a dark cloud for too long, Mr McLear, its eating away at the both of you."

"We didn't do anything wrong," Jimmy said.

"I didn't say you did," Clara replied. "Yet, it still eats at you, doesn't it?"

"I think we should tell them, Jimmy," Miss Heath added. "I am so tired of pretending it did not occur. I feel as if a weight presses down on me all the time, getting heavier and heavier with each passing day. I hate it."

Jimmy dipped his head and was silent a while.

"Why don't we go to the cattle byre," he said. "It's quiet there."

He moved on the cows and enabled them to walk to a low stone building filled with straw. It was cosy inside and they could sit down on hay bales. Jimmy limped around, making sure they were comfortable as if they were in his own parlour, then he sat down on a bale.

"I have this feeling you have guessed most of what happened," he said to Clara.

"I have my suspicions," Clara nodded.

"Can you tell me what my uncle's body was like when it was found?" Miss Heath asked solemnly. "Did he drown?"

"I can't tell you that," Clara answered. "Only an autopsy could determine that, but he looked as if he had just fallen asleep. He had a stab wound in his side, which made us think he was murdered."

"We didn't hurt him," Jimmy said angrily.

"I know," Clara reassured him. "I have a good idea of what happened, since we nearly had a repeat of the incident last night. A gentleman stumbled in the bog, fell and was stabbed by a broken peat cutting blade. He then tumbled into a deep patch of water and could have drowned had we not been able to reach him swiftly. As we helped him out, it struck me how easily he could have ended up as another mysterious body in the bog just like Mr Tennent. I asked myself, what if there was no kidnapping, no murder, but a tragic accident?"

Jimmy was nodding his head.

"That bog has claimed a lot of people over the years. There is this old local story that because of what it was once used for the waters have a taste for blood and lure people in when they are hungry," Jimmy moved his bad leg uneasily. "I've seen for myself how a man can get sucked down in that place."

"We heard about your accident," Clara said. "How it shook you so badly, you could never go back to peat digging."

Jimmy ran a hand over his face, dragging at his chin until the skin seemed to extend and the bags under his eyes briefly disappeared.

"No one believes what I say happened that day."

Miss Heath glanced up.

"What happened Jimmy?" she asked.

His look towards her was filled with surprise and perhaps just a hint of resentment that she did not know.

"You never heard?"

"I don't talk to people, much," Miss Heath said, a quaver of emotion in her voice.

Jimmy snorted.

"Thought everyone knew the story and got a good laugh over it. They said it was my comeuppance, I had it coming. No man deserves what happened to me."

"What happened?" Miss Heath asked again, her expression full of concern.

"Your uncle came for me, that's what happened!" Jimmy snapped. "No one believes me, but I heard his voice calling my name as I was working the bog. I had heard it before, and I tried to ignore it. Told myself it was just my imagination. Then my foot slipped and went into the water and I swear, before God and the Angels, something grabbed my ankle and tried to pull me in. I was stuck, being dragged deeper and I knew it was Edmund Tennent come for me! I struggled so hard, thrashed about that they say I must have dislocated my knee in the process. It has never been right since, but it would have been a lot worse if I had not been rescued. He was going to take me, I know it!"

Jimmy glowered at them, daring them to deny what had happened to him. Clara did not believe in ghouls or the dead coming to collect a debt, but she did think the human imagination could play clever tricks on a man's mind, especially when he was suffering a guilty conscience.

"I never went back to the bog after that, never. Wild horses couldn't drag me there!" Jimmy said staunchly.

Miss Heath seemed at a loss for words. Clara filled in the silence that followed Jimmy's revelations.

"What actually happened the night Mr Tennent disappeared?"

Jimmy had become morose again, his temper fading to nothing. He was a beaten and destroyed man, who had lost his fight long ago.

"You guessed most of it," he said. "I suppose the only part missing is what were we all doing in the bog that night?"

His eyes swivelled to Miss Heath.

"Do you want to tell them, or should I?"

Miss Heath sat up a little straighter. Her voice sounded slightly forced, as if she was trying to keep her emotions from breaking through.

"We were eloping that night," Miss Heath said. "I came back from Dublin sooner than I said. I knew my uncle would be at the golf club until late. My plan was to go into the house, pack a few things and then leave with Jimmy. No one would even realise we were going until after the weekend and by then we would be wed."

"Mr Tennent didn't approve of me," Jimmy added. "He thought I was just after his money and that I thought I could get to it by marrying his niece. That weren't the way of it."

Jimmy slumped further as he thought about how maligned he had been by the world. Everyone had seemed against him.

"It would have gone smoothly, except my uncle came home earlier than usual. He must have felt unwell, I suppose. When I heard him enter the house, I hid in my room so he would not know I was there," Miss Heath continued. "I waited until he had gone to bed and then I slipped downstairs to meet Jimmy at the back door. It should have been fine, only the wind had got up and as we were arranging to leave, it slammed the back door against the wall. We thought at first my uncle didn't hear, then we heard footsteps. We ran, it was all we could do, but he pursued us."

"Hence the footprints in the mud around the back door

and the house," Clara nodded. "Not from people trying to break-in, but people running away."

"He probably thought we were burglars," Jimmy added. "We ran towards the bog and we were quite far ahead. He was behind us, shouting. Then suddenly it went quiet."

"I was sure I heard a splash," Miss Heath said with tears in her eyes. "I turned and there was no sign of my uncle. He was just gone. We went back to look for him. I insisted. But we could see no sign of him, it was like he had just turned into smoke and blown away.

"After that, I couldn't elope with Jimmy. I went back to Dublin and carried on as normal. By then Mrs Kelly had raised the alarm and there was a search for my uncle without success. You don't know how much I hoped to come back from Dublin and find him sitting in his study. To think he just vanished like that, it seems impossible."

Miss Heath turned her gaze to Jimmy.

"We guessed he had been sucked into the bog. Afterwards, I felt so guilty that I had caused his death by my actions. It soured things between me and Jimmy."

Jimmy looked miserable.

"I implicated the Lynch brothers, not because I wanted to save myself, but because I thought the Royal Irish Constabulary would search the bog and find Mr Tennent," he said. "But they were more interested in the guns they found there."

"It was just an accident," Miss Heath added. "No one intended it."

"But we have been paying for it ever since," Jimmy said softly.

His gaze met Miss Heath's and there was silent understanding of a shared and unnecessary guilt. They had finally revealed the truth about the night Mr Tennent vanished, but in that moment, neither felt it had done them any good.

Chapter Twenty-Eight

Clara invited Mrs Kelly to join her in the dining room. The housekeeper looked nervous at the sight of Professor Peabody and his dig party being present, along with Susan, Andrew, Peg and Clara's companions. It was not often Mrs Kelly looked troubled by anything, now she seemed anxious.

"What is this all about?" she demanded.

"I thought you would like to hear what happened to Mr Tennent," Clara answered.

Mrs Kelly's eyes widened.

"You know?"

"I do," Clara said. "I know everything that happened that night."

O'Harris offered Mrs Kelly a chair. She was hesitant to sit down but he smiled and promised it would be all right, so she reluctantly consented.

"Thank you, Mrs Kelly," Clara smiled at her. "I feel we have learned a lot lately about Mr Tennent and his love for this part of Ireland. I am sure, if he were here, he would be perturbed that the discovery of his body has put in peril ancient Irish history."

"You have found Mr Tennent?" Mrs Kelly said.

A Body Out of Time

"Yes. We found him in the bog," Professor Peabody explained. "Truly a disaster for us."

Mrs Kelly, fortunately, did not pick up on this statement.

"Those Lynch brothers did for him!" she declared.

"No, Mrs Kelly, they did not," Clara explained. "In fact, no one hurt Mr Tennent. No one kidnapped him or murdered him. He succumbed to an accident."

"Nonsense!" Mrs Kelly declared. "Why was he out in the bog in his pyjamas?"

She folded her arms over her chest and glared at Clara. It was a fair point, they had to all agree with that.

"He was chasing after Miss Heath and Mr McLear, who were in the process of eloping," Clara stated bluntly.

Mrs Kelly was so stunned by this declaration she fell silent.

"Who is Miss Heath?" Peabody said moodily.

"Mr Tennent's niece," Clara informed him. "That night, she planned to elope with McLear, thinking that her uncle would be late back from the golf club. However, Mr Tennent returned earlier than expected. In attempting to slip out of the house, Heath and McLear disturbed Tennent and he came down to investigate. It's possible he thought the noise was burglars. He followed the errant couple outside and chased them to the bog. Whether he had realised by then it was his niece he was following, we shall never know. He was shouting at them, Miss Heath remembers that, and then everything fell silent."

Mrs Kelly gaped.

"What do you mean?"

"Mr Tennent fell into the bog. We surmise that he tumbled hard onto a peat cutting blade sticking out of the ground and this stabbed him in the side. He then slipped into the bog. Possibly he was dazed in the fall, but he appears to have made no effort to extract himself."

"I saw it happen during the war," Tommy said darkly. "A man was running across the battlefield beside you and suddenly he was gone, vanished into a shell hole filled with muddy water."

A morbid silence fell over them all as they contemplated this information. Mrs Kelly finally cleared her throat and spoke.

"Did they look for him, even?"

"They did. They could not find him," Clara explained.

"We nearly lost Lethbridge that way," Jason said. "Had we not reached him when we did, he could have drowned. That bog seems to suck a man in."

"At least…" Mrs Kelly said. "At least it was just an accident. Not someone wishing him harm."

"It also had nothing to do with the Lynch brothers," Clara pointed out. "Mrs Lynch has been maligned all these years for helping her grandsons, when it turns out she was right to look out for them. They were innocent of any crime against Mr Tennent."

Mrs Kelly twisted her lips together. She was not a woman who admitted she was wrong easily, but it was obvious that a pang of guilt had entered her heart. How many wicked things had she said concerning Mrs Lynch and her grandsons? How often had she wished her ill?

"It is about time this village took better care of their oldest resident," Tommy said, and he did not mask the sternness to his tone. "Mrs Lynch may not have always agreed with her neighbours, but she is not evil, not to be treated like a pariah as she has been. You have believed her guilty of conspiring to protect the killers of Mr Tennent and it turns out you were wrong. You have to make amends."

"You speak about what you don't understand," Mrs Kelly said.

"I think I understand better than you realise," Tommy countered. "In any case, this is about Christian kindness. God wants us to forgive each other, doesn't he Mrs Kelly?"

Tommy had hit on a right note with the woman. She considered herself a good Catholic, after all. And a good Catholic ought to look after people, even when they were thine enemy. That was just good grace and it surely earned you brownie points in the afterlife. Mrs Kelly considered this long and hard. The news that Mr Tennent had not been a victim of the Lynch brothers had rather mellowed her mood and she was feeling rather charitable all of a sudden towards Mrs Lynch. She wasn't going to admit to herself that this was partly to alleviate her guilt over misjudging her all these years. Instead, she puffed herself up with the notion of doing something righteous and good.

"Mrs Lynch is an unfortunate old woman," Mrs Kelly said thoughtfully. "Sadly neglected by her family, though these things tend to only happen after a falling out and Mrs Lynch is strong in her opinions."

Tommy kept his mouth shut, but he could see Annie across the table barely containing her outrage over this statement. The only reason she was holding her tongue was because she did not want to destroy the fragile opportunity for Mrs Kelly to take care of her neighbour.

"Thank you, Mrs Kelly," Clara said to the housekeeper. "I am glad to know that the air has been cleared regarding this terrible tragedy. It is just unfortunate that the truth was not told sooner."

"Miss Heath always was afraid to speak out," Mrs Kelly sighed. "Maybe now we all know the truth she will stop hiding away in that cottage. I saw that things between her and McLear fell apart, well, I can't say I am sorry for that. He was not the sort I would want her to be with."

Mrs Kelly's shoulders relaxed and some of her permanent fire seemed to have dampened down. She released her folded arms, and it was as if she was taking in the room properly for the first time in years.

"Well, dinner won't cook itself," she said to no one in particular. Then she walked off to the kitchen.

"Horrible, self-righteous, pompous woman!" Annie declared the second she was out of earshot.

"Say what you feel now, Annie," Tommy grinned at her.

"You heard her, making out Mrs Lynch somehow deserves her isolation," Annie was breathing fast, having been holding her breath to avoid blurting out what she thought of Mrs Kelly. "I can see now why Mrs Lynch has had so much trouble. It isn't her, but these people."

"Calm down Annie, things are resolving themselves now," Tommy reassured her.

"It seems to me," Clara interrupted. "That the person who could really benefit from Mrs Lynch's friendship and wisdom would be Miss Heath."

She had thrown out the comment to see where it might lead. Annie grabbed at it.

"Miss Heath certainly is similar in some ways to Mrs Lynch, being an outsider."

"And she would not judge Mrs Lynch for her forward-thinking ways," Tommy added.

"Mrs Lynch would surely benefit from having a younger person about who was of a similar intellectual calibre," Clara added. "And if there was ever someone who would not judge Miss Heath for keeping her secret all these years it must surely be Mrs Lynch?"

"We could introduce them," Annie nodded.

"It's about time Miss Heath became part of the world again," Tommy agreed. "She could only benefit from Mrs Lynch's recipes too."

This seemed to satisfy them all and a new aura of hope filtered over the table. Things were going to get better for Mrs Lynch and Miss Heath, Clara was sure of it. Jimmy McLear she was less confident on, she felt his problems stemmed from a dark place inside that only he could fix.

"If Mr Tennent wasn't murdered," Rufus spoke, a look of consternation on his face. "Then the interference of the police was not really necessary. There was no crime, other than the fact Miss Heath and Mr McLear never spoke about what occurred."

"I don't think it's a crime to fail to report someone disappearing into thin air," Professor Peabody frowned. "They didn't actually see the man drown. For all they knew, he could have just given up the chase and gone home."

Clara wasn't sure what legal consequences there could

be for what Miss Heath and her lover had done. She doubted the matter would go further, in any case, she had no intention of revealing what she knew to Inspector O'Connor. She didn't trust that man and she was unconvinced by his abilities as a policeman. She felt no good could come from telling him what really happened. Miss Heath and McLear had certainly suffered a punishment all these years that was worse than any penalty the courts could impose. McLear probably would never overcome his guilt.

Rufus was sitting very still and looking incredibly miserable.

"Our site has been ruined because a man accidentally fell into a bog," Peabody puttered. "It beggars' belief. All those years of work brought to an end because a poet stumbled out of his house and drowned over a decade ago."

Rufus dropped his head further in despair.

"The worst of it is, if Clara had been just allowed to do as she was, we could have told the police it was all an accident and they would not have had to make such a fuss," Susan sighed.

"I confess I was angry you prevented me from going to the police at first," Clara said to Peabody. "I felt I was doing something wrong remaining silent, but having seen the reaction of the police, I have come to the conclusion that you were correct. Inspector O'Connor couldn't find the back of his hand if you asked him to, he certainly isn't capable of solving a crime. In any case, there was no crime, at least not the sort we imagined."

"Damn Lethbridge!" Peabody spluttered at the amateur archaeologist who was sitting quietly opposite him and had so far not said a word. "If you had kept your mouth shut…!"

"I never spoke to the police," Lethbridge told him firmly. "What good did it do me? I can't get on with my work anymore than you can."

Peabody glowered at him.

"Well, who else would do such a thing? It was spite, wasn't it? Because I wouldn't let you take readings around trench three."

"It was nothing of the sort. I tell you again, I had nothing to do with it!"

Peabody was about to bark back at him when Rufus butted in. He looked utterly despondent, as if he had just heard the world was ending. He slammed his hand down on the table to get the professor's attention.

"I did it!" he declared.

Everyone snapped their attention to him. Peabody had a look of amazement in his eyes that was swiftly turning to anger.

"You?"

"It seemed wrong to pretend a man had not died in the bog," Rufus said miserably. "His body was sitting in the finds tent, for crying out loud! Didn't anyone else find it distasteful?"

The young archaeologist looked around his companions, but he was going to find no compassion there. There reached a point when you dealt with bones and bodies a lot in your line of work when they started to become familiar and less disturbing. The archaeologists had not been bothered about the presence of Mr Tennent. They had been looking for a body in the bog, after all. It just happened they found one that was a little more modern than expected.

It also had to be said that the archaeologists were a little lost in their own worlds when it came to these things and tended to think harder about events that had happened a century ago than that which was happening right now.

"Well, I did!" Rufus declared to them all. "I have a conscience, unlike you fools."

"Who is the fool now the bloody Civic Guard has marched all over our excavation and damaged unique artefacts? They will probably prevent us from returning to the dig site! What do you think will happen to all that history once the peat diggers are allowed back? Why do you think I was doing this?" Professor Peabody was up on his feet and leaning over the table, bellowing at Rufus.

A Body Out of Time

Tommy grabbed his arm, just to be sure he wasn't about to launch at the lad. He had seen Peabody's temper in action before.

"I'm sorry," Rufus said. "If I had known he was not murdered…"

"Your apology is worthless now!" Peabody jabbed a finger at him. "Don't bother coming back to university when we are home. You will not be welcome in my classroom!"

Rufus hung his head grimly. Clara waited to see if one of his colleagues would jump to his aid, when they didn't, she decided she must.

"Professor Peabody, while I fully appreciate your outrage, I think you are going too far. Rufus acted as I wished to do. He felt it was the right thing to do, to report the body and if Tennent had been murdered, he would have been utterly correct. He could neither foresee that my investigations would discover Tennent died accidentally, nor could he know the police were such imbeciles."

"That is no excuse…"

"Actually, it is a very good excuse and Rufus is not to be penalised for doing what he felt was right," Clara said firmly. "You shall not exclude him from your course, do you understand?"

Peabody stared at her agog, but Clara had made up her mind and was not going to be deterred.

"Miss Fitzgerald is right," Jason said quietly. "Rufus was only doing what he thought best."

"And I now regret my decision heartily," Rufus added quickly.

"You…!" Peabody was still pointing that finger at the lad. "For crying out loud!"

The professor flung himself back from the table and marched out of the room. Shortly they heard the slamming of the front door.

"He'll come round," Susan consoled Rufus who looked utterly desperate.

"Yeah," said Jason. "He'll come around."

He glanced towards the doorway.
"Probably."

Chapter Twenty-Nine

It came to the final day of their holiday. They had spent the last week free from any form of detective work. Clara had gladly gone sightseeing with O'Harris in the car, while Tommy and Annie had repeatedly visited Mrs Lynch and put her house in order. It was noticeable that the village of Little Limerick was starting to wake up to their responsibilities to their neighbour. Mrs Kelly had begun the transformation, having reconciled her misplaced outrage, and being spurred by a quietly simmering guilt within that, if anyone cared to mention it, would be denied heartily. She had visited Mrs Lynch every day that week and had gone inside the house, rather than just left things on the doorstep. This had been noticed by everyone who cared to see, and they had passed on the news to everyone else. Having Mrs Kelly cross the threshold of Mrs Lynch's home was rather like the breaking of a curse and it was suddenly apparent that more than one resident had a slightly guilty conscience when it came to the old lady.

News had, of course, spread widely about the confession of Jimmy McLear and Miss Heath. It had reached the ears of Inspector O'Connor and he might have caused the couple trouble, except he was in hot water himself.

Information had reached one of the senior members of the new Irish Government concerning the desecration of an ancient Irish sacred site by a member of the Civic Guard, including the severe damage to unique and highly valuable artefacts. This particular minister proved to have a strong inclination towards history and the preservation and promotion of ancient Irish culture. In short, O'Connor was trying to answer some very difficult questions and failing.

No one knew who had informed the minister about the incident, but rumour around the dig site was that Rufus' family was well-connected with some of the Irish gentry who were taking a firm interest in politics and Irish heritage. If it was Rufus who had spread the word in an effort to redeem himself, he was keeping very quiet about it.

The good news was that the interest of the government in the dig site meant that work could be resumed. The talk was that the whole bog was going to be earmarked as a national heritage site and protected for future generations. The bad news was that the government was insisting that Irish archaeologists excavate the site, not Englishmen.

Peabody was surprisingly calm about being turfed off the dig site. When asked what he thought about his life's work being snatched away from him after all he had done to get the site opened up to historians in the first place, he was prosaic.

"At least the history is being preserved for future generations," he said. "In the end, that is what matters most, not the ego of a single man."

He hadn't mentioned that he happened to know the new Irish archaeologist in charge of the dig, that they had gone to university together and that they were working in secret to secure a place on the excavation team for Peabody – some sort of advisory capacity. After all, Peabody was the leading world expert on the preservation of bronze artefacts, and a lot of bronze was coming up from the bog and needing preservation.

Possibly some of Peabody's contentment was also due

to the knowledge that Lethbridge had been kicked off the bog once and for all. Not only was he English, which held no weight with the ministers in charge of Irish heritage, but they had very little time for his curious methods and bizarre talk of a horse carving somehow made out of channels in the bog. Their own experts had sneered at the idea, leaving Lethbridge out in the cold.

Finally defeated, Lethbridge left for England with vague talk of testing out his theory of pixie carvings in Cornwall. Clara felt a little bit sorry for him, he was just exploring history in his own misguided fashion, and he had not really done any harm. Better a man like Lethbridge loitering at your dig site than a man like O'Connor.

Clara felt she was leaving Ireland well rested, despite everything that had happened and felt ready for whatever lay in wait back home. They were all looking forward to returning to Brighton as they paid their last call on Mrs Lynch.

"She has taught me so much," Annie said as she knocked on the door. "I am going to miss her."

Annie looked quite bereft. Her own parents and grandparents were deceased, and it had been nice to have Mrs Lynch filling the void Annie had not realised had sat inside her all these years. She had a tear in her eye as they entered the house and headed to the kitchen.

There they had a surprise, for sitting at the table, talking to Mrs Lynch about Barmbrack cake was Miss Heath. She looked less grey all of a sudden, not least because she had ditched her usual cardigan and was wearing one that was a soft lavender purple.

"Hello," she greeted them with a smile.

"Ah, you'll be being off then?" Mrs Lynch said, rising from the table with only a slight hint of stiffness and giving Annie a warm hug. "I'll miss you."

"I'll miss you too," Annie snivelled.

"Now, gal, what's this?" Mrs Lynch scolded her gently. "No tears for me. You are taking my legacy back to England with you, right you are."

A Body Out of Time

Annie nodded, but couldn't speak for tears. Mrs Lynch squeezed her hand.

"And look what you have done for me, eh? You have made the house beautiful. You have warmed the hearts of those around me and made them reconsider their treatment of me. And you have introduced me to this delightful young lady who is going to learn how to embark on a new journey of independence through me."

Mrs Lynch motioned to Miss Heath.

"Mrs Lynch is going to teach me to cook and we are going to start promoting my art. She thinks my paintings are wonderful," Miss Heath blushed as she confessed this.

"But they are," Mrs Lynch told her firmly. "They are alive with atmosphere. Don't listen to what the folks around here know about art. They think a fuzzy print of a cottage cut from the newspaper is a masterpiece. There is something about your paintings, something powerful. They need to be shown to the world."

Clara admired Mrs Lynch. She was fast approaching one hundred, yet her enthusiasm for life was just as strong as when she had been twenty. She seemed more dynamic than many people half her age. She was glad they had placed Miss Heath under her wing, for she could see the pair benefiting each other no end.

"Don't forget, when you have your international tour for your paintings, you must bring them to Brighton," Clara informed Miss Heath.

Miss Heath blushed even deeper. It was going to take a long time for Mrs Lynch to help her overcome her shyness, but if there was anyone who could do it, it was her.

"We all need a cup of tea and cake," Mrs Lynch declared. "I want to say goodbye properly."

Tommy left the ladies to their farewell ceremony and wandered outside to take one last look at the place he had become quite fond of over the last couple of weeks. Little Limerick was the sort of village that seemed frozen in time, as if nothing in the outside world could touch it. He liked that. He wondered if he would ever come back. A part of

A Body Out of Time

him thought that would not be a wise idea. Time would seep into this place after all, things would change slowly but surely and, ultimately, he would find a sense of sadness and loss in the place instead of peace and contentment. Some places you were only meant to visit once.

Andrew was walking down the street, dressed in workman's overalls and with a stack of wooden planks on one shoulder. Tommy stared at him curiously.

"What are you up to?"

Andrew paused before the wall of Mrs Lynch's garden and carefully lowered the planks of wood.

"We never got around to fixing up the wood store for Mrs Lynch," he said. "I plan on doing that today."

"Aren't you leaving for home today, like the rest of us?" Tommy asked.

Andrew cleared his throat thoughtfully.

"That's the thing Tommy, I took time to think over what you had said concerning myself and Glorianna. It seemed to me I had a choice. I could carry on being a fool and risk my father one day discovering what was happening and turning against me, or I could make the decision to end things with Glory and go back to the way things were," Andrew said. "Only thing is, I know I am a weak-willed man, and if I remained in the house with Glorianna, eventually my resolve would fail me. Instead, I have made the decision to run away from things and stay here in Ireland."

Andrew gave a lopsided grin.

"Father has agreed to continue renting Mr Tennent's cottage, on the assurance that I shall at last do something with my life. I haven't quite decided what that shall be yet, but I rather like being a handyman, so I am going to try that for a while."

Tommy felt a weight lifting off him. He hadn't realised how much he was concerned about Andrew and Glorianna's illicit affair until that moment.

"I think that is a very good idea," he said.

"I dare say somewhere along the way I shall make

another terrible decision that muddles up my life, but one can only try," Andrew shrugged.

"I think it is your impulsive decisions that are your downfall," Tommy told him. "Perhaps only make decisions when you have had time to sleep on them."

Andrew chuckled.

"Well, I think this is the right sort of place to take my time over things."

"On that I think you are right," Tommy agreed. "Best of luck, old boy."

"Feel free to come visit anytime," Andrew added. "I might even take up poetry."

Humming to himself, Andrew headed around the back of the cottage. It struck Tommy that for the first time since he had known his cousin as an adult, Andrew seemed happy. That cheered him no end. It might have been a very strange holiday, but one thing he was sure of, they had left the village a little bit of a better place than when they had arrived and that was surely the best way of things?

Feeling content about life himself, Tommy took in another deep breath of air and headed back indoors to get his cup of tea. He was beginning to appreciate just why Tennent had been so enamoured with this place.

He was even beginning to like his poetry.

Printed in Great Britain
by Amazon